LEAVING ORDINARY

LARGE PRINT

BILLIJO LINK

BONETRAIL MEDIA

Leaving Ordinary. © Copyright 2020 by Billijo Link
All rights reserved.
For more information contact,
Bonetrail Media
www.bonetrailmedia.com
Cover design by Books Covered
ISBN 978-1-7342870-3-5 (ebook)
ISBN 978-1-7342870-2-8 (paperback)
ISBN 978-1-7342870-4-2 (large print)

Bonetrail Series

CHAPTER ONE

1999

Today Louise would visit the land. This trip would return her to a past she brushed against almost daily. It could happen when she filled the blue speckled enamel roasting pan used to make years of meals, dusted a color photograph of the farm framed by wheat fields and grass pastures, or heard violin music. The moments could generate cheer or reflection, and, at times, land emotional wallops.

The stretched doleful coos of mourning doves voiced her melancholy. Louise's knee hooked the bedsheet as she rolled away from the North Dakota summer sunrise that spread from between the white pull blind and the window frame.

She told herself to stop being so mopey.

Get up. You can't get out of this.

The hem of her lace-trimmed blue nightgown dropped low as she left her bed. She raised the blind seeking the hush-filled planned and pruned senior community's landscaping. Dwarf shrubs squatted in oblong beds of pea gravel or rusted brown mulch surrounded by a brochure-ready lawn.

Louise thought it was all tidy and dull.

Why can't there be more flowers around this place?

Turning from the view, Louise questioned if there was an easier way to go back. She gripped the dresser top, and her 89-year-old knees lowered her like an antique, overworked elevator. She tugged the heavy bottom drawer an inch at a time as wood scraped wood. The smell of mothballs stung the air.

I haven't looked at his violin in years. What if seeing it makes the missing hurt more?

Louise saw the travel-worn violin case. Her mind wanted to fast swing away, but her heart locked on and looked. When Louise moved into her apartment five years ago, she placed Leo's violin in the drawer of the oak dresser. Storing away the instrument had quieted memories, but their magnetic pull had not lessened: a life created by two when now there was one. Her age-spotted hand caressed the case's cracked and wounded leather. Her thumb stroked the handle.

"I miss you."

Louise let the instrument be and moved aside newer

photo albums with the plastic pockets until she saw the ebony scrapbook with the ragged gilt edging. The book had the heft of longevity built into it. Louise hoisted this scrapbook and herself and went to the kitchen.

I'll make coffee first.

She brewed strong, tongue-burning coffee like all the gallons she had made before. Louise settled in at the small kitchen table that her children had given her when she'd moved into the apartment. The newer dining set wasn't as sturdy as her old farm table, but it fit the space.

Taking a few sips, she steadied herself before reaching for the memory book.

This is silly. Nothing in there is going to bite me.

The coarse, ebony sheets crackled as she pulled apart and turned pages of old-timey black-and-white photographs bonded into place by paper corner brackets. One picture showed the farm's wooden windmill that creaked and swayed in the gusty prairie winds. Another, their first automobile: a third-hand used Ford truck. Family and friends grew up and grew old in the flip of pages. Grainfields and vegetable gardens in different stages of growth and seasons were kept static. This stop-and-go chronicling continued until she came to a photograph that was years out of order.

Framed by scalloped white borders, the photo showed a young couple sitting outside on uneven wooden high-back chairs next to a white clapboard house.

Louise recalled that house party. She had been eighteen, and Leo was nineteen. They'd been married a short time.

Leo's brash smile tight-lipped a cigarette. He held a violin. Leo rarely turned down an opportunity to play. Louise, next to him, smiled softly and posed in proper posture. She was not wearing a hat. Mother said ladies were supposed to wear hats outdoors. Louise never did like wearing one.

She stilled. The music was faint, but she could hear it nonetheless. It was no song in its entirety but instead a high-spirited compilation of chords, melodies, and crescendos.

She whispered, "I want the music."

Sometimes when Louise was washing her few dishes, she fantasized she could hear Leo playing. Foolishness, she knew. There was the radio or television, but she ached for him and his music. When Leo held his violin and gripped his bow, it was as if the dirt on his palms disappeared, and his musician's heart came out to play. Back on the farm, on the silent evenings when there was no music, its absence was so loud it reverberated all over the house. A person could reach out and touch the missing.

1926

Wheatville's town hall doors were propped open in wide welcome. Late April evening breezes attempted to cool the steamy makeshift dance hall of that western Minnesota farm town's Annual Fireman's Dance.

The salt and pepper mustached band leader's voice boomed. "Folks, welcome! We are the Midwest Musicale Extravaganza. We hope you have a grand time. Boys, let's begin."

Like a train leaving the depot, the Musicale's quartet eased, then chugged until they picked up steam and raced along the rails. Rotating on and off the dance floor were ladies wearing short-sleeved cotton dresses whose mid-calf hemlines floated and snapped as men wearing their Sunday button-up-best trousers or bib overalls spun them in polkas and waltzes amongst a fragrant fracas of rose and lily perfumes, sweat, and rolled tobacco smoke.

Sixteen-year-old Louise looked good-girl charming in her homemade flowered red and blue voile dress. Her below-the-knee hem showcased her legs, stepping and whirling across the tongue-and-groove oak floorboards. She shined from her short bobbed brown hair, held back by a green apple brainbinder headband, to her black patent leather shoes.

Her eyes were drawn to the fiddle player, not much older than herself, and his slicked-back hair.

The musician's talent pushed and pulled jubilant notes across his instrument, revving up the crowd.

The fiddler's pant cuffs hung above his ankles, making his slim five-foot ten frame appear taller. The black wool fabric matched the snug suit coat gaping and straining its button threads. Early into the music show, the musician removed his coat and rolled back his shirtsleeves, displaying muscled forearms and a torso outline. The man's suit didn't fit, but it didn't display "farmer." The verve of his music and rascal smile kept her sneaking looks. She wished he'd ask her to dance.

He held his back straight, then tilted back, and then leaned into the rhythm's vigor. His left foot planted firm. The right foot tapped the beat. The violin player grinned at the horn player, who threw a smirk to the drummer, and the drummer beamed at the crowd as the band showed off their up and down swings of tempo and musical swagger.

At nine o'clock, the bandleader stood up from his piano and called a break and announced that the Homemakers Club was serving a meal. Wives, widows, and daughters hurried to organized positions at long food tables offering home-baked bread and cooked-to-a-blush ham. Similar to the upright pipes of a church organ, the famished and tipsy partygoers lined up to choose homegrown lettuce and cabbage salads, coffee, and water. For something stronger, a

person sidestepped Prohibition and located Jacob
Swansen's automobile.

Several matrons shooed back residents so the musicians could fill their plates first. Louise's insides fluttered when she saw the violin player approach her
dessert table. Smiling, Louise asked, "What would
you like?"

The musician's mouth corners hooked high, and
then his gaze moved over the tall chocolate and
vanilla cakes, juicy apple and sour cream raisin pies,
and flat, brown-speckled Norwegian lefse. "Ahh...
how about some of everything."

"Was that your approach at the other tables?"
Louise asked nodding at the two plates he carried
laden with golden fried chicken, sliced bread, sour
pickles, and sharp white onion-seasoned chunky
potato salad.

"Hard to pass up food like this. Plus, I don't want
to offend any of the ladies."

She filled a third plate for the musician. "That's
smart, and a potential bellyache."

It was then Louise noticed he was staring at her.
The hall was overheated, but the added recognition
of the man's interest made Louise want to fan herself
with a plate. She must have been distracted for too
long because he raised the plates in his hands.

She glanced down, up, and stopped at his grin.
Their shared laughter skipped with nervousness.

Louise asked, "Would you like me to carry this to where you're sitting?"

"Please. Ladies first."

Louise scanned the hall. "There's the band," and moved towards the table.

The musician stretched his step to walk alongside her. "My name is Leo Zint. A pleasure to make your acquaintance. You are?"

Her keen hazel eyes noticed his sparking brown ones. "My name is Louise Miller."

"Are you enjoying the evening?"

"Yes. The music and dancing have been wonderful." She noticed him stand straighter.

"Are there any songs you would like us to play?"

Delighted, Louise said, "I like what I've heard so far. Keep doing that."

They reached the seated band members. The horn player, who appeared a few years older than Leo and wore his suit like a city slicker, pulled out the chair next to him. "Miss, this seat is for you."

Louise raised an eyebrow. "Isn't that for Mr. Zint?" Good manners dictated she address Leo formally, but Louise already thought of him as Leo.

The musician laughed. "He can find another seat. I'm Erik..."

Leo interrupted, "Don't pay him any mind. He can't help himself when a pretty girl is around."

"Is that so?" Louise said.

"You're welcome to join us."

"I'm Colson, the bandleader, singer, and all-around musician. Nice to meet you. Erik is our horn player. Karl here is our drummer. Of the four of us, he's the loudest musician and talks the least."

Karl's quick head nod bounced with shyness, and the rest of the Musicale chuckled.

"I'm Louise Miller. I've been enjoying the music."

"You're my kind of gal," Erik said.

Louise heard Leo say under his breath, "Not tonight."

She set Leo's plate down. "I have to return to my table. It was nice meeting you all. Enjoy the food."

Louise could feel Leo watching her stroll back to the desserts. She added a frisky swish to her glide. Her rash behavior made her hands twitch. To calm herself, she rearranged platters of desserts. Throughout the meal, Louise peeked at Leo. The boisterous band ate, laughed, and invited anyone who strayed near to join their party.

When the musicians returned to their instruments, the cooled-off townspeople reassembled on the dance floor. Soon enough, the dancers wore damp clothing and high spirits, including Louise. When she looked in Leo's direction, she flashed him flirting smiles, and he reciprocated.

Colson yelled, "Last song!"

The rambunctious finale rocked the revelers who clapped and hooted their appreciation. The Musicale began packing their instruments, and the town hall cleanup followed. As Louise wiped a table, she saw Leo amble towards her.

"Did you like the rest of the show?" Leo asked.

"I did. Most everyone stayed until the end."

"I like hearing that. Tonight's crowd had a good time. When you're standing on stage, you get to see what the audience likes and doesn't. People-watching makes the music better. Helps too if there's trouble brewing."

Louise held the rag in her hands and tugged at the ends. "You sounded good to me. Have you been playing long?"

"I bought my violin when I was thirteen. You have the long, pretty fingers of a piano player."

Louise looked down at her hands. On one hand she spread out her fingers. "Thank you. Does the Musicale leave today, or will you stay around for a couple of days?"

"We'll sleep for a few hours and then head to the next gig."

"It must be exciting to go places and play for audiences. See something other than the hind end of a cow."

Leo let loose a fast laugh. "Playing music is more fun than plowing a field. I started with the Musicale when I was fourteen. The band gave me a job and a suit that was too big for my bones. That was three years ago, and now there's more of me, and my suit still doesn't fit."

Louise giggled. "Maybe you could find someone to sew you a new suit?" and then, with a searching tone, asked, "Do you like life with the Musicale?"

"I can't imagine doing anything else." Leo cupped his hand on the back of his neck. "We're headed out. Could I...write you?"

Louise swallowed so she wouldn't stutter on her next words. "I'd like that."

She hoped Leo's request was more than a traveling man's empty flirtation.

CHAPTER TWO

Six weeks had passed since the dance. On and around Louise's parent's farm, green sprouting spring wheat busted through bare brown topsoil. The scent of backyard lilacs wafted round the two-story house, into the screened, long front porch, and through open windows. Daylight pushed dusk to nine o'clock.

Near supper time, Louise stopped short of entering the house's back door to knock the field dirt from her shoes. She had one clean when she heard her mother's no-nonsense tone calling her.

"Coming," Louise said.

Her mother, a farmwife in perpetual practical motion, and who did little bending, appeared on the other side of the screen door. "You received a postcard from a man named Leo Zint."

Shock turned Louise's face towards her mother's questioning look.

Mrs. Miller wasn't done. "Who is this Mr. Zint?"

Louise felt a heated red crawl up her torso into her neck. "I met him at the Fireman's Dance. He plays violin in the band. You heard him play."

Mrs. Miller's forehead furrowed, and the skin between her eyebrows accordioned into a number eleven shape. "Why is he writing to you?"

"We spoke about music, and he asked if he could write to me."

"Louise! It is not proper for a stranger to write to you."

Louise's red color receded and surprise transformed into anger. "How is receiving a postcard improper? I'm sure you read it."

Mrs. Miller stiffened. "I can read any mail that comes to my home. Especially if it's addressed to my children."

From inside the house, Louise's father called, "Mother."

"I'm in the kitchen speaking to Louise."

Mr. Miller approached mother and daughter. "What are you doing talking through the screen door?"

"Louise received a postcard from a man we don't know. He's part of that band who played at the dance."

Mr. Miller raised his eyebrows, and a guffaw

sprung from his barrel chest. "Louise, did you attract a love-sick bull?"

Mrs. Miller's apoplectic expression punctured Mr. Miller's teasing.

"Come inside. You have chores," Mrs. Miller said.

Louise entered and guided the screen door, so it would not smack itself closed and annoy her mother further.

"May I please have the postcard?" Louise asked.

Mr. Miller presented to his wife, "I don't see how reading a postcard makes trouble."

Her mother delivered the postcard and her verdict. "You may have this, but you will follow my rules and behave as a young lady should. Help your sisters in the kitchen."

"Thank you," Louise said and slipped the postcard into the pocket of her day dress. Her mother would be monitoring her. Her younger teenage sisters, Martha and Rose, would want to know what the mail said. Louise would have to wait if she wanted to read it alone.

After supper, Louise, her parents, sisters, and older brother Charlie, who was home between his road crew jobs, sat in the parlor listening to the radio. Each time Louise felt the card bump against her body, she relished the accompanying zing of excitement. Her opportunity arrived when her youngest sister, thirteen-year-old Rose, asked where the Montgomery Wards' catalog was.

Louise stood up. "It's in our bedroom. I'll get it." She soft-stepped up the stairs and into the bedroom. Unadorned whitewashed walls surrounded the three girls' shared bed. Louise sat on a pieced-together homemade quilt of fabric scraps and read the postcard's precise block printing.

Hello Miss Louise Miller,

How are you? Hope you can still hear my violin. The Musicale has been in Kansas for a month. In Kansas City, we visited Union Train Station pictured on the front. It has a high ceiling and windows to match its grand size. On the second floor, you can look at the trains and across the city like a bird on a roof. Saw a bull get loose in a town near Topeka and folks had to catch him. The bull was faster. Our next gigs are around St. Louis, M.O. Please write and mail your letter general delivery. Cordially, Leo Zint

Louise traced the stiff paper's edges. An ecstatic tingling in her fingertips sped up her arms and about her shoulders.

Leo wrote to me!

He had written to her. She returned the postcard to her pocket, wanting to keep Leo's attention close.

The next afternoon, Louise hid behind the chicken coop. Sitting on an overturned bucket, she considered what to write to Leo. Slight dismay ruffled her happiness. What does a small town farm girl write to a traveling musician?

She wrote,

Hello Mr. Zint, How are you? My school year is done. I'm working more around the farm as the growing season continues.

Leo isn't interested in farm life. Louise erased all the words after the question mark. Her life was dull. What could she say to him? She tried again.

Hello Mr. Zint, How are you? It's been quiet since the dance. I miss being in school and all the activities. Field and garden planting are done.

Again, she made words disappear. What if Leo thought she was a ninny? What if he was no longer keen on her? What if he didn't write back?

Louise stared at an adjacent field of corn. Green leaves hung like hound dog ears on the young corn stalks awaiting their forthcoming yellow top tassels and cobs. She looked past the nearby and towards the horizon, trying to see farther than the vanishing point. Louise knew there was more beyond that perceived limit. A correspondence with Leo could import events and a livelihood that wasn't tethered to agriculture and weather. He was also a charmer that she desired to know better.

Hello Mr. Leo Zint,

I hope you are well. Thank you for sending me a postcard. Kansas City sounds exciting. I would like to see the city from a bird's perch. I've only traveled to the neighboring counties. Someday, I would like to see more of the nation.

My junior year is complete, and next May I graduate. I have not yet decided what to do after high school. If I go to college, I'll be able to leave the farm and live in a town or a city.

Planting is done. My chores have grown faster than the wheat. This week's excitement was Mr. Olmstead's cows getting out. He was worried about them straying into the neighbor's pasture.

What new songs is the Musicale playing? I can still hear your violin. We have a radio and sometimes listen to music programs, but it isn't the same as hearing it in person, especially your violin. How is the band? What is St. Louis like? Please write soon and tell me about your gigs and travels. Louise Miller

She mulled over if the 'write soon' was presumptuous. Louise was willing to risk it.

July arrived and turned up the days' heat. Louise was outside taking the wash down from the clothesline when Rose burst like sunshine through overcast clouds in-between the gap of a pink summer dress and blue jean bib overalls to announce, "I have a surprise for you."

"You're going to help take clothes off the line?" Louise said as she folded a button-up shirt and dropped it into the basket at her feet.

"That's work, not a surprise."

Louise rolled her eyes. "There's always work around here."

Rose threw out her arm as if she was about to curtesy and proclaimed, "Let there be more fun, movies, and no work."

Louise clapped. "Thank you, Miss Hollywood. Help me with the wash."

"I came to give you this. Mother doesn't know." Rose whipped a postcard from her dress pocket and thrust it into Louise's hand. The action distracted Louise, and before she knew it, her sister skipped away.

The postcard showed the Mississippi River shoreline in St. Louis, Missouri.

Hello!

How are you? I hope you and your family are well. Is the corn knee high? Last night we played a wedding in a small town south of St. Louis. Lots of Irish and spirits. Played loud fiddle with an Irishman. Another had a flute that he could make whistle. People danced and sang until sunrise. A man knows how the Irish walk and mourn by the sound of their music. The band is good and busy. We head to Iowa City, I.A. next. Please mail your letter general delivery.

Leo Zint—standing by the Mississippi.

Louise tried to imagine what an evening of Irish music would be and sound like.

I wish I had been there.

She pretended to hear sweet yearning and

promising melodies, quick jigs, and popular Tin Pan Alley tunes. Leo's violin played in it all. Louise raised one arm and rested it on an imaginary Leo's shoulder, and her other hand palmed his invisible hand, and together they danced between hanging shirts and drying sheets.

Leo's postmarks wandered the Midwest, and Louise's imagination and letters followed his musical migration. Years before on a Sunday, Wheatville's young people were congregated in the churchyard when a traveling circus passed through. Louise and Rose had run shouting and waving alongside the caravan of flatbed trucks hauling equipment and exotic animals. Several circus workers waved back. At the town's boundary, the circus kept going and she and Rose had to stop.

"I wish I was going with them," Rose said.

"Me too," Louise agreed. She felt Leo, and the Musicale, was like the circus. Again, Louise had to remain within the limits of her small town, but Leo's letters brought exhilaration even if it was secondhand.

In fall, the blustery air currents carried the smell of decaying musty leaves, and empty dirt clod fields waited for snow. It was Louise's senior year, and she was closer to adulthood. School had released for the day, and as Louise stepped into the house she heard her Mother say, "Louise. Come into the kitchen."

"Coming." Louise smelled the beef broth and

pickling spices before she saw her mother minding a simmering pot of bobbing cubed potatoes and carrots.

"A letter came from that young man," her mother said pinching a dirt-smudged envelope.

Surprise had Louise asking an unspoken, not a postcard?

"His name is Leo. May I have my letter please?" Louise held out her hand palm up.

"You need to tell this Leo to stop writing you. First it was postcards, and now a letter."

"We're pen pals. He tells me about his life. You've read the postcards," Louise said.

"Your father and I know nothing about him Neither do you." The paper waved back and forth with each strong annunciation. "Do not give me, or your father, any reason to open this letter."

Louise's bubbling irritation began to roil. "Leo has been a gentleman. He's states away from this farm. Getting kicked by livestock is the most danger I'm near. May I have my letter please?"

Her mother held out the envelope. Louise noted the nail indentations her mother had scarred into the paper.

"Aren't you going to read it?" her mother queried.

When I'm away from you, Louise thought, but rather said, "Later. I have chores to do."

Before the evening milking, Louise snuck behind the red painted barn. Her head curled around his words. The envelope's corner touched her bottom lip.

The dryness of the paper and her mouth's moisture made the two stick together.

Dear Louise,

How are you? Postcards don't have much room, so I'm writing you a letter.

How are your classes? Have you decided what you'll do after graduation? You're smart. I can see you going places, even a big city. Maybe Chicago.

We're in Chicago now. This place moves fast. Erik has a new gal, and Karl spoke to one. Saw the gangster Al Capone in a club. Lots of people here and even more music. The jazz slides into a man's ears and down into his bones to stay forever. The blues roll around the heart and head looking for home. We've been going to the Southside clubs to hear all the music we can. The men from New Orleans are the musicians to learn from. Wish we could play more jazz. Colson says that many audiences don't like the color of that music. Those people are missing something special.

I know you'd like the music. If you were here, I'd take you to those clubs, and you could hear for yourself. We could go to a restaurant and try fancy food. Maybe one day?

Good luck with your classes. Your days are probably full of school goings-on and dances. I like seeing your letters.

The Musicale will be here through the new year. Please mail your next letter to the address below.

Write soon and tell me about your days. Leo in Chicago.

Louise looked up. The setting sun split the western sky into bands of orange, pink, and blue.

Leo said he'd like to show her Chicago. Like a courting couple.

The next day while Louise waited for her sisters to finish their school play practice, she wrote Leo.

Dear Leo,

How are you? I hope the days and shows are going well. Does Erik have the same gal or a new one? Does Karl have a gal? Is Colson lining up next year's shows?

Your letter made me happy. I would like you to show me Chicago. I would like to hear its jazz. What new places have you seen? What are the city people wearing? Dapper suits and glamorous dresses? Do you eat in restaurants every day? I've eaten in a restaurant a handful of times.

I wish I could write to you about something exciting happening here. My semester is half over. I graduate next year. It all seems lonely. My mother asked what I intend to do after graduation. I have no answer, and that upsets her. The woman likes a plan. Preferably the plan she makes.

One of my teachers suggested I consider teaching or nursing school. I've not told my parents about either of these. I would have to go away for more schooling, and that would upset them. The ordinariness of this life may well plow me into the ground until I disappear.

My mother is concerned about us writing to each other. She believes it's not appropriate. She may begin reading your letters. Please continue to write but don't include anything that will make her withhold your letters.

Stuck on this farm, dreaming about Chicago, and waiting for your next letter, Your Louise.

Through Leo, Louise was learning about a world different from the stationary spot she pivoted. Sometimes a niggling of brash behaviors climbed into her mind. What happens at those gigs? Do other gals catch Leo's eye? Were those girls prettier, cleverer, and funnier? Were their skin and hands smooth like stockings and not roughened up by farmwork? Who else may he be writing? She shrouded those stinging thoughts and waited for Leo's next missive.

Louise was beginning to pin hopes on a man whom she had met one time.

CHAPTER THREE

Clouds like soap suds, filtering the smallest patches of blue sky, tented over towering bricked grain silos and their snowed-in farmsteads as the new year and winter claimed the calendar. Another letter arrived for Louise. Her mother handed over the dispatch with stern sentry regard.

Louise sought the enclosed shelter of the chicken coop. Surrounded by dusty straw and fowl feathers the hens' low clucks were the background vocals to Leo's letter.

Dear Louise,

Happy New Year! I know 1927 will be a lucky year for you. Has your last semester started? Don't worry about what comes next. Things will work out.

Did you have a Merry Christmas? Around here it

was nice seeing stores put holiday decorations in their windows. It put a shine on old man winter.

The fellows and I had a party at our boarding-house. It was a pile of musicians and new friends. There was a dame who had small silver bells sewn onto her hat. A guy dressed as Santa. We sang carols around the piano like a family does.

On New Year's Eve, we played a roaring party for a rich guy. Besides our music, there were fireworks and a boxing match. The guests and the hired help toasted the new year. The boss got pickled and gave the Musicale a big tip when it was over.

We'll be working across Indiana next. We won't be staying in one place long. Please send your letters to Indianapolis, I.N. We arrive there in a few weeks.

Hope your family is staying warm and well. Save me a turn on the dance floor. Your Leo

He signed the letter 'Your Leo.' Louise wanted to shout and spin in her joy, but that would rile the hen house. She scrutinized the sentences making sure she hadn't missed anything. With the Musicale's no-madic schedule, Louise knew it might be some time before Leo's next letter. The thought took a swipe at her elation, but she wasn't going to let go. Maybe next Christmas she'd sew bells on her dress.

Over the winter months, Leo's sporadic letters shared more details of the Musicale's hobo life. Louise learned of audience antics like when a vigorous dancing couple crashed into Colson and pulled him off stage, towns the band traveled through and to, chasing jobs and accommodations, and even sleeping in their car. Louise wrote about school and family, her repeated pleasure of seeing Clara Bow in the silent film 'It,' and how winter could make her feel boxed in.

Warmer spring temperatures began to melt the silent snow drifts, and the honks and shadows of returning Canadian Geese rippled over the flat fields. A postcard in early May gave Louise a big surprise. Hasty scrawl said the Musicale was working their way west and would be in Minnesota in June. Louise wondered if, and hoped that, she would see Leo again.

She wrote Leo the day after her late May high school graduation.

Dearest Leo,

I graduated from high school yesterday. Mother made a special supper. My older brother Charlie and his new wife Yvette came from their farm the next county over to join us. My parents gave me a suitcase which was generous of them; and also, a strange present to receive since they expect me to stay here.

I'm an adult now and need to decide what comes next. I've thought more about going to teaching school. Whenever I speak about this option, my parents ask why I think I need to go so far away. I've stopped talking about it, but it hasn't left me. I need to make a plan for my future. It must be comforting to know that the Musicale is your future.

Are you in Minnesota? Will you come see me? I hope so. Your Louise

She could not send the letter as she did not have Leo's latest address. Had their correspondence courtship ended? Both her heart and head hoped not.

June passed and there was no word from Leo. Louise tried to keep her disappointment and melancholy hidden. The July heat and humidity had her family, except for her mother, trying not to stick or prick each other.

One morning Louise's mother announced, "Louise, Rose, please take the dairy herd to the south pasture. Bring them home for the evening milking."

"Yes, ma'am," the girls chorused.

"Rose, did you roll your eyes at me?"

"No mother."

"In this family, everyone works. My children will not be layabout lazy daydreamers."

When their mother turned away, the sisters shared a mutual eye-roll.

Louise would rather be doing almost anything else than minding cows. She followed Rose who loped across the farmyard.

Their father and his bow-legged stride exited the barn. He called out, "Morning Louise."

"Morning."

"You're scowling. Must have been talking to your mother."

"She was talking. I was listening."

"Your mother is who she is. That's how it goes. It's going to be warm today." He gave one of her humidity curls a gentle tug, and added, "Don't you and your sister run the cows back. It gets them and their milk stirred up."

To keep cool, the appointed shepherds rigged up a gunny sack tent. In the earthy burlap shade, Louise's eyeline was filled with black and white spotted grazing cows. Rose napped with her arm thrown across her face.

Louise saw field dusted lace-up oxford shoes. Her vision rocketed up to see Leo's grin. He mouthed, "Hello," and extended his hand. Louise grasped it, and with a gentle tug, he pulled her up and out. Still holding hands, they sidestepped manure piles and moved far enough away not to wake Rose.

"Leo, you're here!" Louise said in a giddy whisper. Bashfulness made her take a step backward. "You came to the farm."

Leo held her hand. "I wanted to see if you still looked the way I remembered."

"Still the same. Who told you where I was?"

"Martha. Your mother was nearby when I asked for you. She didn't look too happy to see me. I think the only reason I was able to come on my own is that your sister is with you."

Louise's heart jigged. "Musicians and strangers aren't on my mother's list of potential beaus. You're not even a traveling salesman or a town desk man."

Leo tipped his brown fedora back and head forward. "The only time I've been a desk man is when I had to move a desk. Do you want a desk man?"

Laughter spilled out of Louise. "I want a man who can stir up a room of people with his violin. A man that makes me want to dance and laugh."

Leo laced his fingers through hers. "There are roads all over this country going towards people wanting to hear the Musicale's music. And we're ready to play. There's something I have to tell you." Leo shoved his hands into his trouser pockets. The day was warm, but Louise's insides dropped degrees. "You know those letters I've been writing to you? I didn't write them. I had Erik write them for me. I mean, those were my words, he just did the scribbling."

"Why?" She paused. "Do you know how to read and write?"

Leo's face turned up to the sky. "I know some words. I can count. The thing is my ma died when I was six, and after her passing, my dad couldn't take care of the farm and me, my brothers, and sisters. We were farmed out to relatives. My dad made his cousin promise to send me to school. Once I was on his cousin's farm, there was too much work to do, so I couldn't go. I went a few times but going a day here and a day there doesn't add up to much."

"You were a farm boy! How did you learn to play the violin and all those songs?"

Leo looked Louise in the eyes. "I listen. Then I pick out the notes until I have the song put together. Some sounds just fit."

Louise wasn't quite sure what to say. She was embarrassed that someone other than Leo had read her private thoughts. The feeling began to wane when she considered Leo's efforts to write to her. "You sure like me."

"More than like you. I'm not school smart, but I know how to work hard. I can take care of you. Will you marry me?"

Louise exhaled a "yes," and Leo leaned in and pressed a kiss to her lips.

She rounded her lips and kissed back. "My mother will not be pleased."

CHAPTER FOUR

Louise and Leo swung their interlocked hands as they and Rose followed the hip sway of the herd back to the farm.

Rose asked Leo, "How long are you staying in Wheatville?"

"Only a few days. The Musicale has a gig on Saturday."

Louise added, "A house wedding will be quick."

"Are you sure you're okay with that?" Leo asked.

"Yes. Other than my family, nothing is keeping me here."

Rose interjected. "Does this mean Louise will be part of the Musicale?"

Louise felt her shoulders tighten.

"Yup. The Musicale hasn't had a woman in the band before. We'll figure it out as we go," Leo said.

Yes, we will Louise thought.

At the barn door, Leo said, "I'll go speak to your father."

Louise hunched her shoulders. "I'll tell my mother."

She passed the flowerbeds that her mother had planted next to the house and kept safer from wind, wildlife, and winter. Yellow fishing pole-straight gladiolas, fanning blossoms of purple irises, tissue paper-petaled orange poppies, and stiff white daisies were filling space. Her mother was in the large vegetable garden kneeling among straight rows of tomato plants picking weeds.

"Mother, I have something to tell you," Louise said and pulled a handful of weeds.

"I'm listening."

Louise was glad her mother was preoccupied. "Leo asked me to marry him. I said yes. We'll marry and leave on Friday."

Mrs. Miller straightened up like her daisies and crossed her arms over her chest. "There's no need to rush into marriage. You barely know this young man. We don't know his family. Being a musician is not a dependable job. How's he going to take care of you? What if something happens to you so far away?"

Louise did not answer. She knew her mother's advice and questions were sensible. But the urge to get away from this farm and small town overpowered reason and risk.

Mother and daughter waited for the other to speak. Around them, birdsong and insects moved about and did not care about the standoff in the garden.

Mrs. Miller's arms uncrossed and she rubbed her palms over the large pockets of her floral bib apron. "Our town is prosperous. It's not necessary to runoff to parts unknown."

Louise's wheel of fortune had turned, and she was ready to move.

"Leo has a job, and I'll be traveling with them." In an attempt to appease the tiniest part of her mother, Louise said, "Leo grew up on a farm. He knows how to work."

"If that man had sense, he'd be on a farm working and not moving from place to place. What kind of home will you have? I'll tell you. No home."

"I've made my decision. Leo and I can stop at Minister Hadelsen's before leaving town if necessary."

Her mother lashed out, "You don't know what you're doing! You're not thinking about your future. If this foolish decision ruins you, do you think you can run back here?"

Louise thrust out her chin. "There will be no running back."

Over the next two days, Louise's mother spoke when necessary, and the family shied away from the matriarch's silent anger. For Louise, there was relief in the rush of wedding preparations.

Her wedding day started early in the morning. A little after nine, Louise stood in her mother's kitchen and listened to her sisters assess the Musicale through the window.

Martha said, with a hand over her smile, "I remember that handsome horn player from the dance."

Rose bumped Martha with her hip to get a better look. "They're all handsome. Well, except for Colson. He's old like Father."

Louise walked over to her sisters but stood far enough away so that if anyone turned to the window, they would only see the younger girls gawking.

Rose sighed long and loud. "To think our older sister is marrying a traveling musician. You'll get to see exciting places. I wish it were me."

"Rose! You watch yourself." The girls turned to see their apron-wearing mother standing with her fists on her hips and nose pointed down. "Come away from that window. Finish helping with the food."

"Yes mother," Martha replied. She walked over to a bowl of boiled cold potatoes without a backward glance. Rose groaned and followed.

The day before, the four Miller females had baked several dozen yeasty rolls and two chocolate frosted chocolate cakes. As Louise was already wearing her best party dress, a sleeveless lilac airy creation with a flower flounce at the hip, her mother had dictated that Louise would not have to help with the remaining preparations.

The ceremony would start soon. Louise fidgeted with her flounce attempting to keep her giddiness inside.

"Girls, finish up so your father and Charlie can carry the table outside. Then we'll need to take the plates, silverware, and glasses out. The hams are out of the oven and resting. I made a coffee cake too."

Louise spun around to look at her mother. "Why? We already have the chocolate cakes."

"Louise, just because this is a small family wedding doesn't mean we do not host properly. If you would have waited, we could have gone to the church and then had a reception at the town hall like Charlie and Yvette's wedding. This is where we are, and we will make the best of it."

Louise bit the inside of her cheek. *Mother is mad that my wedding is not going to be a big display. Martha and Rose can be paraded about. Martha especially will toe the line.* Instead, Louise said, "There's no time. You know the Musicale has to get back on the road."

Louise's father walked into the kitchen. "Mother, is the table ready to come outside? Minister Hadelsen is here."

"Girls, clear the table so your father can get it moved."

The younger sisters moved mustard colored

thick-rimmed stoneware mixing bowls, utensils, and curled potato peelings from the table. Louise used her frustration to hard-scrub the wood's pin knots and swirls.

Mrs. Miller redirected orders to Mr. Miller. "Offer the minister something to drink. Check to see if we need more root beer and water taken out."

"There's plenty to drink out there. Does this table need a tablecloth?" Mr. Miller asked.

"Martha will bring the tablecloth outside. Louise, go finish getting ready." With that order, Louise understood that the present quarrel with her mother was over. Each woman knew the other's feelings, but neither would change course.

Louise looked through the parlor window memorizing her family as they moved about the yard setting up. She listened as her mother directed the activity with efficiency, even putting Leo and the band to work. Her mother's rose bushes beneath the sill perfumed the air. The thorns of the words from the kitchen exchange poked Louise.

Her new life was beginning, and her mother's reign was ending. Louise was determined to have a future with Leo. Whatever direction the wind carried her, it would be far from this life. A breeze passed through the open window, and she rubbed the goosebumps on her arms.

Her father called from across the room. "Louise, the minister is ready."

She walked over to a side table and picked up her cloche. "I have to put my hat on."

Yesterday she had replaced the hatband with leftover lilac dress fabric and silver ribbon. The hat capped her bobbed hair in cream, and she pushed her shoulders back, and chest out.

"You look pretty," her father said.

"Thank you." She linked her arm through his crooked, sturdy arm. He smelled of plain soap and hay, and she inhaled deeply. As they passed through the front door, she saw her mother waiting on the porch. Their eyes met, and her mother said, "You'll need these."

"Thank you," Louise stuttered as she accepted a bouquet of petite, ivory and lemon colored roses and her mother's temporary truce. The hand-off complete, the Millers walked toward the guests standing like a triangle with Leo and the minister at the top.

Louise felt euphoric and knew she radiated this at her groom. Leo, grinning, lifted his heels rocking back and forth. Directed by the minister, each said their vows swiftly and easily.

The minister lifted his hand above their heads confirming the union of holy matrimony. Then he said, "You may kiss your bride."

This was Louise and Leo's second kiss, and it made her feel dizzy delight. She grasped firmer onto Leo.

"May I introduce Mr. and Mrs. Leo Zint." Familial polite claps and an unruly shivaree from the Musicale ended the ceremony.

Louise didn't think her happiness could go any higher. She sought Leo's eyes and savored his open-faced pleasure.

Leo announced to the assembled, "Louise and I want to thank you for being here today. And thanks to Mr. and Mrs. Miller for putting on the wedding. Since I've played so many other people's weddings, I had to play at my own. After lunch, the fellows and I would like to play for you."

More clapping followed, and then people lined up at the food table. Her mother had been determined to give the handful of family and closest neighbors a lavish, hot meal for her oldest daughter's wedding. Louise suspected her mother hoped to offset whispers. People would talk about her quick marriage to the man in the band, but she didn't care.

Rose bounced over to the newlyweds. "Congratulations! What songs will the Musicale play? Our mother doesn't like some of the popular tunes. She gets this pinched look, so ignore her." The Zints watched the teenager take a breath and then yell, "Come here, Martha. Oh goodness, mother's giving me the look. I'll be right back."

Leo pointed at Rose as she scampered across the yard. "Rose sure is a talker. She doesn't take after your mother."

Louise gave his arm a playful swat. "Let's eat, then music."

As people finished eating Louise heard Leo say, "You boys ready to put on a show?" and then whisper, "Erik, put that 'shine away. My mother-in-law is a prohibitionist and today is not the day to make her more upset."

The Musicale began with an upbeat shoulder-swayer then reached high-feeling heights in the second song. Guests tapped their feet and slapped their thighs. It was the third tune when people stood up and foxtrotted around the yard. It was during a dance with their old neighbor, the light-footed Mr. Alderhof, that Louise spun the quickest. It was here through spinning glimpses that she saw her father offer his hand to her mother. Her mother shook her head no, but her father waited, arm extended. At the next song, her parents began a slow waltz to an old country tune.

Several songs later, Leo said, "Folks, thanks again from Louise and myself for being here today. Here's something special for my bride, Cole Porter's 'Everybody Loves My Baby, but My Baby Don't Love Nobody But Me.' Leo winked at Louise and began playing while Colson sang.

Louise absorbed the song's loving sentiment and the attentive serenade. The early minutes of marriage were beginning well, gamble, or not.

Soon after that and close to their one p.m. departure, Colson called out, "Last song."

Louise's father stepped in front of her and asked, "May I have this dance?"

While dancing, Louise peered over his shoulder and noticed her mother standing next to the food table with clasped hands and a stoic expression. She knew her mother wanted well for her. The obstacle was each woman's definition of "well".

Her father offered, "If you wanted to stay here, I could put Leo to work on the farm. You wouldn't have to rush off."

Louise swallowed back a knot of sadness. "Thank you, but Leo already has a job."

"If things change, you two come home."

The music was calling and would carry the Zints into their new coupled life. As the reception wound down, Louise went to her shared bedroom to change into her traveling clothes.

She was folding her wedding dress when she heard her mother scold, "Be careful with that dress, so it doesn't get ruined."

"I am."

Then Louise turned and watched her mother scrutinize her. Her eyes, so like Louise's, closed and then opened. "You're getting ready to leave for some gypsy life far from your family and town. What if something happens to you?"

"I'll be fine. I may not know exactly what my life

will be like, but I know some things from Leo's letters. I'll write to you and the family and let you know
what's about."

Louise turned away and put on her wedding hat.
"Leo and the band are waiting. I need to finish."

Her mother was quiet, but Louise heard her
breathing and could imagine what the matriarch
was thinking: this is a risk. Letters are different
from living. She'll be far away. Louise's internal
voice acknowledged her mother's concerns. But the
risk of the imagined life trumped the mundane life
here.

The sound of the doorknob turning told Louise
her mother was leaving the room. Before going Mrs.
Miller said, "Change out of those fancy t-strap heels
and into your everyday brown shoes. I'll send your
father upstairs to get your suitcase."

When Louise was again alone she looked around
her childhood bedroom, memorizing the blocked
quilt, the tied rag rug, and the feel of three girls who
had shared a bed for as long as Louise could remember. She knew she'd miss Rose, and maybe
Martha too.

A quick one knock and her father called,
"Coming in! Is my girl ready?"

"All set."

He cast around the bedroom like he did when
looking for a stray calf. His voice lowered an octave,
"Your suitcase is packed."

She bit her lower lip. "This town isn't big enough to support a musician, let alone a band of them."

Or me.

Her Father took her hand and turned it palm up. He placed in it an envelope she knew contained money and then folded her long fingers around the bulky paper. She stared at the patches and cracks of his dry, chaffed farmer skin which no gloves could prevent. He squeezed her narrow knuckles and then let go.

CHAPTER FIVE

The Musicale's instruments and luggage were stacked and cinched to the Ford Model T's rooftop and body. The car looked less sleek luster and more bumpy, broad box. Louise sat in the back seat between Karl and Leo whose arm curled around her shoulders.

Erik hung over the front seat. "If we all get a gal we're going to need a bigger automobile."

Colson in the driver's seat said, "With you, we'd need a bus to ferry all your lady friends. Let's see how it goes with Louise traveling with us."

Louise speculated if Leo had to convince the Musicale to let her come along.

Rose jumped onto the running board. "Be sure to write. Don't forget us."

Louise blinked back tears. "I will. I won't." Then

she looked at her parents. They stood next to each other, one's shoulder touching the other's shoulder. She waved, and her father waved back. Her mother nodded.

The engine knocked and shuttered, and the sedan started down the dirt driveway. Louise looked back at her family. The balloon tires rotated, and a trailing ribbon of dust hindered her view until acceleration and distance made them disappear.

Louise was on her way. Was she sure about this? It was too late to change her mind.

Leo squeezed Louise's shoulder, then kissed her cheek. "This will work."

The vehicle turned onto the county highway, orienting east to the larger north shore town of Abigail, Minnesota.

Erik asked Colson, "Are you thinking to look for a quick job tonight in Saint Paul since we're going through?"

"Yeah. Make a little money and have some fun if we can."

In the next hours, Louise watched fields and fencing appear and recede with occasional interruptions of small towns and speed limits while listening to the men's conversation. She was keen to see the capital city. Being Leo's wife was making her feel braver and bolder.

When the Musicale was on the periphery of downtown Saint Paul, Colson pulled over. "I'll ask around if anyone needs a band tonight. You all wait here. If I can't book something, then how about we eat and keep driving to Abigail?"

Louise wasn't sure if she was supposed to make and voice a choice. She said nothing and followed Leo's agreement to the plan.

Colson went hunting for a promising prospect. The remaining Musicale leaned against the Ford.

"What do you think?" Leo asked.

Louise made slow visual passes of the stone and brick buildings and watched horse-powered steel and sinew move up and down the street. "I want to see more of it all."

"On its way. This country is so big it would take a lifetime to travel it."

"Do you want to see it all?" Louise asked.

"Sure. I like looking at tall city buildings that shadow the small ones, rolling prairie that doesn't want to stop, mountains that take your breath away, and small towns like Wheatville."

Louise took in the men wearing suits or delivery uniforms and the women whose dresses didn't have a hint of homemade. To her, everyone appeared fashionable.

I want to be like them. I want to dress like them.

Her mother, opposed to most anything city-related, would have prejudged the passersby to be missing the good sense God gave them.

"I know what small towns and prairie look like. I'll take the cities and the mountains," Louise said.

Forty minutes passed before the group heard Colson's sharp alerting whistle. When near he said, "Got us a late gig at Reynold's Supper Club. The pay isn't much, but the manager said we can keep any tips and get a free midnight supper."

Louise wondered how much "wasn't much."

Leo asked Colson, "Where are we sleeping tonight?"

Colson, with an arched eyebrow, said, "We could sleep in the car after the show before heading north. I suspect the local law would frown upon that. Or leave right away and pull off onto some country road and bed down. I asked the Reynolds manager about places to stay around here. He suggested a house down the road owned by some Romanian matron. Says it's not a palace, but it's cheap and clean."

Louise kept her expression neutral. Would they all sleep in the car? She had not slept in a car before. From Leo's letters, Louise had presumed there was almost always boardinghouse or hotel rooms available. Clean was relative after growing up on a farm.

"Let's get a couple of rooms at the boardinghouse. This is my wedding night," Leo said.

Louise knew blushes striped her cheeks and forehead.

Erik asked, "Colson, are you going to make us

bunk up triple, so we only have to pay for two rooms?"

"Yup. We talked about this before. Now that there's five of us, we'll have to decide about the lodging as we go along."

Colson drove several miles and stopped at a weather-worn multi-story lopsided Victorian house. The left side sloped up as the right side sunk into the ground and the front porch had detached from the house. Louise's mother would never have stayed in such a place, but Louise loved the adventure of it all: her wedding day, the city, tonight's show, and this eccentric boardinghouse.

In for a penny, in for a pound.

A leg stretch gap separated the porch from the front door. The band surrounded Colson as he swung his suitcase forward and knocked it on the weathered grey-brown door.

An older woman, inches taller than the doorknob, with a tidy bun wearing a faded, starched corseted dress opened the door and rumbled a smoky "yes?"

"I'm Colson, and this is my band. We need two rooms for the night."

"You have money?"

"Yes. You have rooms?"

"Goot. Then we have agreement," the Romanian said and swung back the door.

"Ladies first," Leo said.

Louise marveled at this strange and ridiculous entrance into the house.

"Sweetheart, you can do it."

With a laugh and leap, she was over and in. Leo and the men followed.

The landlady escorted them through shabby rooms permeated with stale smells of cooked cabbage and potatoes, faded flowered wallpaper, and mis-matched, minimal furniture. "This room is dining room, but we do not use. We eat in kitchen. Through there," she pointed down the hallway toward the back of the house. "Breakfast is between six and eight o'clock. Be late, food gone. We have indoor plumbing, but sometimes it doesn't work, so we use outhouse out back." The matron marched up the staircase and commanded. "Follow."

"We have a pair of newlyweds—married today," Colson said.

Over her shoulder, the landlady eyed Louise. "In Romanian, we say, casa de piatra. Means...stone house. Strong. Doesn't blow away in wind. I put you in back room. You sing? Play instrument?"

Before Louise could reply, Colson assigned, "Louise helps with the managerial aspects."

Louise was surprised to hear Colson's response. She wondered what 'managerial' meant.

I'll ask later.

She followed Leo into a closet of a room. Inside was a short bed a little bigger than a cot. A black-spotted silver mirror hung above a chipped white pitcher and washbowl with hand-painted peonies that sat on a scratched wood dresser.

Leo said, "This isn't so bad. The rooms come and go." He placed their suitcases next to a heavily varnished curved-back wood chair in the corner.

"I like it," Louise said.

Leo grabbed ahold of her hand. "That's my girl."

Louise preened. She liked his new endearment.

He gave a soft tug towards the door. "We have a few hours before the show. Let's have a look at the city."

After Leo showed Louise how to board the streetcars, they rode the lines, passing window shop displays, and admiring the city's motion and commotion and hopping off to saunter around Lake Como before returning to the boardinghouse. Louise was caught in the wonderment of her hour and a half honeymoon and the miles of sidewalks.

Back in their room, Leo turned, and with his back to her changed into his Musicale suit. Louise averted her eyes and stared hard at the water pitcher's painted pink peony petals.

"I'm dressed. I'll wait outside so you can change by yourself. Then we'll go downstairs," Leo said.

"Thank you," Louise whispered.

Leo opened the door. "I know we're still getting to know each other. We'll take it slow."

She felt reassured by Leo's promise to ease into

the intimacy of marriage. Her butterflies then shifted into a dilemma when she changed back into her wedding dress. Louise was certain it wasn't sophisticated enough for going to a club, but it was her best dress. She'd need to buy new dresses for Musicale gigs.

Louise opened the door. "Hello, Mr. Zint."

Leo stepped in front of her. "Hi, Mrs. Zint." He touched her wrists and glided his hands up to rest at her elbows. Desire rushed up from Louise's belly causing an electrified ripple across her skin. They came together in a kiss. A sweetness flooded her making her hot from the inside out.

The yell. "Zint, let's go," interrupted. Louise sighed, and Leo swore.

Colson yelled again, "Evening's started. We gotta go!"

It was Louise's first night with the Musicale.

CHAPTER SIX

Karl drove the band to the restaurant. While stopped at an intersection Colson and Erik's boisterous singing roared out of the automobile.

"Where's the party?" a driver a lane over hooted.

Colson hollered, "Reynold's Supper Club. We're playing tonight. Come on by."

Several automobiles behind the conversing cars honked their horns attempting to move along the conversation. Erik and Leo hung out of the vehicle whooping and waving. Louise laughed and joined in.

They parked near the restaurant and began unloading. Colson, a watchman for any-moment marketing, let his baritone fly suggesting everyone misbehave. The rest of them harmonized in the chorus. They traipsed after Colson carrying instrument cases and a drum kit. Louise kicked up her heels as she paraded along with the minstrel preshow. Their musical circus attracted the attention of sidewalk strollers and street drivers.

After two blocks, Colson stopped at a neon basement sign that said Reynold's Supper Club. With a flourish he said, "Here it is."

A cramped entryway led into a long narrow room that started as a dining room wallpapered in burgundy brocade, pushed past a mahogany bar area, and ended with a ten-foot space between the last table and an upright piano pushed against a painted black brick wall.

Colson pointed towards the piano. "That's our stage."

"How do you want us to set up?" Leo asked.

Erik looked around the half-occupied dining tables. "Might have to take a seat at some gal's table. Maybe a redhead tonight."

Colson ignored Erik and began directing the band. "Karl in back, I'll be at the piano, Leo next to me, and Erik on the other side of Leo. Louise, find a spot nearby. Now let's talk about the set. Leo, I'll need you on the piano for some songs. We'll adjust the song list as we need, but let's get something ready for the first hour."

The men settled onto the stage and began tuning their instruments. Standing offstage Louise reveled in it all. She didn't know Leo played piano too. The show would start soon! Louise couldn't wait to hear

Leo play again. What kind of crowd would show? Who would misbehave?

A bow-tied waiter no older than Leo or Karl approached the band. "You fellas want a drink before the show starts?"

Erik answered, "Bring five glasses. We're celebrating."

Louise knew her eyes were big and shocked. The law said no drinking, but this speakeasy paid no heed.

"Do the drinks make you nervous?" Leo asked.

"Yes," she whispered. "It surprised me. I'll get used to it."

"That's my girl."

The waiter returned carrying a tray of drinks. "This is the state's specialty: Minnesota 13 whiskey. First round is free. If you want more, you'll have to pay for it."

Colson raised his glass. "To a good show and good years. Cheers."

Leo clinked his glass with Louise's. Her first swallow burned her lips before dropping like a geyser down the hole. She sputtered and coughed. Leo rubbed circles on the small of her back.

Louise croaked, "I'm all right. You better get settled." She studied the speakeasy's layout. She wasn't sure where to sit.

"There's room at the bar end where you can sit and still see the band," Leo said.

Louise heaved relief. "I like that. Good luck tonight."

Stationed nearby and out of the way, she asked for a glass of water to cool the whiskey. In Wheatville, homebrewing beer and wine had been moved out-of-sight but kept on hand. Public drinking would take getting used to.

The Musicale started their show with easy-does-it, sliding in songs. Louise tapped her foot and bounced to the music. Her body tightened and flexed with the sounds of Leo's violin. He regularly swiveled towards her with cocky grins and winks.

When the restaurant was full, the band swung free and wild. Waiters moved tables out-of-the-way to create a larger dancefloor. The occupancy, plus the energetic musical showmanship had the band wiping sweat with their handkerchiefs.

Louise studied how Colson measured the audience for every degree of revelry accepted, demanded, or denied. Colson adapted and redirected to satisfy and elevate the patrons. Those Saint Paul diners responded the loudest to the hot beats of jazz and the sizzling standards.

Erik played his various horns and smiled at the good time girls. Karl watched the crowd listen, linger, and let loose. Leo appeared to mirror Colson's attentiveness and at the same time feed the audience and tempt them with more.

A slowed, weighted closing time tempo had the

merrymakers pulling partners close and swinging like grandfather clock pendulums. The Midwest Musicale Extravaganza finished on tired, inebriated applause. The musicians put away their instruments as the restaurant nudged the last night owls out the door.

"Attaboys," Colson called.

Louise walked over to where the sweaty, pleased men were talking. Leo stood up and kissed her, then asked, "What did you think?" and before she could answer, "Fun, isn't it."

Erik closed his horn case. "I need to see a man about a dog?"

Colson slapped him on the back. "Fine idea."

Louise asked Leo, "Why would Erik need to see a man about a dog? It's past one in the morning."

"He's getting booze for the road," Leo said.

"Let's find out what kind of food this joint feeds people and something to wet our whistle," Colson said.

The manager, a blond hair, blue-eyed Scandinavian tree of a man, approached and said, "follow" and led them to several tables pushed together. "Sit," he commanded. They sat, and he walked away.

Colson yelled, "What are you feeding us?"

The manager yelled back, "Food."

A waiter set three plates of sanguine German sausages whose salt, black pepper, garlic, and mustard seed smelled bold, along with heavy boiled potatoes and fried translucent buttered onions. Cold beer came next and cooled the heated spice. The men cheered when they saw Erik return carrying a cardboard box. He pulled out two bottles of Minnesota 13 and set one at each end of the table near empty plates and foam-dripping beer glasses.

"Courtesy of Corn Cob Nick's," Erik said.

Colson belted down more whiskey and then out in song. The other musicians followed his lead. Louise clapped and sang along when she could. The band resurrected their instruments and the supper table transformed into an impromptu breakfast dance.

A cigarette girl began dancing with a waiter. They high-stepped a fast pace. The bartender refilled the beer glasses, and the Musicale played and drank while arms and cigarettes flashed about.

Louise tipped back her whiskey glass. In those last sips, the fire of what her mother called the devil's drink cavorted along her limbs. She stood and stepped forward, tap, stepped back, tap, and arms up in the Charleston swing. A busboy jumped into partner with her.

Later the manager called out, "It's after two o'clock. One more, then we all go home."

The rhythm switched to a slow burn. Louise watched Leo put down his fiddle and walk to her. His index finger tapped the shoulder of her dance partner. Holding his left elbow squared and his right hand up they eased into each other's arms and space for their first dance.

Leo's catgut string-calloused hand pressed flat on her back. His smoother bow hand held her farm-worked calloused hand. His breath fanned across her ear and neck. When the music ended, they did not step back but stayed touching a few seconds more.

"There'll be some more dancing after this show," Erik razzed the newlyweds.

Leo lifted his head. "You're just jealous. Go find your own gal."

"Thought I had, but she had to go home to her mother."

"You mean her husband. Heck, she thought you were a traveling salesman."

Good-natured hoots flew with the banter.

"I am of the more romantic variety," Erik said and then took a sip of whiskey.

Karl inquired, "What type of wares were you displaying?"

Erik tipped back on his chair and the front two legs lifted off the floor. "The impressive kind."

Karl twirled a drum stick with his fingers. "Are you sure the ladies weren't just interested in your horns?"

Leo tossed on, "You mean the ones sticking out of his head?"

"I am devilishly good looking," Erik said.

"Gather up, boys," Colson interrupted. "And

Louise, too. Settle down. We don't want to have to stop and answer questions from the city's good servants."

The band returned to the car with more stagger than swagger.

The jawing dwindled but did not terminate. Louise wondered if they were often this rowdy or if being in the capital city, the luck of finding a paying job, the evening's libations, or her and Leo's wedding had launched the men into higher celebratory moods. The Zints settled into the Ford's backseat thigh to thigh and shoulder to shoulder. Leo picked up Louise's hand and held it in between both of his. She shivered at the connection.

At the house, Colson ordered, "Be quiet and get the instruments inside. Stand up straight and walk ordinary. That landlady does not appear forgiving."

The behave order was forgotten. The band spoke in loud whispers and accelerated into noisy pea-cocking boasts and insults.

The landlady opened the door wearing her heavy blanket robe and a reprimanding expression. "Vhat are you doing? Quiet. This is goot neighborhood."

They jumped the porch gap and entered half stumbling across the threshold.

Erik threw an arm around the squawking woman's shoulders and planted a smacking kiss on her cheek. "Found my new gal."

Laughter congratulated. The woman didn't

throw off the arm but instead slid out from under with pink spotted cheeks.

Colson bowed to the landlady. "We apologize for the ruckus. Too much celebrating the newlyweds."

The landlady sniffed. "More celebrating can be done later in daytime." Then, directing a raised eyebrow and knowing smile at Leo and Louise, "Everyone bed."

Louise swallowed hard. Her heartbeat accelerated, and her hand shook in Leo's as they walked up the stairs. She considered if Leo was scared too.

Their steps slowed to the bedroom. Leo turned the brass doorknob.

Through closed bedroom doors, Louise and her siblings had heard their parents' private moments. The care and raising of livestock had taught her about the mechanics of sex, but she fixated on how she and Leo would fit together. Would it hurt? What if things didn't work right?

Louise walked to the center of the bedroom. She stood there and bit her lower lip.

Leo put his arms around her waist and touched his chest to her back. "It's going to be okay."

Louise's arms hung by her sides. "Will they hear us?"

"Doubt it. After all that booze, they'll fall into beds and be snoring up a storm."

She tried to relax into Leo's embrace. "What do you want from me? I mean, what do you expect?"

Leo circled to Louise's front. "I expect that since this is your first time, we'll go slow." Then his hands and tongue caressed hers. Their bodies pressed and flattened the air molecules between them.

Louise stepped back, pulled her dress over her head, and draped it on the chair. Leo watched, his eyes gleaming in the faint illumination of the gaslight. Turning her back to Leo, she undid the hooks and fabrics of her undergarments. She could hear him remove his clothing and waited until all undressing sounds ceased.

She had to turn around. Leo was her husband.

Louise swiveled back and looked from high to low at Leo's hair, clavicles, ribs, the intimate in between, and stopped at his feet as he did to her.

Leo stepped to Louise and curled his hands around her shoulders. Holding the slim columns in a light grasp, his thumbs swept back and forth over her pebbled skin. He put his forehead to hers until she stopped shaking.

Louise unlocked her arms and rested her hands on Leo's waist. Their heads angled and lips touched. He guided her to the bed. Their kisses, caresses, and limbs learned the anatomy of the other.

After, they lay intertwined on the narrow mattress. Leo slept while Louise thought about their lovemaking. It had been more fumbling and patience then fluidity and finesse. The care Leo had taken reassured Louise that this part of their marriage had started well.

They woke to the band's footfalls pounding downstairs to breakfast and sunlight cutting through the threadbare curtains. The noise began to crack the intimate chrysalis that the Zints had created a few hours earlier.

Leo kissed her. "Morning."

Louise's eyelids fluttered from sleepiness.

Leo's finger stroked her cheek. "Are you okay? Did I hurt you?"

"I'm well."

"I'm glad. We should get dressed and go downstairs. Abigail is waiting."

Louise watched Leo rise up from the bed and begin to pick up clothes. "Will tonight be like last night?"

Leo chuckled. "I hope so."

CHAPTER SEVEN

Mrs. Louise Zint had been traveling with the Musicale for three months. She adopted the band's night owl routine of evening gigs and after-parties, afternoon band rehearsal and exploring, clumps of days waiting for work, and a travel schedule mated to change. Colson delegated bookkeeping, uniform mending, and catchall tasks to Louise. She became a relied-on band member. Louise enjoyed her new job and the lifestyle her marriage and the music provided.

To save money, and sometimes without lodging options, the band camped. Many of these nights included the buzz and nuisance of mosquitos and crickets competing with the Musicale's jam sessions.

In October, they were driving from South Dakota to Chicago for an extended temporary engagement at a speakeasy who suddenly lost its house band. They stopped for the night near a grove of tall cottonwoods.

A midnight blue deep darkness encircled their campsite. Erik and Leo set up tents around the wiggling and snapping campfire. The cloudless sky allowed the twinkling stars and a warm white full moon to spotlight the campers. Sitting on a blanket, Louise and Karl played two-handed gin rummy. Leo on the violin and Erik on the guitar pressed and plucked spirited ditties.

Colson added his harmonica to the night sounds. It's flutters and wheezes levitated and hovered in the air. That palm-sized instrument's vibrations brushed their souls and burned away travel fatigue, fickle rest, and close quarters.

Later the moonlight shone through a rip in the top of the Zint's tent.

"Look at that moon. Hard to see that in a city," Leo said.

Louise wriggled closer to Leo for more warmth. "That roof barely keeps the rain out. Why should moonlight be any different?"

"I like that it's our roof. This tent is our home."

Louise waved her hand upward. "Our home is on the road. If we want to keep that canvas over our heads, we'll have to patch it."

She was fond of their put-down and pick-up shelter. She savored the magical nights under starlight, and also by electrical light. Rural electrification had not reached Wheatville, her hometown. Louise enjoyed the use and convenience of electricity. In a few days, they'd be in Chicago. Louise relished Leo's letter promise to show her the city.

Leo brushed his hand up and down her forearm. "Sometimes it'd be nice to stay in a place longer. Have our own address."

Louise snorted with laughter. "A traveling band doesn't need an address. We'll be in Chicago for three months. That's a long time for the band to stay somewhere."

"It is. I'm glad we can stay put there for a while. That city is something to see."

Louise smiled in the dark. "I can't wait."

The Musicale took up temporary residence as the Vines Club's house band. The interior included bowtie waiters, pressed white tablecloths, and painted murals of grapevines, stone arches and skinny, peaked trees. Before their inaugural performance, the Musicale had two days to learn the chorus girl's routine music and work out any kinks. In the interim, substitute musicians played a cobbled version of the evening revue.

Louise thought the Chicago women were the most glamorous yet. More so now, she knew her working wardrobe needed city airs. On her first afternoon at the Vines, a showgirl named Polly invited Louise to use the ladies dressing room. "Listen hon, if you need to get away from those men of yours, you just come to our dressing room. It's crowded, but you can relax. I have to get gussied up. Bye."

A "thank you" tumbled out of Louise. The next night before the Vines' evening entertainment began, she found the offered-up room.

At the doorway, shyness and homesickness squeezed Louise. She missed her sisters and several former classmates. The Musicale's moving invited acquaintanceships but made it difficult to make friends. Spending most of her time with Leo and the band created a vacuum of girlfriends.

Posters of past shows, magazine pages, and news-paper cutouts decorated the walls. Scattered on the floor were all colors and sizes of feathers and sequins. Glass perfume atomizers, lipstick tubes, glittering headpieces, high heeled shoes, and show clothes were hung and flung throughout the room. This feminine nest of ladybirds showcased sorority and sass. Louise wanted in.

"Hey girlie, any reason you're stuck in the door-way?" a cigarette-smoked voice asked.

Louise turned to the speaker. Near the door, a long-legged showgirl with bobbed black waves and a matching oriental silk robe was seated in front of a dressing table and mirror. Louise mumbled, "I was just looking around."

"Come on in. I'm Cleone. What's your name?"

"I'm Louise Zint. My husband Leo is the Musi-cale's violin player."

Louise watched Cleone eye her then take a deep puckered pull on her cigarette and blow out a small comet of smoke. "So, your man's in the band. What do you do?"

"Assistant manager," Louise claimed at that moment.

"Smart choice. Before that?"

"A small farm town."

Cleone turned to her reflection. She pressed a makeup puff into a jar of powder and then patted her face. "Country girl heads for the big city?"

"Something like that."

"Welcome to Chicago. I gotta finish getting ready. See you around."

Louise stared with envy as the exotic woman added more black mascara to her already darkened lashes.

The next morning in their rented boardinghouse room, Louise woke Leo early and said, "I'd like to use some of my father's wedding money to buy a dress."

With a sleepy frown, Leo said, "Why are you asking? If you need a dress, buy a dress."

"A dress like the women at the club wear will be expensive."

With twinkling tender eyes, Leo said, "Make sure you can dance in it."

"Of course."

"We can go downtown this afternoon," Leo suggested.

"How about now?"

Soon enough they passed grocers, pharmacies, and all other varieties of storefronts. Louise pursed her lips in a flat line of firm intention as she and Leo canvassed dress boutiques. Then she saw it. 'Lady Lennox's Dress Shop.'

Louise stood in the shop alcove and admired the coin-sized porcelain ivory and onyx floor tiles. Daylight reflected a high-quality polish. Through the tall shop door window, she saw hanging daisy shaped lights and a hip-high glass counter that displayed silver and gold tubes and compacts, evening gloves, handbags, and other beauty accessories. Dress racks lined the walls. A giddiness pulsed in her hand and she pushed open the door before her brain could hesitate.

The tiles ended at the door's threshold and honey wood herringbone parquet pointed Louise deeper into the shop.

"Good afternoon. Can I assist you?" a sales clerk a few years older than Louise asked. The woman reminded her of the wild swans that summered on the lakes around Wheatville. Her carriage supple straight as she glided in her pale green crepe blouse and matching paneled skirt.

"I'm looking for a party dress," Louise said, presenting in what she hoped was Cleone's statuesque poise.

The clerk dipped her chin and replied, "Does Madame have a particular color in mind?"

"No, but I'm in a band, and the dress will need to be appropriate for the club."

"We have many fine dresses that would complement your slim size. This way, please."

Louise realized Leo was not beside her. She twisted around and saw he stood next to the front door. His fedora in his hands, he waited. Louise returned to him.

Leo began, "I'll go up the street while you find your dress. When should I come back?"

"Two hours will be fine."

Leo brushed a quick kiss to Louise's check and sprung out of the shop.

Louise squeezed her hand over her mouth to keep her belly laugher from escaping. She walked through the clerk's trailing rose perfume to a rack displaying four dresses.

"Madame, here are a few selections that you may wish to try on."

Being away from the farm had softened and smoothed Louise's hands, but she was almost afraid to touch the beautiful, expensive clothing. The most elegant and intricate was a drop waist gold beaded Egyptian evening gown. The next was a muted robin egg blue silk with four white Fleur de Lis panels. The third was a sleeveless dark royal blue satin.

The last was an art deco ebony sleek satin with a

bright white geometric triangle on the left front torso. Nipped arm cuffs closed with rounded pearl buttons and a hem that would land at her knee. The last dress was all lady and go. Louise gestured to it. "I'll try that one, please."

"Wonderful. Please follow me."

After Louise stepped into the dressing room the clerk pulled closed the heavy drapery privacy curtain. Alone with the dress, Louise's muscles buzzed with electrified anticipation. She dropped her ordinary light blue dress to the floor, then slipped on the black and white creation. Louise's hands skimmed like a waterfall across her collarbone, over her breasts, sliding overtop her stomach, and past her hip bones. Louise knew this dress would be her touchstone uniform for the Musicale.

The clerk interrupted her dreaminess. "How is the dress? Would you prefer to try on the black and gold?"

Louise pushed aside the curtain. She strode over to the shop's trifold mirror and studied herself. Lifting her chin, she succumbed to the sophisticated women reflected. "I'll take this."

"Excellent. You look beautiful and stylish. Our seamstress will measure you. When do you need the dress?"

"As soon as possible."

"If you have time to wait, we can attend to the alterations immediately. Do you require accessories? We have a selection of stockings and lipsticks."

"I can wait. I'll need new stockings, please."

After Louise's measurements were taken, the women moved to a table of silk and rayon stockings. Louise pulled the fabrics between her fingers. The silk's soft texture produced goosebumps. Louise wavered between the fine and delicate silk and the less expensive and practical rayon.

Later as Louise paid at the counter, an internal voice that sounded akin to her mother's prudence said *the ebony dress is yours, the rayon is enough, don't dwell on silk.*

The Lady Lennox in training said, "Thank you. Enjoy your new dress."

Louise walked out of the shop and did not stop until she moved beyond the boutique windows. Exhilarated and wobbly, she pressed herself against the brick building next door and looked up at the sky. A distance, not just measured in miles, separated Louise from that small town farmgirl that Leo had first met. The happiness within her wanted to bust out.

Leo found her staring upwards. "Sweetheart, are you okay?"

Louise twirled. "I like my dress!"

"It must be some dress. We need to head back. Tonight's the night."

Back at the boardinghouse, Louise said, "You get

ready first, then go shoot the breeze with Erik while I change. I want to surprise you."

"He's going to rib me some about being kicked out of the bedroom so soon."

"Yes, but you get to come back in."

Alone, Louise slipped into her new dress. The satin made her skin prickle and shiver. She fluffed her hair, applied the black mascara and red rouge and lipstick her mother had prohibited, and dabbed lily of the valley behind each ear. Louise knew Leo would be dazzled.

He knocked on the door. "Are you ready?"

Crossing the threshold, Louise sauntered into the hallway with one hand placed on her waist. Beaming a thousand-lumen smile at her husband, she spun smooth as if she was standing in a molasses puddle.

Not saying a word but taking her in from crown to heels, he raised his eyebrows and said, "You're beautiful. That's some dress."

"Thank you. It's a big night."

Leo offered his tuxedo clad arm. "Time for the Musicale to entertain Chicago."

On the way to the club, a masculine fretting of tight-lipped silence and occupied thoughts damned the easy flow of before show banter. The men looked polished and dapper in their new band uniforms. These Chicago audiences were used to first-class music. Louise knew the band wanted to win the customers' adoration and repeated attendance.

The Musicale's overture launched high and fast. Their music flew up and through the low-ceilinged room lighting up ears and eyes like fireworks. Playing solo and as the soundtrack for the chorus girls, the evening displayed swank, silhouettes, and musical theater.

Due to the volume and velocity of this job, there was an hour break at eleven o'clock. A comedian took the stage as the band went backstage to replenish for their second set.

Louise handed each musician a towel and a glass of whiskey. "The music was flying out there. Charles Lindbergh would have had a hard time keeping up,"

"Lindbergh stopped in Chicago earlier this year on his goodwill flying tour. Wish I could have seen him fly," Karl said.

"We need you here on the ground," Erik said.

Colson began to pace. "You boys are doing great. Let's keep up the energy and push. It's going to take everything we have to satisfy that crowd. This isn't a small town barn dance. Leo, lighten up on your strings. Erik, make sure you're on pitch. Karl, no holding back."

"I'm on pitch," Erik snapped.

Colson's focus was directed towards an unseen list. "Our transitions aren't quick enough. We have to start rethinking our arrangements. Pick up a few extra players while here."

"Extra players would build up our sound. We could experiment more," Leo said.

Colson nodded. "We'll keep to the playlist we have and make changes tomorrow."

Later as the band returned to the stage, Leo lagged behind. He asked Louise, "How do you think we're doing out there?"

She straightened Leo's new black bowtie. "I love what I'm hearing. Colson's right about your strings. Make those fancy people want more."

Leo kissed her. "See you after the show."

"I'll be waiting."

CHAPTER EIGHT

A week later, the band and Louise sat at the Vines' bar having post-performance breakfast drinks when she saw Cleone leave the main room and head to the showgirls' dressing room. Louise admired the sashay and tone of Cleone. This was a woman who lived in the bigger world.

Louise knew having a baby could limit, or end, her life on the road. Several dancers in Milwaukee had whispered about stopping a pregnancy, but Louise wanted to prevent. Her mother would be aghast at such a desire. Louise hadn't come this far to be deterred.

She wound her way to the showgirls' room and found Cleone and the other dancers depluming the feathers and sparkle off their bodies.

In a private voice, Louise said, "Cleone, can I speak with you?"

"Hey, Louise! Did you like our show?"

"Yes, you and the girls have a bang-up revue. I was wondering if you could help me with something?"

Cleone leaned forward. "Spill."

Louise tensed and she squeezed her elbows into her sides. "I need...I need to know how...what...I need to know how to prevent getting pregnant?"

Cleone nodded.

Louise kept speaking. "Getting pregnant would change things. I like where Leo and I are going. Settling down can wait. I need to know how to keep things as they are?"

Cleone tapped her lips with a finger. ""Small town has more smarts than I realized. There are few ways to do this. There's what's called a diaphragm. It's a piece of rubber you put up inside when needed. That's probably your best bet."

"How do I get one of those?"

"I have a special friend I can ask. Give me a day or two. When was your last monthly?" Cleone asked.

"Last week."

"Good. That keeps things simple."

"How much money do you want?"

"Let's wait on that."

Louise's shoulders sagged. "Thank you. I had

better go. Leo is probably wondering where I am. Enjoy your morning."

Cleone threw up her arm like a pageant queen. "Ha! The night's not over."

As Louise walked the hallway back to the main room, she felt the taut concern within her was being loosened with Cleone's help. Louise and Leo hadn't spoken about family planning. She didn't know how to bring it up. If she started using the diaphragm or whatever he would know. Louise wasn't sure what to do.

On Monday evening, the Musicale had the night off. She and Leo went to a club he had visited the last time he was in Chicago. They walked down an alley and entered through a backdoor into an empty shop. Nailed wood sheets covered windows and faded Arabian carpets the walls. Mismatched small tables and chairs were scattered about the room.

It was the first time Louise had seen an all-black band perform. Louise, Leo, and a few other white people were the minority in the place. Instead of feeling unwelcome, she felt special listening and dancing to improvised jazz, swing, and ragtime riffs.

After the show, as they exited the alley, Louise said, "Thank you for taking me there."

"My pleasure. I know the place looked different, but I didn't want us to miss some of the city's best music. Were you uncomfortable?"

Louise considered the question. "A little at first.

I'll go back again and again if I can hear that wonderful music and see all that dancing."

The comfort of their conversation made Louise want to tell Leo about the birth control. It's now or later.

"Leo, I need to tell you something." The seriousness in her voice stopped their meander. "I like the life we're living, and I don't want it to stop. If I had a baby, our lives would be different."

"That's true. Living on the road is no home for a kid."

"We agree. Cleone said she'd help me get something to prevent me from getting pregnant until we're ready."

"Is it dangerous?"

"I don't think so. I trust Cleone."

Leo squeezed Louise's hand. "I knew I found myself a smart girl."

"You're not mad?" Louise asked.

"More relieved. I've been trying to be careful, but mother nature can be wily."

Three days later Cleone found Louise alone sitting at the bar while the Musicale practiced on stage before the Vines opened for the night. "I have something for you," then she batted her eyelashes at the bartender, "Two Southside gins, please."

Then back to Louise, "We'll take our drinks and head to the dressing room. It's early. Most of the girls haven't arrived. Grab your drink, let's go. Thank you, Mister Bar Man."

Louise smelled the fresh juniper before taking a sip. The showgirl held her drink aloft and waved to the staff calling out "heys" and "evenings" until they reached the room.

"Who's here?" Cleone called out. No one answered. "I spoke with my friend. He was able to get ahold of a diaphragm for you, plus he included a little book. Have a seat there. You can look at the how-to's now and ask me questions. I have to get ready for tonight. When you're done, you can help get those stinker side hooks on my costume."

The brown paper bag Cleone handed her felt light and misleading in its significant weight. Louise sat down and withdrew one of the two items. She read the small 'Marriage Hygiene' book as if it held a skittish secret.

When Louise looked up she saw Cleone watching her in the mirror. The showgirl asked, "How you doing there?"

"This will do. Thank you."

"Any questions?" Cleone asked.

"No."

Cleone stood, and the apple red fringe of her costume beads knocked and shimmered in the movement. "A woman doesn't get a whole lot of choices in this world. When you get married, the law says, your husband's in charge. Take care of yourself and, if you can, have a good time while it lasts. A dame has to have moxie. Try not to take guff from anyone. Now help me with these dress hooks."

During the evening show, Louise thought about what Cleone had said. When Leo asked to write to her, Louise said yes. When Leo turned up on the farm and proposed marriage and the Musicale life, she said yes. Louise was saying yes again to having a say about her future. Louise didn't know if she had moxie, but she was taking this opportunity too.

To Louise living in Chicago was like being in her own happy personal movie. There were music numbers, chorus girls and flappers, parties, touring city sights, and access to the latest inventions and fads. Her family on the farm would not have easily recognized Louise.

Late in the afternoon on Christmas Eve, the Vines hosted a private party for employees and friends of the club. Louise had stitched small silver bells to the hem of her pine tree colored dress. She jingled and shimmied about the party of staff, gangsters, gals, and bohemians. When Leo wasn't playing, he partnered Louise in fast-stepping knee kicks and waving arms. It was a holiday of high spirits.

The New Year's Eve show was a larger holiday celebration. Everyone in the place wore paper party hats with their fine clothes, the drinks flowed like an unstoppable river, and the Musicale and the club's other acts delivered a razzle-dazzle show. Just before midnight, Colson announced the start of the ten second countdown to 1928. Louise joined the band and a myriad of performers on stage. Leo put his arm around her waist and her arm encircled him.

Karl thumped his bass drum each time the crowd yelled out decreasing numbers. When "Happy New Year" thundered in the room Louise and Leo shared a tipsy, happy kiss. The partiers tooted their paper horns and cheered. Leo let go and the band started playing 'Auld Lang Syne'. The assembled sang along. To Louise, the jumble of people somehow harmonized into a beautiful rendition that she wanted to remember forever. She thought of her Wheatville family and wished them well.

The new year meant the Musicale's Vines subbing residency was over and they would be moving south. Louise would miss the club, Cleone and the performers, and swing and spirit of her Chicago life. In a few days, the Musicale would leave and go to the next place. Earlier that day she and Leo had bundled up and walked along the lakeshore. Tonight, the Musicale had been invited to a club that Louis Armstrong was secretly playing.

Similar to the back alley place Leo had taken her to, this club was jammed full of folks, high and low smoke, and musicians whose nexus was Armstrong and his sounds that blended, bent, and bloomed for the crowd.

Armstrong's mouth filled his trumpet like a bicycle tire and his fingers moved up and down like a bank of elevators. His voice was like honey that dripped into the scratches and holes of people's souls. Entranced by the entertainer, Louise and Leo sat as if in church listening to Armstrong's version of divinity.

The place kicked everyone out at six the next morning. Leo, with his arm around Louise's shoulders, followed Colson, Erik, and Karl back to their rented rooms.

Louise hummed snippets of the evening songs and then said, "Armstrong is dynamite. His music is something not of this world. The wildman blues is accurate. Plus, we have Lou in our names."

Leo gave Louise a loving squeeze. "He blows his horn and sings like he's announcing to the world that it's time to shake the bad away and ride the music as long as you can."

Louise agreed. "That's good advice."

CHAPTER NINE

The Musicale's bookings sent them south across the snow-buried Midwest Plains. In late January, they halted in Kansas City, Missouri.

Louise wrote her family.

Hello Everyone!

Happy New Year from Kansas City. I hope the box of Christmas chocolates arrived in time. Leo and I are fine. December was as busy as expected. We ate Christmas Day dinner at a Chinese restaurant called the Noodle Parlor. Red and gold paper lanterns hung from the ceiling. We ordered chicken chow mein which is like spaghetti noodles with cut up vegetables and sauce.

We stopped in Iowa City and picked up a one-night gig at the local armory. The Musicale played a dance marathon called a bunion derby. During the

*morning hours, the dance promoters used a phono-
graph. I don't know who won. We left town before the
last couple dropped.*

*We have several February shows booked. I'm not
sure how long we will be in Kansas City. Late winter
is slow for business. Colson is making arrangements
for upcoming jobs. We saw Charlie Chaplin's movie
'The Circus.' It was funny and swell to see a movie
that showed summer days instead of the winter blues.
Say hi to everyone. I hope 1928 brings you all good
things.*

Love, Louise and Leo

She was certain little was said in the Miller
household about her and Leo's livelihood. As far as
her family knew from occasional letters, the Musicale
tended to play in town halls and barns. Any wildness
was edited out. Louise had met assorted entertainers
and people about town in her new life. The variety of
unconventional ways of living would have shocked
her family.

After she posted the letter, she returned to the
band's hotel and found the men in Colson's room
talking.

"Let's stay put for the next few weeks. The rooms
are cheap even if the weather is ugly," Colson said.

Leo tilted his head back and lifted his chin. "If
we head north, we can scout out for work. Someone
needs a band."

Erik who had been sitting on the window sill

stood up. "Why don't we have a rent party? People already pay to hear us play. What do you think Karl?"

Karl drummed his fingers. "Something will work out."

Leo rubbed his head. "I'm tired of this town. Nothing is going on."

"Plenty is going on; we just need to open some doors," Erik said.

Colson slapped his thigh. "Well then, it's time to open our door. I'll be the doorman and singer, you boys will play, and Louise will sell refreshments."

Erik whooped, then said, "When should Karl and I tell people to start coming by?"

"Around 9."

Louise asked Leo in an incredulous whisper. "We've been to rent parties, but now we're going to set up a makeshift club right here in our hotel rooms and charge people?"

"Yes. We'll need to pack up our things and move the furniture."

"I don't know about this."

"Don't worry. The Musicale has had rent parties before. Colson will make a deal with the hotel manager. Erik and Karl will work the streets inviting people. We'll get the place ready. Find all the glasses you can."

"Why?"

"For selling drinks."

Louise laid her hand flat on the wall. "We're selling booze? What about the police?"

"Leave that to Erik and Colson."

Louise goggled at her husband as he crossed the room and pushed the bed against the wall. She wanted to yell out that they were about to break the law, several laws. "I know it hasn't been easy getting gigs this month, but we're just in a slump. We don't need to get ourselves arrested."

Leo moved Colson's comb, hair cream, and other personal possessions from the dresser top into a drawer. "Replacing the Ford and all the other expenses, plus not having as many shows, we need to make some dough."

"If we're caught bootlegging, we could go to jail."

Leo pushed the dresser into a corner of the room. "We're not going to get caught. What's the difference between us selling and all the places we've played selling it?"

"Because if they're busted, they go to jail. Not the band."

Leo walked towards the door. "Trust me. Nothing bad is going to happen. We have to set up the other rooms."

He ignored her protests and concerns. Leo presumed she'd get over her angst and get to work. He didn't think they could get into trouble.

At eight-thirty p.m. Colson sang out, "Furniture

moved, booze ready, now let's get the instruments tuned. No band suits tonight."

Louise felt Leo's hand touch the small of her back. "Don't be sore. This will go off without a hitch. You'll see."

"This is risky."

Leo held out his hand. "Small risk. We need the money. I'll be keeping an eye on you. If something comes up, I'll see it before anything starts."

Louise slipped her hand into his, and he pulsed his grip a couple of times. "You might even have fun tonight."

She watched him saunter over to the impromptu band area. Louise wasn't one for church, but her need was such that she sent out a silent prayer to whoever would listen.

Louise walked to the corner table of liquor bottles and sandwiches they'd set up. Colson stood at the doorway greeting people with, "Come on in," "Welcome," and "Are you ready for a good time?"

Louise leaned against the table and watched Leo. Karl's measured drumbeat was the background for the light-hearted dueling strings of Eric's guitar and Leo's violin. He played proud and sure. His confidence boosted her some. People were crowding into Colson's room and through the connecting doorway into Erik and Karl's room. Some danced, most talked, and no one appeared concerned. Louise reconsidered that maybe this evening would go without a hitch.

Two young men threw their outside coats towards the wall. In long-sleeved button up shirts and suspenders they approached Louise's table. She asked, "What would you like?"

"Two beers."

Louise handed over the bottles and as she was accepting their money, a couple behind them asked for two whiskeys. Business at Louise's table was fast and easy. Her worry watered down with each drink she poured. She danced and sang as she served and imbibed.

Early the next morning. Leo and Louise stood in the middle of the main party room and watched the last trio, the hotel manager propped up by a man and woman on either side, wobble through the doorway into the hall. No instruments or windows were broken. The smells of spilled booze and crushed cigarettes complimented left behind debris that included a navy suit coat, red feathers, and one black high-heeled shoe. Colson slumped on the floor emitting loud nonharmonic snores.

"Good turnout. Did you have fun?" Leo asked.

Louise giggled. "Ah huh. I thought my heart was going to crash to the first floor when I saw those two police officers."

Leo stretched his arms over his head. "Their appearance did put everyone off for a moment or two. Thank goodness Erik yelled out, 'Come in fellows, we're all having a good time.' I suspect he asked them to come in uniform. Give people a little extra show for their money."

"Erik could have told us they would be stopping by. People got their money's worth. Tonight was fun, but selling booze rattled me. If we never repeated that, it would be fine with me."

The Musicale threw nine more pay-to-party hotel room shows before leaving Kansas City. Louise's fear decreased with each hosted evening, but the possibility of being arrested tinged her good-time. She was relieved when they moved on.

In the late spring the Musicale was in Denver. They played a bar which refused to pay them for two weeks' work. Colson and the owner shouted and threatened while the band and the staff froze in place.

Louise asked Leo, "What happens if they don't pay?"

Leo squeezed her hand. "Colson will get the money."

"What if he doesn't?"

This city had been an expensive stopover. The roads had put the newer vehicle into the repair shop, they'd had problems finding clean, cheap rooms, and the locals had given them suspicious appraisals and kept watch as if the Musicale were bank robbers.

"Louise, stop worrying."

She didn't stop. Louise heard worry huddled underneath her husband's stoicism. There was a meanness on the owner's face that reminded her of a bull ready to charge. She could smell the sourness of her fear sweat.

The charge came when the owner told Colson, "You have two choices: I let you leave, or you can stay, and you won't be walking upright ever again." The bar owner's hired goons pulled out their handguns.

Without breaking eye contact with the owner, Colson told the band, "Boys, get your instruments. We're leaving."

The Musicale left Denver that day and found rooms in a mountain mining town north of the city. Late that evening, Louise sat cross-legged on a creaking hotel bed. Leo slouched against a tarnished brass headboard smoking a cigarette. The tobacco dulled the musty damp that also chilled the room.

"Leo, are you okay?" Leo rarely smoked, and he seemed to be in an isolated contemplation.

He extinguished his cigarette. "What happened today can't happen again. I like making music but having gangsters point guns at us is dangerous. Playing for free isn't going to feed us or keep a roof over our heads."

Louise snuggled into Leo's shoulder. "We always have the tent. Too bad about our money. That bar was a lousy place. Colson won't let the Musicale play there again."

Leo pressed his face into Louise's hair. "What if you had been hurt today?"

"I wasn't. No one was."

Leo rose from the bed. He went to the window and stared out. "I've been thinking about what comes after the Musicale."

Surprise made Louise rear up. "That is years away."

"We need to start looking for our next opportunity."

Louise squeezed a handful of quilt. "What happened today was a one-time situation. The speakeasies and rent parties we've played, booze haul side hustles, and all the other risks we've taken have worked out."

Leo looked at Louise. "Luck can change."

Louise saw an expression on Leo's face she could not interpret. She wanted Leo to stop the serious talk and resurrect the playful musician. "It's late. Let's get some sleep."

Leo continued standing by the window. "You can. I'm not tired."

Louise slipped under the covers and blocked the conversation and concern that her life might be changing.

CHAPTER TEN

The Musicale traveled a small town meandering circuit up into Nebraska, swerving into eastern Wyoming, clipping the southwest corner of North Dakota, and hiking across Montana. The summer weather allowed the band to camp, and sometimes the townspeople put them up in their homes and barns.

In August, Western Montana flipped between warm days and cool nights. Last night the Musicale had played a public dance at a former military fort turned town. Louise woke with a cold nose and she questioned if it wasn't blue, and burrowed into Leo's armpit. She was thankful that the band had been allowed to sleep in a barn instead of their tents. If a farmer kept a clean barn, they were sure to get paid and this barn was tidy.

Leo kissed the top of her head and murmured, "Morning. Last night was a barn burner."

"Careful. We're in a barn." Louise gave Leo's belly a soft pinch.

"Hey!" He hugged her tight. They could hear the waiting cows below step and stomp. The farmer and his children would be along soon to milk. The cozy quiet would be exchanged for the sounds of working people and milk squirting into metal buckets. An occasional moo and the dryness of crushed straw floated upward and joined the nasal snoring of the other musicians.

Minutes passed. Then Louise said, "Last night was a good time. These folks like the old country and ragtime tunes. Maybe you could learn more of those Czech folk songs from Karl."

Leo rubbed his chin across her hair. "Some of those are downright haunting. You don't think those would make people too sad?"

"Put them in before breaks to wind people down."

Leo hummed a few bars and then asked, "Do you think about where we'll be this time next year?"

"I know where we'll be. On the road."

"Don't you ever want to stay in the same place... where you can call it home? Not just a rented room or tent."

Louise flashed back to the Colorado holdup. "What are you getting at?"

"It's time for change. The band is doing alright, but we can't be traveling the Great Plains for our whole lives."

"Not our whole lives, but we have a good thing going." Louise folded her lips inward and laid back down. Leo was talking change again.

"The country we've been driving has acres full of wheat fields. The bushel price of wheat is high. Maybe it's time for us to settle down and be part of it. Make a home with real walls," Leo said.

Louise's heart waited, and she asked the question that she did not want to ask: "Do you want to quit the Musicale?"

Leo leaned over Louise and stared into her eyes. In the dim light, she could make out Leo's biggest smile. Louise knew from all the times before that his eyes would be shining too. "Yes. Start something new. Get a farm. Get our share in this boom."

Louise flinched. She didn't want to stand in a field or a kitchen. She wanted to be in the clubs and the dancehalls.

"Leo, we can't afford to buy an automobile, much less a farm."

"But we could put down stakes, work, and get a foothold. We can rent. Save until we can buy," Leo said in a fired-up whisper.

When had Leo's ambitions changed? How had Louise missed it? Was there a farmer tucked away in his fiddle case all along? Louise exhaled. "How long

have you been thinking about this? Since Denver?"
She stared at the barn's rafters.

"What happened there made me think harder
about what could be next for us." Leo propped himself up and leaned over her. "Don't worry sweetheart.
When we settle down, we'll be in the land of milk
and honey. Let's get a little more sleep before the
farmer comes in."

Louise felt numb. Her hands seemed too heavy to
lift. Why this now? Maybe Leo needs a rest from
traveling? Maybe the price of wheat has him seeing
bushels of dollars instead of endless hours of fieldwork? Was it because winter was coming? He told
her he wasn't a desk man or a farmer. Just a musician.

She hadn't realized that Leo had been reorienting
his internal compass in another direction. The needle
that swept in all directions while traveling with the
Musicale now had a new singular path, and it was the
life Louise had left behind.

Two weeks later Louise brushed scarlet nail
polish onto her fingernails in the Billings, Montana
sunshine that streamed into their boardinghouse
room. She closed one nostril and then the other to
lessen the chemical odor. Leo and his violin dallied
with popular songs that stretched the year's playlist.
During a pause he said, "There's a pond in the town
square. Let's go have a look."

"My toes will be dried in twenty."

Later when they strolled the sidewalks, Louise,

wearing her metal round frame tinted sunglasses asked, "How about a movie instead of the square?"

Leo shook his head. "Let's start at the square and see where that takes us."

"Or we could start at the theater and go to the square after."

Leo's chin paralleled the ground in a straight line. "I wanna walk."

She threw out a flirtatious giggle. "We could find a radio and dance."

Leo kept looking straight ahead. "You can listen to the Musicale's rehearsal."

Louise stopped and put a hand on her hip, "Who put a bee in your bonnet?"

Leo turned to Louise. "I want to quit the Musicale. We need something more we can count on."

Louise was shocked. If Leo left the Musicale then so did she. Louise said, "I don't want that."

"We could have a life that's more solid and dependable. Where you don't have to move from job to job."

Exasperated, Louise bit out, "You sound like my mother. I like our life."

"We need something different. Besides playing the violin, the other thing I know how to do is farm. It doesn't take much know how to plow a field, make hay, and pick up rocks."

Louise shook her head as if a mosquito was buzzing in her face. "You haven't worked a farm since you were a kid. Get a job in a city instead." She and Leo reached the square city park with a painted white gazebo in the center.

"We need a change," Leo said.

Louise wanted to shout: Where'd my Leo go? She instead reminded him of the work. "You and I both know farming is a hard life. It's long days with always more to do, hoping for good weather and prices, and holding your breath that a bad season doesn't come. There's little time to play music."

Leo crossed his arms over his chest. "The show's over. The Musicale's next gig is in Sioux Falls. We'll be driving through North Dakota to get there. Bonetrail is close by."

"What's in Bonetrail?"

"The Musicale once played a wedding near there. It's a good town with plenty of farmland. There're fields of wheat, alfalfa, corn, and good-looking pastures of cattle. I liked the look and feel of the town the first time I saw it. We can make a good life there."

"Sounds like a graveyard. We can't just up and leave the Musicale. There are upcoming shows."

"We can. Say you're with me in this."

She wanted to yell no! But Mrs. Leo Zint said, "How can I stop you if you've decided to quit the Musicale."

"Louise, don't be that way. I'm doing this for us."

Louise felt limp. She started to walk, though it

felt like she was dragging her feet. If she stopped, she'd sink onto the park grass. Leo's new choice meant she became a farmer's wife locked to the land. She never wanted that life. Louise's mind jumped to the possibilities that once Leo was in Bonetrail, he'd realize he was mistaken?, or Bonetrail was boring?, or farming was a bad idea and want the Musicale back?

Leo picked Louise up at the waist and swung her around. "We'll make this a success. I'll tell them tonight at supper."

He had planted himself on new land, but the earth below Louise spun until all she could do was close her eyes and swallow back nausea.

When the Musicale sat in front of steaming roast beef sandwiches and mashed potatoes, Leo told Colson that the couple was leaving. The band leader's first response was a quiet question: "You sure about this?"

"Yes. It's time to settle down. The Musicale is headed to Sioux Falls. We'll jump out at Bonetrail."

"Son, I'm not telling you what to do, but this is a big decision." Colson considered Leo, nodded slowly, and then said, "Alright then, we'll drop you off in Bonetrail. You can change your mind before then."

Erik thrust his arms over his food and with his fingers targeted at Leo. "That's a lousy decision. You're a musician, not a farmer. You and Louise don't belong on a farm. We're a family."

Leo postured like a boxer. "Sometimes families

separate and go different directions. I was born and raised on a farm. I know what to do. Louise and I can't be like the wind blowing from place to place."

Erik pushed back his chair and stalked away.

Karl put down his fork. "I'm sorry to see you both go."

A whimper built up in Louise's chest. She placed her fingers over her lips to keep it inside. She didn't want to go either.

CHAPTER ELEVEN

Leo packed for Bonetrail in an excited dash. Louise said little. He knew she was upset, and he idled down in her presence. Leo kept his distance from Erik and found reasons to engage Colson or Karl in conversation about travel routes and gas stops.

When it was time to climb into the Ford and start the trip to Sioux Falls via Bonetrail, Louise did not want to sit next to Leo. She tried to not touch Leo and yet not make it obvious she was avoiding him.

The Musicale had lived and worked together in close quarters. Leo and Louise's different desires were obvious. The other men kept their thoughts to themselves. Louise watched the mountains recede as they drove east and entered the undulating foothills of the Rockies.

At Glendive, Montana, they stopped to eat at a

restaurant and then found a camping stop. The long driving day and late hour had the group skipping the campfire and setting up tents. Inside the Zints' tent there was no bedroom talking.

Louise rushed out a terse good night setting the lock on the invisible door between them. She turned over with her back to Leo. Going to Bonetrail was not what she wanted. Louise's relationship with the Musicale was through Leo. When his dream changed, so did her direction. A wife went with her husband.

She knew Leo wasn't asleep as his breathing didn't have deep intakes.

"Are you going to stay silent all the way to Bonetrail?" Leo asked.

Louise didn't want to answer. She wanted to punish with silence. Leo slept in the tent, would ride in the car tomorrow, and still be her husband in Bonetrail.

Leo shifted. "I'm trying to make things better for us. I wish you'd understand."

She stayed silent.

"I want this for us. I want a home and child."

It was the surprise mention of a child that jangled Louise's lock. She said, "I know you want this. But I didn't get a say. You decided, and I have to go."

Leo rolled onto his side. "I know."

"Yet you still did it."

Leo flopped onto his back, jostling Louise. "What more do you want me to say?"

"That you will ask me what I think before making an important decision."

"A husband's supposed to make the important decisions."

Louise had been taught that growing up, and the greater world concurred. While traveling with the band, she observed many ways of living. Louise longed for more of a say in her life. She rolled onto her side to face Leo. "Our marriage has been different from most. We can keep doing it the way we want."

Leo rolled over and their eyes met. "That's what I'm trying to make for us. We can buy land and run our own farm. No need to drive the country drumming up work and always under someone else's roof. No one pointing guns or giving us suspicious looks because we're outsiders."

Fat, hot tears of frustration and sadness rolled down Louise's cheeks. She wanted to yell and disturb the night. Causing a ruckus wouldn't persuade Leo to backtrack.

"I need time."

"Are you going to ignore me tomorrow?" Leo asked.

Louise wanted to say "yes" but instead said, "Let's get some sleep."

The next morning, the Musicale hooked southeast, crossing the North Dakota state line. Grassy buttes jutted from the land like the cruise ships Louise had seen in the newsreels played before movies. They began to diminish into rolling hills, making room for flattened prairie checkered with fields, miles of barbed wire fencing penning in clumps of cattle, and sparse trees.

Erik yelled out, "You were supposed to turn at that last right."

Colson hard braked and then looked back. "What right?"

"Where all those cows are standing. See the break in the fenceline? That's the turnoff."

In Louise's quiet mutiny she had seen the turn, but said nothing. She thought, if Leo wants to go to Bonetrail, he can get us there.

"Why didn't you tell me sooner?" Colson said.

"Thought you saw it coming," Erik replied.

Leo piped up, "Swing the car around and head back. It's not like there's anyone around to get in the way of changing directions."

Colson shifted into reverse then jabbed at the gas. The band members were pressed back into the seats as they careened towards the missed turn.

Leo stuck his head out the window and laughed into the vehicle's wind. "We're going the right direction now."

Louise kept her vision downcast and pinned to the front seat.

"Where do you two want to be dropped off?" Colson asked.

"On the main drag. Stop by the restaurant up ahead," Leo said.

When the vehicle stopped, Louise saw a one-story brick building with a glass front door and windows on either side.

Colson turned to Erik. "Unload the luggage. Leo, you get your instruments."

Leo jumped out and hustled to his task. Louise sat a few seconds longer, not wanting to leave. When she stood in the street, she looked around. Bonetrail resembled many Midwest small towns she'd been in. It didn't appear to be as prosperous as her hometown of Wheatville. Still, there was a grocery, doctor's office, church, butcher, a combination funeral parlor furniture store, and a grain elevator reaching for the sky.

After the luggage was set on the dirt road, the Musicale stood looking at each other.

Leo cleared his throat. "Fellows, this is goodbye."

The other men said nothing. A sudden gust flew down the street and a metal store sign creaked.

"Not goodbye. We'll catch you down the road. You never know where the Musicale will turn up," Erik said.

"Sure thing." Leo croaked out, "We'll all play together again."

Louise didn't say they wouldn't. Seeing this musical family again would be like finding a gold mine in the backyard.

Colson mumbled, "We'd better get back on the road. Long drive. You take care, son. You too, Louise."

Leo put his arm around Louise's waist. "We will. Thanks again. Next time you're in Bonetrail, stop in and see us. We'll play together for old times' sake."

Louise felt Leo's warmth press into her body. That and the early fall afternoon sunshine did not alter the cold upset residing inside her.

Karl pulled his fedora low. "The Musicale won't be the same." He turned away, paused, and turned back. "Good luck."

In a funeral whisper, Louise said, "Thank you."

Erik said to Louise, "Don't miss us too much," and then he thrust his hand out to Leo. "Good luck."

Leo shook. "Same to you, friend. Slow down some."

Erik chuckled. "Why'd I want to do that? Lots to do in this world."

"Stop jawing and get in. Daylight's burning," Colson said. Before he stepped into the car, he rested his hand on Leo's shoulder. "Good luck you two."

The Zints watched the band drive away, fraying the strings between the Musicale and the couple. When the band was out of sight, an invisible snap busted the bond. Each waited for the other to initiate the next step. Leo lowered his hat making it harder for Louise to see the wetness in his eyes before picking up his suitcase and accordion. Louise picked up her travel-worn suitcase and Leo's violin.

"Do you want to walk around some and see the place? Or we can get some coffee and ask about lodging?" Leo asked.

Exploring Bonetrail did not interest Louise. She said, "The restaurant. This town looks like all small towns."

As they walked inside, a silver-haired waitress called over, "Welcome to the ka-fey. Sit anywhere that's open."

Seated in a booth, Leo reached across the table and held Louise's hand. "Strike up the band. We're here."

Louise knew that Leo wanted her to respond in a similar exuberance. She raised her eyebrows and served up a dry smile.

The waitress came to their table. "Hello, what can I get you?" she asked in a cheerful tone.

Leo said, "Two coffees, please."

"Right up."

When the waitress had placed the coffees on the table Louise noticed the firm muscles in the woman's stout arms.

"Thank you. I'm Leo Zint, and this is my wife, Louise. We're new in town. I passed through a long time ago and always remembered this place. We thought we'd give Bonetrail a try."

"I'm Clara. Nice to meet you both. Welcome to Bonetrail."

"You wouldn't by chance know of any place to board?"

"Mother Shields rents rooms. She's strict, but her house is clean, and she's fair."

Leo raised his mug in salute. "Thank you. Much appreciated."

"It's good to have new people in town. Don't let Mother Shields' bark scare you away."

After coffee, and now possessing the boarding-house address, the Zints walked three streets west and stopped at a two-story, white painted wood plank house.

Leo said, "This must be it. Looks taken care of." He knocked. "Hello?"

No one answered. Leo knocked and called out again. Louise sighed inward. Of course, no one was home. They're probably wishing they were some-where else too. She sat down on the steps to wait.

Louise rested her chin on her fist and gazed at the blue sky with lake-sized clouds. The sunshine would have been too warm if not for the breeze that rose up and died and repeated. She guessed at how far away the band was.

Sitting next to her, Leo shook out the pebbles in his shoes, straightened his socks, and then adjusted his shirt cuffs. Avoiding commenting, Louise brooded over why Leo couldn't stay still. Eventually, Leo slipped into a posture that mirrored his wife's.

At thirty minutes, he grabbed Louise's hand and

squeezed. Louise wanted to shout, I don't want to be here! You can't pass your feelings to me and make them mine! This change in Louise's life made her feel grabbed by the throat. Speaking out seemed hard, and useless. Her only option was to wait this place out. Maybe Leo would change his mind before too long.

Near an hour, they saw a mature woman striding down the road with arms close to her sides. Her hat stayed put as her day dress whipped about her legs attempting to keep up. In one hand, she carried a sturdy black handbag and in the other, a paper sack.

The landlady stopped and, standing as straight as a newly placed pole, looked at a sitting Leo and Louise. In one syllable she said, "Yes?"

Leo jumped up and whipped off his hat. "Hello..."

Before he could continue, the woman interrupted. "I'm Mother Shields. Can I help you?"

"I'm Leo Zint. This is my wife, Louise. We would like to rent a room. We arrived in town today."

Louise eased up for the introductions.

Mother Shields looked them over inch by inch. She took in their clothes, their luggage, and the instrument cases. She squinted the longest at Louise's crimson lipstick and matching nail polish. Then she asked, "Where do you come from?"

"All over the place. Louise and I were in a band

but now we're settling in Bonetrail. Hope to get a farm real soon."

Mother Shields lifted her chin. "You don't have a job. Do you have any money?"

"Yes, ma'am."

Louise thought the landlady might make Leo withdraw his wallet and count out the money for her inspection.

The matron ordered, "Come inside."

Mother Shields stepped between the Zints and walked up the steps. The screen door banged as the young couple picked up their bags and followed. The inside of the house had the stuffy hot of being closed up. Louise questioned why the landlady hadn't left open a window.

Mother Shields pointed. "Are those instruments?"

Louise eyed the woman's tight, dull, grayish-brown bun. The hairstyle had the effect of making the woman's eyebrows arch and her thin face appear almost skeletal.

Leo reached for his violin and opened the case buckle. "Yes, they are. Would you like to see? I play both violin, accordion, and some piano and guitar, though, the violin is my first choice."

"I do not care for music in my home. Inappropriate music leads to profane behavior."

"But ma'am...," Leo crooned, "they're just instruments. They don't do any harm."

"Those are my rules. If you would like to find somewhere else to rent, please do so."

They all remained quiet until Leo said, "We hear your rules."

Mother Shields nodded her head once. Then her footsteps thumped across the scrubbed hardwood floors. An unembellished parlor led into a similar dining room. She motioned with her hand that the couple should sit at the large dining table.

The Zints sat down. They watched the landlady walk through an open double doorway into a kitchen that Louise guessed occupied the back part of the house. She inventoried the rooms. In the parlor were a faded sofa with two embroidered pillows, two sitting chairs, and starched white curtains. A few books were on a bookshelf, which, of course, included the family bible and no dust. To Louise's surprise, there was also a radio. In the dining room, besides the oak table and chairs there was a squat China hutch with two photographs of a sour-faced man and woman dressed in last century clothing reigning from high.

Mother Shields set a glass water pitcher painted with peaches on the table then took three glasses from atop the hutch. Neither Zint reached for a glass. Then the landlady sat down, folded her hands, and in a clear and precise tone stated, "I expect my lodgers to follow clean living and quiet hours. Curfew is nine o'clock. No alcohol, tobacco, or guests. Louise, you will help make meals, and Leo, you will help with chores. There will be no tomfoolery under my roof. Do you understand?"

The Zints nodded.

"Very good. I'll show you to your room. Be careful not to scratch my furniture and walls."

Mother Shields led the Zints upstairs and stopped in front of the first door. "This is my room, and I keep my door locked."

She pushed open the next bedroom door. "This is the room you are renting."

Inside was a bed with a handmade, unadorned bed quilt, an oil lamp, a closet, and a dresser that held a water pitcher and basin. The room was as matter-of-fact as Mother Shields.

Louise pointed down the hall. "Wouldn't putting us in the bedroom on the back side give everyone more privacy?"

"This is the room that is available."

Louise closed her eyes so she wouldn't roll them, opened them, and then said, "I think the back bedroom would be best. Leo is a snorer. And you did say you wanted quiet."

Mother Shields examined Leo. Leo gave a noncommittal shrug.

"Fine, but if there is any funny business, you will be asked to leave."

"We understand," Louise said.

Mother Shields walked to the back bedroom.

"Supper is at five-thirty, and I expect you to be on time," she said and went downstairs.

This bedroom was a sibling to the first. Neither Leo or Louise said anything, each taking in their new home.

Leo broke the silence. "I'm a loud snorer?"

"Not really. But as far as that woman is concerned, you have recently become the loudest snorer in the tri-state area."

Leo set his suitcase next to the dresser. "A burden to bear. I like this bedroom better. Further away from Mother Shields."

Louise went to the sole small window and stared out at a backyard that contained a vegetable garden and a chicken coop. In close proximity were other houses that resembled this house. In other yards, she saw late-summer velvet purple petunias and sunshine yellow brown-eyed susans.

She shook her head at the thought that they would be living under that contrary landlady's roof. Louise hoped that Leo misremembered Bonetrail and that the reality he saw here would change his mind. She heard Leo unbuckle his suitcase.

"That woman won't allow you to play your violin. Are you sure you want to stay here?"

He yanked open a drawer. "It's a strange rule. We'll only be here a short time."

Louise couldn't believe this man. Her Leo would

have found a way to play his violin. "It's not fair. We're paying good rent money."

Leo set his violin case in a corner. "No use getting upset. Why don't we walk around the town and see what we can find?"

Louise set Leo's accordion next to the violin. "I suspect this place looks like most small towns. I had better wear a hat or that woman will be offended."

Leo held open the bedroom door. "Keep an eye out for help wanted signs. In a town like this, we may have to talk people up to find out where the jobs are."

They strolled several streets of small family homes with attached sitting porches and tidy yards with clotheslines. At the intersection that turned either right to downtown or left to the grain elevator, Leo said, "There's the elevator. I should introduce myself. Meet you back at Mother Shields for supper."

It was harvest time. Farmers were hauling their grain loads to the elevator filling the railcars headed for mills in Bismarck, Minneapolis, and Chicago. A spontaneous desire to climb onto any of those trains shot through Louise's heart.

Louise said, "Alright," as calmly as she could.

Leo kissed her cheek. "Wish me luck."

She wanted to yell that he was going the wrong direction. She squeezed her hands into fists and ground her shoe bottoms into the dirt. Louise asked herself where she could go?

CHAPTER TWELVE

Louise rambled along Bonetrail's main street in the fading heat. She swiped her fingertips along the rough and bumpy brick and smoother wood of buildings.

What would she do here? She needed to find a job. When Leo realized the fantasy he made up about Bonetrail was wrong, they needed more savings to leave and start elsewhere.

Being a shop clerk or waitress held little interest for Louise after the glamour of the Musicale. What else could Louise do in a small town when most women worked at home or on the family farm?

Across the street was a little bare plank church. The building seemed to have been positioned with definite intent between two fields. Louise walked behind the church. In the back, a knee-high black painted scrollwork metal fence surrounded a scattering of upright headstones. Wild prairie roses climbed through the fence as late-season bluebells pushed up and around the bushes.

Louise looked around and seeing no one, knelt down. She snapped a bell off its stem and sucked the cupped nectar into her mouth. Her mother had taught her about the blossom's liquid sugar. She reached for another and continued until all the bluebells within reach were decapitated and laid in a pile next to her knees.

How had Louise ended up in Bonetrail? This was not her dream.

She fantasized that she looked out a train window, watching the fields pass from one state to the next, leaving Bonetrail far behind. Louise had left home for a life less ordinary, and here she was on her knees in this last stop churchyard wondering what had happened.

How long will we stay here? What if we make a success of it and never leave? Or fail. Where do we go next?

An engulfing disappointment tired Louise. In a space the roses didn't occupy, she pressed her back into the metal fencing. The slight discomfort felt solid and reassuring. Birds chirped and called, and Louise heard an occasional automobile drive down the street.

It was peaceful here. No one to make her leave.

When the sun rays had softened to an evening butter yellow, it was time to go back to Mother Shields'.

At the house, the landlady was in the kitchen cutting up a roast beef. The meat would probably appear at breakfast the next day, too. The smell of vinegar stuck in the air. On the dining table was a bowl of wrinkled green beans that must have spent months marinating in a jar.

Before Louise could offer to help Mother Shields, the woman ordered, "Wash your hands. Go to the hutch and get out the plates and silverware to set the table. Not the expensive china. Don't break anything."

As Louise set the table, she surmised the older woman's insides were vinegar filled.

Mother Shields set down dense homemade oat-flaked bread and baked russet potatoes onto the table. "Where's your husband? It's time to eat."

"I'm sure he'll be here shortly. He's probably talking to someone."

Mother Shields harrumphed. "He's late."

Louise thought, *come on Leo, get here faster*.

She could hear the clock atop the hutch tick the minutes as they sat at the table waiting.

Why do I have to sit here with this mean old turkey? That woman is getting colder with the food.

"We could put the food in the oven until he gets here," Louise suggested.

"Supper is at five-thirty."

"Hello ladies," Leo called out as he bounded into the house. "Let me wash my hands, and then I will hightail it to the table. I apologize for being late."

After Leo sat, Mother Shields folded her hands and led the table in prayer. When everyone had begun to eat, Leo said, "I got a temporary job at the grain elevator. I work every day, except Sunday, through the rest of the harvest."

Louise gave Leo an adequate smile. Already. It was too fast.

Mother Shields' lips pressed into a line. "A man needs steady work. None of that gallivanting around the country business."

Leo reached for the platter of roast beef Mother Shields passed to him. "But that gallivanting showed me Bonetrail and brought me back. I'm ready to make my mark on this land. In the end, it worked out swell."

When supper was finished, cleared, and cleaned, the Zints went for another stroll. Most evenings had been for performing. Tonight there wasn't a channel for that reserve of habituated nocturnal energy. Neither said much to the other, and there was a gap between their bodies.

At bedtime in the back bedroom, as Leo's sternum cradled Louise's upper back, he said, "We can make this work."

A few minutes later she could tell by the push

and pull of Leo's chest that he was asleep. Louise's tears soaked Mother Shields' starched, white pillowcase. Leo's newfound dream of farming had become her future waiting to unfold. She would be stuck on the farm again.

Louise didn't have anyone to whom she could confide her struggles. Never to her sisters or her mother. If her mother learned about Louise's predicament then the other woman would be proved right. She had warned Louise. Louise could hear her mother speaking: What did you think would happen when you left with some music man? That you'd live on the road forever? Step out of that dreamland that you've made up. You grew up on a farm, and that's where you belong. A person does not dash off thinking that the real world doesn't find you.

The next day after breakfast, Leo went to the elevator. Louise told Mother Shields that she needed to unpack. She laid on the bed staring through the windowpane at the blue sky. Louise sought afternoon solace in the graveyard and returned in time for supper preparation.

When Leo arrived home from work, Mother Shields refused to let him in. "You're too dusty to come inside. Wash up and change your clothes outside."

"Mother Shields, how am I supposed to clean up if you won't let me inside?"

"You should have thought of that earlier. I will not have you dirty my house."

Louise interrupted. "I'll bring you some water and a change of clothes. Meet me by the backyard shed."

To whittle down her afternoons, Louise moped around Bonetrail until she had to return to the boardinghouse. Sometimes Louise followed the train tracks that cut through on the northside of town. She watched the trains arrive and depart, the steam whistle a beckoning promise.

Their life with the Musicale had meant a consistent togetherness for Louise and Leo. It was rare that they were far from each other. If they were apart, it was for short hours. When Louise lived with her parents and siblings, she had wanted distance from them. It hadn't been so with Leo during the band days. He was her husband, playmate, and best friend. Louise missed him.

Before supper, Louise would go to the shed and wait for Leo. As Leo washed the heavy mix of grain shaft, dust, and sweat plastered above and below his clothing, he told stories of his day and the residents he met.

Louise's boredom and loneliness began to step around her anger. Several weeks after arriving, she offered to help Mother Shields finish harvesting the rest of her garden. Together the women picked, cleaned, and canned in a quiet but cordial reprieve.

She enjoyed the feel of tomatoes sitting in her palm. She liked watching the dirt fly as she shook clean the onions. One afternoon, Louise slipped off her shoes and pressed her feet into the soil, making heel dents. Dirt crept up between her toes. She let the earth began to discharge her discontent at the loss of her old life and the move to Bonetrail for Leo's wild hair idea. Louise closed her eyes and stood in a temporary peace.

The comfort was interrupted when she opened her eyes and saw Mother Shields staring. The landlady's perplexed expression exhaled a derisive loud "hmmm," then she began pulling spent plants.

Louise wasn't breaking any rules by taking off her shoes.

Just because that stiff of a woman thinks it's inappropriate doesn't make it so.

She balked at Mother Shields' judgement. The next afternoon, Louise took off her shoes, stepped into the garden, and moved about barefooted.

To appease her boredom and help build their finances, Louise found a part-time job as a school janitor. The tasks were easy and meant an escape of a few early morning hours before the school day's start.

Leo was hired as a full-time farmhand for Frank Wheeler. Mr. Wheeler picked Leo up on the east side of town each morning except on Sundays. Leo helped care for the livestock, bale the remaining pastures and ditches, and then planted winter wheat.

The snow hadn't come yet, so he and Mr. Wheeler spent hours fixing fence, looking for dipped lines and tilted posts, and picking rocks.

Louise continued to meet Leo in the shed when he arrived home. More often than not, he'd find her in her emerald green winter coat, tan wool beret, and gloves sitting on an overturned earthenware pickling crock reading a drugstore magazine.

"Waiting for me?" Leo asked.

"Seems like always."

Leo smirked. "Hopefully not that long."

"Depends on the day."

Leo reached for the rag hanging on a nail. He wet the cloth in the bowl of water Louise had brought from the house to the shed and then began to wipe away the farm dirt. "Today, we put in new fence over the county line near the Cannonball River. The sky was so blue, and the clouds floated by fast. The weather is ready to change. What did you do today?"

"Cleaned the school. Clara said I could pick up shifts at the café since Irina is moving to Bismarck."

"That's good news. We can put more money towards the farm." Leo wrung out the rag, then reached for the house clothes that Mother Shields demanded he wear. "Mr. Wheeler will keep me on as long as there's work, but I am not sure how long that will be with winter around the corner."

Louise could see and feel Leo's desire to stay in Bonetrail had not waned.

Don't panic. We don't have a farm yet.

The work for Mr. Wheeler stopped for the season, and it was Leo's turn to fill his daytime hours. Monday through Friday, Louise would go to her janitorial job and then spend the lunch hour and some afternoons at the cafe. She returned home in the late afternoon to an always monitoring Mother Shields. A handful of traveling salesmen had stayed at the boardinghouse since the Zints' arrival. The opportunities for guests to talk to each other always included Mother Shields as chaperon. These rare encounters reminded Louise of her previous life and helped to divert some of the landlady's attention.

On Louise's way home one early afternoon in November, she was a block away when she heard it. Leo's violin. He hadn't played since coming to Bonetrail. She stopped and let it fill the known and unknown cracks and holes which had been created when the ground underneath her had shifted and been traded for this farming town. A combination of her anger and the distance of days had begun to camouflage and wall the music until she realized that the Musicale memories were fading.

Finally, the music. Her alert, feminine ears were again being drawn towards the man with the violin. She jogged to the familiar, comfortable, beautiful notes.

When Louise stepped inside the shed, she saw

Leo sitting on her overturned crock. His Cheshire smile telling her how much he relished the music.

"Where's Mother Shields?"

"Not home," Leo said, and he didn't stop playing. He stood up and walked towards her. His eyes twinkled with mischief. He stepped closer, and she stepped back. He stepped even closer, moving Louise to the middle of the shed. Leo circled her and the notes wrapped around them. He picked up the pace and the magic spun faster. Louise threw up her arms, let her head hang back, and laughed. The joyous glee was as raucous as the music.

Too soon the private concert was over. Leo returned the violin to its case. His hand laid on the case's top, lingering a few seconds longer.

"Thank you. It's been a long time. I'm out of breath from dancing. Plus, I shouldn't have eaten so much watermelon this fall." The statement came out of her mouth in such a casual way that Leo cocked his head to consider what had been said.

"What's wrong with watermelon?" Leo asked.

"It's a polite way of saying I'm pregnant."

Leo gaped at Louise. "A baby?"

Louise nodded.

Leo grabbed Louise's hands, and they spun and laughed. They held each other and waited for their vision and lives to stop spinning. "When?"

"The baby will come sometime in the summer."

"Busy time to be having a baby," Leo said. "We'll

need to find a farm soon. I keep looking and asking around, but nothing has come up."

Louise was relieved that Leo had been unable to find a farm to rent. But also within her was a growing longing to leave Mother Shields' house.

That night the supper meal was different. The music and shared news had pushed the couple into a sated state that Mother Shields could not interrupt.

CHAPTER THIRTEEN

Leo used his hours of free time to traipse around Bonetrail at least once a day and talk to people. There would be an odd job here and there, but it wasn't until Roger Keebler, the town's maintenance man, broke his arm that something materialized.

At the café, Louise overheard Mr. Hornsby tell his coffee companions about Roger's injury. She asked Clara for a break and tore off to Mother Shields'. At the house, Leo wasn't downstairs. She raced upstairs, "Leo! Leo! Are you here?"

"Where's your fire?" Leo asked.

"Roger Keebler broke his arm. He's laid up."

Leo shoved his coat under his armpit while tucking in his shirt, and then he and Louise jogged to the municipal office. At the squat building, Louise huffed out a "good luck" and hurried back to the café.

At work, she glanced out the restaurant windows every few minutes trying to spot Leo. Her anxiousness began to lessen when she realized that she hadn't seen him walk by. The longer he spent at the office, the greater the likelihood he would be Roger's short-term replacement. The season and her pregnancy moved deeper into winter, and opportunities for Leo to find work dwindled at the same rate.

She felt sorry for Roger and his family, but if she and Leo were ever going to get out from under Mother Shields' roof, they needed more money.

After the lunch rush, Leo moseyed into the café. Louise knew by his walk that he now worked for the town of Bonetrail.

Her own working hours were split between the café and school. When Louise could, she napped between the jobs. It helped her fatigue and lessened her time around Mother Shields. Shortly after arriving in Bonetrail, Louise began to stymie thoughts of the Musicale life as it amplified her sadness and loneliness. Having a baby meant a job with the traveling band was no longer available. The hope that Leo would change his mind about settling in Bonetrail was shrinking. Louise struggled to envision her future.

One day after arriving home from an afternoon cafe shift, Mother Shields asked Louise to help set the table.

Leo stepped in and told the matron, "I'll do it. What dishes do I put out?"

Before Mother Shields rebuked the offer, Louise fibbed and said she needed to get something from upstairs.

Lying in bed that night, Leo said to Louise, "You know I can help you clean the school."

"I know. I'm doing okay for now. When I get too big to bend over, you'll be the first person I ask."

"I'm the only person you'd ask."

"Good thing we agree then."

Louise enjoyed, and didn't want to pass over, the warming peace of the school. Sometimes she would sit at a desk and rest her palms flat on the tilted hardwood and daydream about her past and fidget around her future.

In December, Mother Shields announced that she would be visiting her daughter's family for the holidays. In her deliberate and no-nonsense approach to all matters, she outlined how the Zints would care for the big house during her absence. None of the tasks listed deviated from the current manner they lived in. The Zints were the only guests that month and into the new year.

Mother Shields' son-in-law retrieved her a few days before Christmas.

Before walking out the front door Mother Shields said, "I will return in the new year. I expect my home to be in the same state when I return. Merry Christmas."

For the first few hours, the house radiated the landlady's prickly presence. Time and the Zints' relaxing cheer began to diminish the energetic imprint. The additional coal Leo added to the stove pushed heat into downstairs corners that hadn't been warm since late fall.

That evening, Louise stood at the dining table. The crisp snip, snip sounds of the scissors cutting out baby clothing accompanied the radio. Leo hovered close to east coast voices to hear new tunes. When the music programs finished he picked, caressed, and crooned the music on his violin. They would need to replace the radio battery before their landlady returned.

This was the first time Louise and Leo lived alone. Louise decided she was going to pretend that this was their house. She left her sewing project on the table and cooked the meals she wanted. No one observed or judged her or Leo.

The next evening not long after supper, three knocks reverberated through the front door. Leo and Louise exchanged a surprised, curious look. There had been a handful of visitors to the house but this close to Christmas Eve, people most likely gathered with family. Leo opened the door. They saw a stocky, tall man bundled in a large winter coat and hat with ear flaps and no gloves.

When the man smiled, the wrinkles at the corner of his lips and eyes lifted too. "Good evening. Don't know if you remember me, but I'm Heinrich Schmidt. Me and the Mrs. live next door."

"Hello! We remember you. Come in," Leo said.

Heinrich stomped the snow off his work boots before entering. "We heard your music a while back and was wondering if you folks wanted to come over tomorrow night for Christmas Eve. I mean, you don't have to come over just to play. We're having a party."

Louise's smile seemed to stretch to her ears and she nodded towards Leo.

"Yes. What time should we come?" Leo said.

Mr. Schmidt rattled off the particulars and turned to leave. Louise stretched her neck out the door like a chicken. "What should we bring?"

"Bring yourselves and that instrument. That'll be fine. See you tomorrow night."

Louise closed the door and skipped around Leo. "We're going out for an evening."

The people of Bonetrail were polite, but making friends had not come quickly for the Zints. Working at the café and elevator introduced them to people, but their newness to the community, and their association with Mother Shields sometimes limited their friendship opportunities.

On Christmas Eve, Louise announced, "I'm going to go change into my black and white Musicale dress for the party. If it still fits, that is."

Upstairs in their bedroom, Louise opened the closet and dug into the back where the dress hung. Seeing it made her miss the Musicale and her family in Minnesota. Both, seemed so far away. When Louise touched the dress her hand tingled. Tonight she'd let some of the old Louise shine and have a goodtime.

The dress was tighter, but it still fit. She swept her hair back with a cherry red scarf. Leo wore his Musicale black slacks, button-up white shirt with gray stripes and gray tie. He slicked and flipped back his hair. It appeared as a wave that moved from his forehead to the back and stayed put.

Leo carried his violin and accordion to the Schmidts. In a small nod to Christmas colors, Louise held a jar of pickled and wrinkled green beans in one hand and a jar of pickled beets in the other. The beets glistened like big, fat, unpolished rubies.

At the Schmidts' door, Leo's knock was firm and cheerful. No one answered. He knocked again with more firmness.

A smiling bosomy, broad-shouldered woman opened the door. A white apron embroidered with poinsettias protected a navy dress. Her brown hair streaked with salt and pepper was pulled into a tidy bun that bumped out in the back. "Hello, hello. Merry Christmas! Get in out of the cold. So, nice you could come. I'm Myra."

"I'm Leo. This is Louise. Thank you for inviting

us. We brought a few things to share, plus, I brought my violin and accordion."

The living room, dining room, and kitchen brimmed full with all ages. They sat on chairs, propped against walls, encircled a table, and gathered in groups. Most were speaking at a high volume. This congregation was connected through family ties, but they all bowed their heads to the church of farming.

Mr. Schmidt sat on a sofa with a pipe in one hand and a glass of rose-colored liqueur in the other. He swung the glass up at the Zints in a sort of half-salute, and small drops of the drink splashed onto the floor.

"Mr. Schmidt, get up and greet our guests," Myra said in a light scold.

"Myra, honey, I just settled in," but Heinrich stood up and shook Leo and Louise's hands. "Glad you could make it. See you brought your instruments. That's good. Heard you playing over at Mother Shields'. I suppose that old battle ax doesn't approve?"

"Heinrich. Don't speak ill of the neighbor. Especially not in front of her lodgers."

"Sorry. Me and Mother Shields aren't the best of friends. The fence is a good boundary line."

"Don't worry. Mother Shields is a taste one tries to swallow fast," Leo said.

Heinrich chuckled, and Myra placed a hand over her smile.

More guests noticed the couple's arrival. What

drew cheers and whistles were the instruments. Some Schmidts moved the furniture, and several chairs were set up as a makeshift corner stage. In a flash, Louise considered where the Musicale was at. She reminded herself to let that go. That life was over.

In a conspiring loud whisper invested with mischief, one of the Schmidt boys said, "Let's go get the church's piano. Pastor Williams is away on his trip. He'll never know."

Young men snickered, and one by one started to put on their coats and exit the house.

The group activity was not unobserved by Mr. Schmidt, and he called out to the group, "Where are you all going?"

"Gotta get something from outside."

"What's outside?"

"Be right back."

"Boys, where exactly are you going?" This time Mr. Schmidt's question and tone demanded a straight answer instead of detour responses.

"We're going to get the church's piano and bring it back for the party," one of the beanpole Schmidt nephews with slicked-back hair said. "No harm."

It wasn't a reprimand or chuckle that tumbled out of Mr. Schmidt but an unrestrained boom of laughter that drew the attention of all in the room. "If anything happens to that thing you're all paying for a new one."

The rest of the young men stumbled over each

other leaving the house before the decision was reversed. Leo, who still had his coat on, waved to Louise and hustled out the door to join the mischievous movers.

Myra put her hands on her hips. "Mr. Schmidt, where are those boys going?"

The patriarch delayed long enough for the wrangling group to climb into the truck and then remarked, "They're going over to the church to get the piano for the party. Now mother, don't fret."

Myra rushed out the front door and shouted as the truck's engine roared, "For Pete's sake, don't break the piano while you're moving it." Turning to her husband she laid fire eyes on the man and crossed her arms.

"They'll be fine. The boys know what to do," Heinrich bellowed. He settled back into the couch cushion, and his pleased smile heralded more of the evening's merry shenanigans.

Thirty minutes and two toots on the horn later, they backed up over the snow-covered front lawn, and all the cheering partygoers pushed out the front door to watch the abducted piano's unloading.

As Leo tossed his coat onto a catawampus pile of coats next to the front door, Louise asked him what happened.

"We whooped all the way to the Bonetrail Congregational Church. I don't think that church has ever seen such noisy parishioners come to call. A few boys climbed through a window, and a couple of others went to the back door."

"Were you a door or a window?"

"Window. We pushed the upright across the sanctuary, out the back door, up a wood board ramp, and onto the truck bed. Took a turn too fast and the piano slid and pinned a Schmidt. The yelper was fine once we got the piano off him."

When the piano was positioned in the middle of the parlor, the Schmidts' teenage daughter Sadie plopped down on a chair in front of the mahogany and ivory instrument. During several of Louise's school cleaning shifts she had seen Sadie, a senior, help the high school teacher.

Leo set his drink on the piano top. Myra rushed over and placed a crocheted doily underneath the glass. Then he hung his suit coat on the back of a nearby chair and sat down. When Leo undid his cuffs and rolled his sleeves back, Louise's body rippled with excitement. He tended to roll his sleeves back when a performance was already in full swing, but Leo was ready to start strong tonight.

Sadie started playing and singing 'O Come All Ye Faithful' in German. Leo accompanied on his violin. Not too many beats into the reverence of the song the entire room joined. Louise had grown up around Germanic and Scandinavian immigrants. Her maternal German grandparents had spoken very little English. Each German lyric thickened the tight knot that formed in Louise's throat. She spread her hands across her belly then crossed her arms and with a gentle firmness pressed into herself.

Louise thought about her family in Minnesota. Several years had passed since she had last seen them. Letters back and forth let the others know about their lives. Her mother would like Bonetrail.

Air currents of convivial cheer flew through the rooms. An improvised dance floor that extended into the kitchen overflowed with quick steppers.

The gaiety of the dancing was the opposite of the intense focus of the two card games. Half the dining table held slices of headcheese, summer sausage, and liverwurst; dense farm cheeses; baked buns; apple and peach kuchen; and powdered sugar-dusted anise pfeffernusse cookies, while the other side was occupied by a Canasta game. Pinochle hands grabbed space on the floor. The card players drilled in tight to their games. A run of points could provoke an eruption of yelling and mumbled cussing. Neither game in this house was meant for the thin-skinned. When a team closed out a game, new blood sat in the released seats.

Louise spent most of the evening near the music. She danced with numerous Schmidts. One of the cousins knew how to play some on the accordion, and someone's daughter played the guitar. It was not long before the musicians went from a duo to a quartet. Near eleven, Myra shooed away the card players and reclaimed the other half of her dining table. In the now vacant space, ladies placed platters of rosy sliced hams, steaming baked potatoes with gold butter, baked beans, open jars of pickled garden vegetables, tangy sauerkraut, and yeasty buns.

"Time to eat!" Myra said.

The party lasted until the early morning. A smaller group of men, Leo among them, reloaded the borrowed piano onto the truck and returned it to the church in a quieter state of mirth. Louise helped the ladies clear the food, pack up leftovers, and wash dishes that had spread throughout the house and yard. A quieter Heinrich directed young people to sweep and return the furniture to its everyday locations. Parents rounded up their children and coats. Guests said good-byes and Merry Christmas. The 'thunk' sound of a closing window signaled that the party was over.

Together, Louise and Leo said goodnight to Myra and Heinrich.

Heinrich patted his rounded belly. "Glad you could come. It's good to have new folks in town."

Myra handed Louise a small paper bag of food. "Here's something for tomorrow. Thank you for coming. Our door is always open."

The new friendship with the Schmidts made Louise feel a hearty happiness that had been absent for many weeks.

Leo and Louise's laughter created puffs of white

air as they strolled across the frozen yards to Mother Shields. Louise snuggled into Leo's chest, the violin case bumping into her hip.

When they entered the house, Louise turned to face Leo. It was dark, but there was a hint of moonlight pushing tendrils of light into the space where they stood. The quiet enveloped her senses as if her entire body was covered by a heavy quilt. Louise lifted her hand and pushed it along and up Leo's cheek. Before her fingertips had reached eye level, Leo had passed his hand over her arm and encircled her wrist. His thumb moved back and forth across her wrist like a heart-paced metronome. They stood there breathing and touching. Lips and fabrics touched in the dark house.

For the rest of the week, the Zints enjoyed the freedom of directing the house's on-goings. Louise worked her shifts at the café, and Leo kept busy shoveling snow off the streets, checking boilers, and completing all the tasks of a winter's to do list. Louise loved every minute of it. But when 1930 arrived, so did Mother Shields.

On her first day back, Mother Shields recounted her litany of holiday dissatisfactions. Nothing seemed to please the woman. Louise heard the words and ignored the sentences. At supper when Louise reached for her fork, Mother Shields began to list the various meals she had eaten while away and the dismay at the selection and taste.

Louise pushed air over her upper lip and considered Mother Shields' poor daughter. Louise was lucky her mother lived so far away. She acknowledged her own mother's commanding personality was a much lighter shade of her landlady's. Louise moved her fork in figure eights on her plate.

Mother Shields snapped her face towards Louise. "Why aren't you eating?"

"I lost my appetite."

"Please stop scratching my fork on my plate."

Louise moved a mouthful of food to her lips. She chewed until the over baked chicken became stringy mush and then swallowed.

Leo redirected. "Has your son-in-law started planning for the spring planting?" This question started a new trajectory of complaints about farmers overworking the land with their newfangled machines.

After the supper meal, Louise stepped past Leo who played solitaire at the dining room table. Once in their bedroom, she laid on the bed in the dark. The absence of light and sound settled into her bones. Her body sank heavier into the quilt. The bed accepted the weight of her discontent and bigger body. Even the baby was still.

To Louise, it could have been minutes or hours later that Leo joined her upstairs. He tripped over the door's transition strip but was able to recover quickly enough to prevent tumbling down. She smiled in the dark at his less than agile entrance.

Louise's voice floated towards him and asked, "Are you all right?"

Leo laughed. "Yeah."

His laugh kept her smile in place. Leo undressed and laid down. His hands reached for Louise as she turned her body and scooted into his arms, and their breathing synchronized.

"Leo, we have to live somewhere else. Get away from that woman," Louise whispered.

"I know," he said into her hair. "We don't have enough money saved to buy a farm, but something will come up for rent soon. Then, we could borrow or trade labor for the supplies and equipment."

Louise wanted to get away. Away from this house. Away from this town. Return to Chicago. Her neck tightened at the thought of having the baby under Mother Shields' roof. Leo wasn't leaving Bonetrail. The realization drenched her heart and head in sadness and instead of crying, she went to sleep. They stayed cupped in each other's bodies as the stars crossed the sky waiting for the sun to catch up.

CHAPTER FOURTEEN

January and February blew into the year on a frigid winter wind that would trap the prairie until late spring. Snowfall had come and stayed, and what remained was a solid pack with sharp jagged ridges that made a crunching sound when walked on. A few precious days gave insincere sunshine but, more often than not, the overcast shadow of smoky-white clouds hovered over the county. The wind grew, diminished, and repeated, but there was always plenty to turn the windmills.

In mid-February, Roger Keebler returned to work. Leo applied at the Kefner Creamery, but there were still no jobs available. During the day he would come to the café and sit at the counter, nursing a cup of coffee and waiting to be available should someone need a strong back. It was during one of those visits that he met Garrett Driscol. Driscol was a local boy who had purchased a farm about six miles up the county highway. He owned a pickup truck and a flashy smile. It only took an off-color comment about the weather to start a friendship between the two men. It also helped that Driscol was spending time with Heinrich and Myra's daughter Sadie. He knew Leo was holding out for a farm near Bonetrail.

On a late-March mid-morning, Driscol strutted into the café. He pulled off his knitted hat and pushed his hand through his flattened hair. Louise set a filled coffee mug in front of him.

"Thanks," he replied and took a gulp. He started half coughing, half choking. Leo slapped him on the back in three quick whacks. Once everyone had settled down, Driscol side-glanced at Leo. "I found you a farm to rent."

"Where?"

Driscol told of a property located five miles north of Bonetrail and several miles west of the county road. The land needed work. There was a farmhouse, a barn, and a small creek that he pronounced as 'crick.' Louise saw Leo narrow his eyes and finger tap a quick cadence. He picked up his coffee cup and stopped at taking a sip and asked, "When can I see it?"

"Let's go now."

Leo called out to Louise, "We'll be back." Before she could say "wait," the men were exiting the cafe.

Louise pressed her knuckles into the counter. She was left behind while Leo went to look at the property. He was about to make another decision for the two of them, and Louise would have to go along with it. Where was her say?

She met up with Leo at the boardinghouse later that afternoon. He paced the bedroom and rattled on like an auctioneer describing the place. Forty acres to rent and live on. The farmhouse was a squat building with an arctic entry to hold back the cold and store coats before entering: a long front room with kitchen and parlor, two back bedrooms, and an attached coal shed behind the house and an outhouse and creek nearby.

He ended his description with "It's not much to look at, but it will hold us. I can take you over tomorrow so you can see it."

Taking on a farm would move them out of Mother Shields' house, but root them in Bonetrail. Louise said, "I have to work tomorrow."

"Maybe you could get off early, or we can go the day after. Clara would give you time off."

Louise rubbed her eyelids and tried to keep her upset bottled. She told herself not to shout and rile Mother Shields. Again, Leo jumped, and she was told to leap and catch up. "How long's the renting contract?" Louise asked.

"Two years. It's the right place for us. Our new start. We leave Mother Shields behind in town."

Louise did not speak the words: *your new start and the baby and I drug along.* She said, "If we do this, we could get stuck."

"We're not going to get stuck. Sweetheart, this is the opportunity we've been waiting for."

You've been waiting for. We're about to spend most of our savings and risk on land that isn't even ours. Crops fail. Animals die. But instead, Louise asked, "What happens if we don't make it?"

A rigidness set in Leo's shoulders. "That won't happen. We're young and strong, and we know how to do this."

"You're making another decision without me agreeing."

"What are you talking about?" Leo asked.

"I didn't want to move to Bonetrail. You told me, but you didn't ask me if this was what I wanted," Louise bit out.

"We couldn't stay with the Musicale for the rest of our lives. It was time to go another direction."

Louise threw up her hands. "Wanting another direction is understandable. You didn't ask what direction I wanted."

"You could have spoken up."

"You're right. I didn't speak up. Though, what was I supposed to say? That you weren't allowed to quit the Musicale? We are going to gamble with Mother Nature and the odds are always in her favor."

A harsh bark emitted from Leo and then he said,

"All life's a gamble. I told you before I'd take care of you. You trusted me enough to marry me. Trust me on this. We're taking the farm. We move in two weeks."

Louise watched Leo leave the bedroom. As pregnant as she was, Louise felt hollowed out. Their blizzard of a fight was finished. Over the next few days, her feelings did not thaw. Leo was tentative around her.

Louise considered what to do. She didn't want to leave Leo. Going to the farm meant compromising and returning to a place that echoed the life she had escaped. Louise knew she would go to the farm with Leo. She also knew that they needed to begin working together as they had with the Musicale. Their new livelihood depended on it.

On the same day, Leo signed the rental agreement with Driscol's help; Louise asked to be the one to announce their departure to Mother Shields. It was something she would relish doing.

Louise waited until the three of them sat down to supper and then said, "Leo and I have rented a farm, and will be moving out."

Mother Shields' eyes pinched. "I already heard around town. I will be watching your packing and making sure you take none of my things. I know what belongs to me."

Louise's grip on her utensils squeezed so tight her knuckles were bone white. She loosened her aching hands. Instead of slamming the fork and knife onto the tabletop, she set them down in straight parallels to her plate. "We won't be needing or taking any of your things."

"I know. I'll be watching."

Later in bed, Leo pulled Louise into his chest for the first time since their argument and murmured into her hair whose fashionable bobbed cut had disappeared three inches ago. "This is our new start. We'll make a good life for our family."

Louise didn't know what to say.

He rubbed her belly. "I know you didn't want this."

Louise stilled his hand. "I don't want to farm, but you didn't want the Musicale anymore, and everything's changed." Within the silence of the drawn-out seconds, Louise could feel their conflicting dreams scraping her heart.

Leo rolled to his back. "I knew you didn't like Bonetrail. I figured you would change your mind and get used to the place. Be excited for something to call our own."

Louise pondered how they had become so far out of tune. Her mother would say she created this mess. There was no going back. Again, each kept to their side of the bed.

With each day closer to moving to the farm, Leo's happiness reached higher and he shared his good cheer with everyone, Mother Shields' behavior became more cantankerous, and Louise said as little as possible and retreated into sleep when she could. In preparation, Leo bought two draft horses and a wagon. People started giving the couple hand-me-downs, including a shovel, towels, and a chipped set of mugs. The Ladies Guild at Myra's church gave them two goose feather-filled pillows and a colorful mosaic quilt of hexagon-shaped flowers. The Zints had occasionally attended Mother Shields' and the Schmidts' church more out of community expectation than any desire for religious guidance. Louise gave her bittersweet notice at the café and school.

Louise's lips lifted almost into a smile when she said thank you to the wishes of good luck and good farming. She'd miss gabbing with Clara, the customers, and the Schmidts. Louise had made real friendships here. Not the 'just passing through' cordial acquaintanceships that she had while with the Musicale. She'd try to see her new friends when she came to town for groceries. The friendships would become twenty-minute catch ups before people moved on to their errands or returned to their farms. A farmer, and thereby a farmer's wife, always had more work to do than hours in a day.

On her last day at the café, Clara released Louise early, but she decided not to return Mother Shields' just yet. Instead, she meandered through Bonetrail. The afternoon was a crisp fifty-five degrees and the sun was bright. The spring daylight hours were getting longer. Dusk had been pushed back to seven o'clock.

Last summer, Louise had grimaced when she arrived in this farm town, and now she was surprised by her complicated feelings about moving beyond its borders. Caught up in her thoughts, she walked herself to the small cemetery.

Louise stepped inside the plot. Scattered among the headstone and crosses were melting snow clumps. She walked the short pathways in tic-tac-toe pattern while her gloved fingertips brushed the top of the markers. After some time, the wet, chilled ground began to creep up into her shoes and tried to invade her wool socks. It was time to go.

As Louise passed the Schmidts' house, she heard Myra yell out her name. Louise turned and saw Myra beckoning her in. She entered the house and found another sanctuary. This one smelled of baked apples and sugar. The oven's heat fogged over the windows.

"Take your coat off and sit down. Come in the kitchen. I have coffee on. The day is turning out warmer than I expected. Not too long now and the snow will be gone."

Louise sat at a red and white checkered oilcloth-covered worktable. A trio of dough lumps interrupted the squares. Myra handed Louise a cup of coffee. "Have you ever made strudels?"

"No. My mother made the dessert on occasion."

"This is no dessert. This is a meal. I'll show you."

Myra picked up a dough sphere. "You have to pull the dough out. Like this." She rotated the dough in her hands while she pulled it outward at the same time. When the shape was almost the size of a pie plate, Myra laid it back on the table and used a flour-dusted rolling pin to flatten further. Next she dipped her fingertips into lard and varnished the dough top. "Now, we need to let it rest and soak in. Wash your hands. It's your turn."

Myra peeled a second lump off the table and began to turn it in her floured and greased hands. "Take this and repeat what I did."

Louise cupped and lifted the warm, sticky dough. When she pulled back her hand some of the dough stayed attached and stretched on its own.

"Add more flour to your hands," Myra said as she deposited baker's snow on Louise's moving hands and then tossed the rest onto the table.

Louise followed and faltered with the dough. With expert hands, Myra guided Louise's.

"Now we pull the first one," Myra said. She made her fingers into soft pinchers and pulled dough towards the table edges until it was almost paper thin.

"That's nice and flat. We'll try to stretch it out some more. You want to almost see through and try not to break it."

The women stretched the dough increasing its surface area until it claimed half the table.

"That's good. Now we roll it up into itself like a rope," Myra said.

Myra held the edge and, using her fingertips, rolled the dough into a rope. Then, like a pianist practicing scales, she rolled her palms across the length, smoothing out the surface.

"Finally, we get to see the strudels." She cut the length into two-inch pieces until there was a jumbled pile laying on the oilcloth. "You finish cutting that one. I'll flatten and stretch the next. Then you can roll it up and cut it into pieces while I take care of the last of the dough. How are you and the baby doing?"

"I'm a little tired. Leo keeps saying this one will need to play a different instrument and eventually, we can have a family band."

A laugh like a bird taking off and soaring lifted out of Myra. "It'd be nice to have more music in this town. Especially for the young people. Stretch that last one a little more before rolling."

"Thank you for showing me this. As children, my sisters and I were only allowed into the kitchen under my mother's watch. She said we made messes too easily if she wasn't around."

"Every woman wants her say in her kitchen," Myra said.

After joining the Musicale, Louise had missed Rose and her father and on occasion thought about her mother and the rest of the family. Her letter writing was sporadic, though she had written to them about the baby and new farm. They'll be happy that she and Leo were settling in one place, on a farm no less.

"I suspect my mother would agree with you. I'm ready to be out of Mother Shields' house and into my own home."

"Mother Shields cannot be the easiest to live with, though she's hardworking and keeps a clean house. She's suspicious of people who didn't grow up in the area," Myra said.

"Ironic that she doesn't like strangers but has a boardinghouse. Why is she so mean to outsiders?"

"Mother Shields' first husband died not too many years after they were married. He left her with a farm and four children to take care of. Story goes that she made a go of it. Did well enough and there came a point when she wanted to either buy more land or equipment. She went to the bank for a loan. The banker, who was new to the town, had her sign a contract that turned over the farm to the bank. You see Mother Shields didn't know how to read then, so she didn't know what she had signed."

"That's terrible."

"It is. Mother Shields lost her home. She cleaned houses and did laundry to make ends meet. Years later she remarried another farmer named Shields. After he died, she sold that farm and moved into Bonetrail. Please roll and cut up the last one. I'll get the potatoes started," Myra turned to her stove.

As Louise rolled another dough cord, she thought about Mother Shields' past. Sun rays of pity began to melt Louise's icy regard for the landlady. No wonder the woman didn't like strangers and the world at large. Plus, not many women would have been able to work a farm and raise their children on their own. Louise rolled a leftover dough fragment between her fingers and enjoyed the moist feel and the fragrance of bursting yeast molecules.

"Louise, come help with the potatoes."

On the stovetop was a cast iron Dutch oven whose bottom was layered with cooking cubes of potatoes and onions. "Add salt, pepper, and a little more lard to these."

"Next we add the strudels," Four hands scooped up ivory chunks and nestled them on the potatoes. When the cooking pan was filled Myra added the pan's lid. "Now we wait and clean."

"Isn't that true for wives?" Louise asked.

Myra clucked. "Among other things. There's always something to clean."

Finished with the chores, the women sat down for more coffee and conversation.

Myra asked about the moving plans and added, "If you need something let me know. I might have an extra or something you can borrow for a time."

Louise's heart swelled at the gesture of help and friendship. "Thank you."

"I know you probably have lots to do over at

Mother Shields', but you and Leo are welcome to have supper here tonight for your last night in town." Myra pursed her lips, then said, "If Mother Shields would like to join us, she is welcome."

Louise suppressed a groan. "It would be a neighborly thing to do."

Myra glanced in the direction of Mother Shields' house. "This being a small town, it's best to be cordial, but that woman is so persnickety. I swear she'll outlive all of us just to show us up." Myra checked her pin watch. "Time to check on the strudels."

Myra lifted the pot's lid. The escaped heat turned the inquiring cheeks a soft pink, and the starched scents of baked dough and potatoes filled the kitchen. "Done. You go over to Mother Shields' and get the rest of them. I'll set the table."

As Louise headed to the back door, Heinrich entered.

"Hello, Louise." Then he greeted Myra and kissed her cheek.

Myra began shooing him away with her dishtowel. "Get cleaned up. We're having company for supper."

Before entering Mother Shields' house, Louise put on a polite face. She had arrived before Leo. Mother Shields was scrubbing potatoes.

"Good evening," Louise said.

Mother Shields harrumphed in response.

"The Schmidts invited all of us over for supper."

Mother Shields propped her fists on her hips. "I've already washed these potatoes. Supper is started."

"Potatoes keep," Louise said. The woman would not bend.

Leo entered the house. "Hello ladies."

"Hello to you too. We've all been invited to the Schmidts' for supper. I helped Myra make strudels," Louise said.

"Like the dessert?"

"No. This is more of a meal. Mother Shields has declined the invitation. Are you ready to go?"

"One minute." Then Leo trotted upstairs. He was back in quick time carrying his fiddle case. He grabbed a hold of Louise's hand, and they skedaddled out, almost skipping to the Schmidts.

Heinrich must have heard them because he opened the front door as they stepped onto the porch's first step. "Come in. We're eating well tonight."

When Myra set a platter of strudels atop the dining room table's yellow tablecloth. Applause followed. Food made small pyramids of bone white strudels, diced buttered potatoes, and spicy blood sausage on their plates.

The dinner was immersed in conversation and laughs that started low in the belly and shot upward through mouths wide open. Farming was always a topic near the beginning, but there were also stories about Bonetrail residents who had become not just names and faces, but friends and neighbors. The Zints had once been outsiders, musical vagabonds no less, but now they were part of Bonetrail, the farm rental was evidence of that connection.

Warm apple pie encored the ensemble. The meal lasted two hours, but felt like a few minutes. When the ladies began clearing that was Leo's cue to take out his fiddle. Heinrich's relaxed cheeks puffed on his pipe and his body reclined in his chair, confident that his world was content.

Louise wiped the table in arm sweeps that accompanied the rise and fall of tuning notes. Once the table was clear, the ladies started their washing in the kitchen. Leo followed and stood in the middle ground between the two rooms. His bow picked up speed and then stopped and hung and began again. Chords floated and flew around their heads and filled the rooms while pushing aside the winter sluggishness. Their breadbaskets were filled, and they enjoyed the last bits of a 'spring is coming' longer-light sunset. Sometimes the notes and pipe smoke blended, infusing a stronger soothing into the foursome.

Louise wiped the dishes and listened while the old dancehall Leo played songs she had heard many times before. Absent was the boyish band musician and instead, mature energy pulsated outward. There was new verve directing the show.

The next morning Louise awoke to Leo shifting

and adjusting in the bed. She knew he was thinking about the farm. She rolled over, and they faced each other.

"Morning." Leo passed his hand over Louise in a jumpy caress.

"Let's get up and go."

The man didn't reply and instead lit the lamp. Together they dressed, pulled together the last of their belongings, and went downstairs. It was a little after sunrise. Mother Shields was still in bed. Maybe she'd stay in her room until they were beyond the Bonetrail town boundary.

Louise cut thick slices of bread, and they each spread honey until their bread was soaked. The clover sweetness coated the tops of their mouths. Louise said a silent wish that such sweetness would stick to them. She closed the door behind them and followed an almost galloping Leo across the yard. They walked four streets to the Roberts' house where the draft horses were stabled.

Leo bridled the horses. Louise guided on one side of the team and Leo on the other, as the percussion of the clop, clop and the small clouds of horse breath accompanied them back to Mother Shields'. There, the workhorses were harnessed and hitched to the Zint's new wagon of household goods. A movement caught Louise's attention, and she saw Mother Shields standing at an upstairs window like a crow peering down. There was neither contempt nor blessing in the older woman's expression but a stiff acknowledgment that the Zints were leaving. Mother Shields would be the last woman to tell Louise how to live within her home.

Leo flicked the reins, and the horses lumbered into motion, advancing the wagon's rolling steel wheels and Louise toward a farming life she had never envisioned.

CHAPTER FIFTEEN

The morning was crisp and clear. March days tended to fluctuate between chilly and freezing. Prairie birds were perched on the spaces between barbed wire fencing or wood posts and were singing and winging between land and sky.

Louise flexed her shoulders back to loosen them. Leo began whistling, adding to the music of the bird calls. The last streaks blue-black sky faded and sunrise pinks and oranges pushed into its place.

"It's going to be a beauty of a day. Once the sun's all up and out, it will warm things up," Leo said.

Louise "hummed" in reply. A pheasant flew out of the ditch, and the horses side-stepped a little, neighed, and returned to the route. She studied Leo. He was a man happy for his future with his eyes and mind focused forward. Leo did not notice the breeze that ruffled the curls that poked out from underneath his wool hat. Louise longed to suck his nerve into her person and banish the fear within. Was she going to try to make this work? Part of her didn't want to make it work. If it didn't, her family was up a creek without a paddle.

The cavalcade turned and began the march down the snow-packed farm roads. When the farm came into view, Leo let out a whoop.

There wasn't much to or in the yard except for drifted snow. On the outer periphery, there were fields and pastures. To the west was a line of bare trees standing six feet at their tallest. There was a definite absence of agricultural machinery. Louise knew she and Leo would have to borrow and rent until they could afford to buy or get a loan.

Leo set the wagon brake. "We're here." He jumped and trotted to the other side, and as Louise was about to descend, he swung her down, and her feet touched the land. "Ma'am, may I escort you inside?"

Louise followed Leo to a paint puckered and peeled white rectangular farmhouse. In-between two smaller front windows, trimmed with black flaking paint, was a patched screen door keeping company with a scratched wood entry door.

"Ladies, first," Leo said.

Louise walked across the threshold and heard Leo utter a faint "home."

The small entryway led into a larger combination room that included the kitchen and parlor and a short hallway to the bedrooms. Louise looked at her new lodgings. The low ceiling shrunk the long room making the room somber in light and feeling. She knew Leo was watching her. The lighting was dim enough that Leo was unable to see the disappointment in her eyes. Louise's one small relief was that the floor was not dirt.

Leo walked to the hallway. "The bedrooms are back here. I figure we can use the one directly behind the kitchen wall so that way the stove pipe can heat our room. The other we can use for storing things until we need to make more space for when the baby is old enough."

At the mention of the baby, Louise rubbed her expanding middle. The baby had been quiet all morning. Movement from her child would have been a good distraction from her resignation and sadness. This farm was the concrete symbol that her old life was history and reconciling to her present and future wasn't coming easy.

Louise walked down the short hallway and peered into each bedroom. The lighting was still murky from the early morning and shadowed the bed frame. She brushed her fingers across the rough, warped wall planks. "Maybe we could paint to brighten the rooms?"

Leo crossed the front room in four strides. "Good

idea. Now that you've seen the house, let me show you the barn. The chicken coop is near the barn."

Louise hastened to follow him. He held the front door open for her as they continued their tour. Louise watched Leo show off the small farmstead with the extended arm sweeps of a salesman. He told of plans and ideas about the buildings and corral and what he would do and where he would put things. The fiddle player who had left the farm as a young, ornery adolescent had now returned as an elated farmer.

Louise saw the various farm areas, but she didn't feel the zoom of Leo's pleasure for animal pens.

She startled when she realized Leo had asked her a question. He must have repeated the question because his head was cocked to the side waiting for her answer. "What did you say?"

"I thought it would be a good idea to start unpacking the wagon. I can bring the crates and boxes into the house and you can start there? Then, I'll take the team over to the barn and unload the rest of it."

"Okay."

Together they unloaded the wagon bed.

"What do you want me to do with your cans?" Leo asked.

"Put them somewhere where you won't be walking."

Leo honked out a guffaw. "I'll do that" and a whistling Leo headed to the barn to finish unloading tools and supplies.

The memory of the tin cans lightened Louise's mood a smidge. After the rental contract was signed, she had begun saving the used tin cans from the cafe. The large Maxwell House coffee and Karo syrup cans would be her most useful. The smaller cans would be used to start garden plants, and the larger cans would protect the established plants. Leo had been pleased with her resourcefulness and the accumulation of the washed tin cans, but he had a noisy run-in one evening after a celebratory night with Driscol and a few other Bonetrail pals.

He had miscalculated his footsteps in their dark bedroom and fell on the flour sacks of cans. By the sound of the racket, it was not a graceful fall but a full-arms-windmilling-every-which-way   crash landing.

Louise lit the lamp. "Leo. Are you alright? Did you hurt yourself?"

"What's going on in there?" Mother Shields, of course, heard and stood outside their door scolding them.

Louise rushed to the door and opened it. "Leo misjudged where my can sacks were and ran into them."

"I expect quiet in this house. If you and your husband cannot abide by my rules, then you can leave sooner. Do you understand?"

Louise nailed down the retort that wanted to fly

at Mother Shields' head and said instead "It won't happen again."

"Better not." Mother Shields marched back to her bedroom and shut the door with a purposeful thud.

Leo's face showed a bewildered look more than an injured one. Louise didn't know whether to be annoyed or amused, so instead she walked over and reached down to help him up. An unsteady Leo grasped her upper arms, swayed a little, and laid his forehead on her shoulder. "Your cans hurt."

Louise brushed his hair. "Then don't fall on them. Time for bed."

Leo pseudo waltzed them to bed and began to move his hands down Louise's backside. "I like that idea."

Louise snatched up Leo's hands. "I think you should get into bed first."

"I can do that," Leo beamed. For more than a little drunk, the man threw off his shoes and clothes and was in bed in record time.

It was a good memory. Louise stood and rested her hands on her hips, then stretched her spine upward until her shoulders almost touched her ears. Several hours later, Louise felt satisfied at the unpacking she had completed. Their few plates, mugs, and the rest of the sundries sat in tidy rows on the open kitchen shelves. The previous residents had left behind a kitchen table, a stove, four chairs, and a bed. The Zints had a place to cook, sit, and sleep.

In a hope chest at her Mother's, Louise had left behind an inherited set of dishware. It wasn't fancy, but she could have used them now. Their future had come into being.

Leo walked into the house. "I'm hungry."

Louise noticed that the sun had moved to the other side of the room and shook her head at the remembrance of how quickly a day can move on a farm. She sliced dense bread and white cheese and put them, along with sour pickles, on wood plates.

It was late afternoon when Louise inspected the black behemoth of the cookstove. She scrubbed it clean and then lit paper and tinder and guessed at the unregulated heating temperature to bake potatoes. Tonight wasn't a celebration for Louise, but it was their first supper by themselves since Christmas. She poured sunset colored peach juice into two glasses—something to sweeten the evening.

Louise yelled from the front door. "Supper!"

As Leo approached, she watched him pull a handkerchief out of his back pocket and wipe his damp forehead. Inside the house, Leo washed his hands in the basin of water Louise had set aside. He had a satisfied, tired look. She looked down and adjusted her apron to hide her dismay.

Leo moved the kerosene lamp to the middle of the table. "I'm ready to eat."

Louise set the butter dish on the table. "We need to buy another kerosene lamp or two. We're also going to have to dig a bigger root cellar hole. That one next to the house isn't big enough."

"That I can do. Maybe this month. I'll have to see how much the ground has thawed but it should be pretty good so close to the house."

"We need to get some hens and a rooster for the coop," Louise added. She felt an immense urge to add more tasks to Leo's to-do-list. To remind him that farm work was never-ending.

Leo buttered a slice of bread. "On Wednesday, when we go into town, we can see if anyone has chickens they want to part with. Otherwise, we'll have to mail order them. Plus, we're going to need to purchase several dairy cows."

Louise reminded Leo about their tentative finances by saying, "We'll need to get on the creamery route."

Leo raised his glass of peach juice. "I already stopped by the creamery and they said to give a holler when we have milk and cream for pickup. They'll add us to the milk run."

Louise was surprised. "You've been busy."

Leo's musician's laugh, energetic and melodic, flew up and joined the Chinook winds passing through their farmstead.

Then Louise rose and put the large tea kettle on the stovetop to heat water for dishes. She'd been busy too, like a farmwife. Her practical side accepted the innocence of the conversation, and the other part rebelled at being on the farm. Louise was more than an ordinary farmwife.

When she began to clear the table, Leo retrieved his violin case. He lowered himself into the chair like a feather drifting to the ground. The case came to rest on his knees and then with a snap the lid was opened. Leo reached inside and, lifting at the neck, brought out the wooden instrument. The flicker of the kerosene lantern skipped across the dark honey varnish of the spruce top. He had once told Louise the violin was very similar to a woman. Both had a neck, belly, and waist. In a boisterous laugh laced with a thread of wickedness, he said there was even a tailpiece. She did not understand, and when Leo explained the double entendre, her internal temperature climbed ten degrees higher.

Louise had washed half the dishes while Leo was still tuning his violin too high or too low. There seemed to be a tension in him that was failing to find his notes.

"Is something wrong?" Louise asked.

"I want to get this right. This is our first night on the farm. The music should be as close to perfect as I can play it."

Leo wasn't one for perfection but instead a man that took the songs and often added his charisma and improvisational feel.

"Whatever you play will be better than anything this house has heard before," Louise said.

"That's what I'm working towards."

More starts and stops came, and then an ease and flow found its way into stringing the notes into a song. The lamplight spotlighted Leo, and the evening dark and cold pushed in close to hear the new farmer.

After the farm was buttoned up for the evening, the couple went into the bedroom and pulled back the church ladies' gifted quilt. With a whoosh, the small triangle of flame was extinguished and the darkness knitted together.

Later, Louise listened to the snoring of a satiated Leo, and she caressed his forearm and thought about her day. She went from someone else's house to her own in one day. Not too far off until a third Zint would need attention and care. Maybe this farm could work out for them, for a while anyway? They knew where their bed was every night. Louise got through today, she'd wait to see about tomorrow.

As her heavy body pressed into Leo and the tick mattress, she imagined she could hear tonight's violin music and the wind playing a performance together. The duo flew with the owls and the stars across the plains and landed among groves of sweet-smelling West Coast fruit trees.

The next day Leo woke up, dropped a quick kiss on Louise's forehead, and was out of the room before Louise muttered a good morning. Dawn was breaking judging by the chatter of the birds. Louise pushed herself up on the bed. The baby was up and awake and matched its father.

Louise's belly had rounded. The pregnancy was less an announcement and more a reality now. She dressed in her heaviest cotton dress that was too tight and tall wool stockings. Much of her Musicale clothing wasn't suitable for Bonetrail much less the farm. Shortly after hiring on at the school, more durable clothing had become a necessity. It was another example of how her world had changed.

Louise acknowledged that complaining about her bigger body was not going to change her situation. She put on her coat and walked to the outhouse. The sky was a gradation of indigo blue and soft blue with a bottom rim of marigold yellow.

When she returned, Leo had lit the stove and put the water on for coffee. The heat rolling off the stove felt good in the cold kitchen. Louise exchanged her coat for an apron and then laid smoked pork in the frying pan. When the fat sizzled and popped, she added eggs and finally, a jar of stewed tomatoes.

Leo scanned the horizon out the kitchen window and watched the yard begin to light up. The wind rustled the grasses and carried away the last stripes of the sunrise. The day would be clear and bright.

When he finished eating, his chair scraped across the wood plank floor. He jogged to the door and grabbed his hat and coat that hung on their new hooks. "Got work to do." The farmer was chomping at the bit to start his second day on the farm.

Louise stared at the closed door. Then she took in the big room she now called home. It was strange to transfer feelings of safety and sanctuary to this weathered wood building in the course of one sunset and sunrise. She didn't have time to ruminate about the house when what she needed was to get her day underway. Louise needed to clean out the coop before any living thing could take up residence.

Before any of that, she placed a weighty crock mixing bowl on the table. Louise added water, yeast, salt, oil, and sugar. Using the wooden spoon, she stirred and slowly began to add flour. No more buying bread or having someone else make it. While she stirred, a shopping list for their next town visit developed.

Louise also needed to sew more baby clothes. She didn't have a sewing machine. Myra did and had said to come over. The two of them could sew baby clothes. Leo, of course, would bring either or both of his instruments. The afternoon was an occasion she could look forward to.

When the dough was the consistency Louise wanted, she draped a flour sack kitchen towel printed with orange tiger lilies over the top. After Louise put the kitchen to rights, she dressed in her coat and gloves and went to the barn. From there, Louise wheeled a shovel, rake, and wheelbarrow over to the chicken coop, which had been nailed together with discarded wooden planks. She hoped the thing didn't fall on her.

Louise opened the rust-hinged door, and the ammonia stench of decaying manure, straw, and rodent habituation made her breakfast jump to her throat. With a thrust of her chin, she swallowed it back down. She closed the rough-hewn door, laid her forehead on it, and gulped in fresh winter air. When Louise turned her head, she saw a large rock nearby and in an awkward sideways movement positioned the rock to prop open the door. She placed her hand on the wood planks and straightened up one vertebrate at a time then wobbled back to the farmhouse and found a faded headscarf.

Back at the coop, Louise stood at the door. "Goodbye, sophisticated lady." Then she double wrapped the scarf over her nose and mouth and carried the rake and shovel into the mess.

Later she yelled at Leo across the yard. "Leo! I need your help." She rubbed the parts of her back she could reach. "The wheelbarrow is full. Please dump it somewhere. I have to go check my dough."

Inside the house, Louise filled a cracked, shallow bathing basin. Cupped tepid water splashed her forehead, cheeks, and chin and rolled down her arms. The rinsing away of the coop carried a small bliss, and rising bread dough replaced the smell.

Louise yanked off the flowered kitchen towel.

She smacked her palms down each time she kneaded the softened, malleable dough. The battered yeast released a smell that reminded her of her childhood house. Her mother made multiple loaves of bread almost every day, and Louise knew she'd be accumulating a loaf count of her own.

She knew there was more to do before suppertime but did not care. Louise decided to sit down for a cup of coffee. The coffee grounds made her think of the café, and she pictured its goings-on. Louise missed it. This morning was the beginning of many solitary hours for Louise while Leo worked around the farm and going into town occurred maybe once a week. Her neighbors were now the western meadowlark, the prairie hawk, and the wind.

CHAPTER SIXTEEN

The second night on the farm, both Louise and Leo were bone tired. Each had worked until the sun went to bed. Louise prepared a dinner of fried egg sandwiches and bread-and-butter pickles. Leo ate three sandwiches before he was full.

Wednesday was livestock sale day, so after morning chores, the Zints would hitch up the draft horses and go into town to buy their dairy cows. They'd leave the farm a little after seven to make sure they were at the sale barn by eleven. The day was overcast, and the temperature stayed close to the mid-forties. Louise carried a Karo Syrup pail of buttered bread and jelly sandwiches and the wool camping blanket and canteen they used during their Musicale tenting days.

Climbing into the wagon for Louise was now a two-person job. "Leo, please help me up?"

Leo finished putting the empty crates and boxes in the wagon bed and then walked around to help her. "Ma'am, could you use a hand?" Cupping her elbow and positioning his other hand on her lower back, he helped boost her into the wagon.

Louise unfolded a travel blanket and then wrapped the edges around her legs, adding to her winter coat, hat, gloves, and scarf and then she gasped, "Your instruments."

As Leo reached down to release the wagon brake. "Already loaded in the wagon."

"We'd hate to disappoint everyone."

"Won't be happening today. I made sure we have the kerosene lamp for the ride home later tonight just in case." Leo began whistling a jovial tune that matched his mood. He gave the yard a last glance to confirm that nothing was out of place and then turned his attention to the road.

Louise looked at the landscape. This country was different from what she had grown up around. There had been acres of trees and stout, pretty brick grain silos. What her eyes could see here were sleeping fields coming out of the deep freeze of winter and cattle huddled together for warmth in snow and dirt pastures. Some farmers had immature tree lines in between fields, but that was a rarity, and the trees were short enough that a person could see the infinite horizon.

A mated pair of pheasants flew up out of the ditch. This time the horses didn't shy away but instead pranced and then calmed. The pheasants didn't fly high, but the height they achieved displayed their long, slender, light brown tail feathers that appeared as if a painter had used a fine brush to make black swipes up and down the shafts. The body feathers were a combination of white, copper, and burgundy. The male's head feathers were a bright red, and his neck ringed in teal and green. Songbirds sat on fence posts whistling and calling to each other. These birds were spots of color against a backdrop of winter white and brown. High overhead a hawk dipped and sailed the wind currents.

"How many head of cattle are you thinking of buying?" Louise asked.

"I thought we would start with ten Holsteins since they're some of the best milk producers. How many chicks do you want?"

"Start with ten hens or chicks and a rooster. Do you want me to come with you to the sale barn in case there's something to read?"

Leo shook his head. "I'll be fine. I can hear. They'll take my money."

Louise had offered several times to teach Leo to read, but he always declined. "I can teach you the alphabet. It wouldn't take much time at all."

"I can sing the alphabet," Leo said.

"What I mean to say is that we can practice the letters. Start with small words."

"No. Too much time has passed. There's other things to do. Plus, you can do all the reading and writing for us, so why go to all the bother and fuss."

"It's not a bother or fuss." They repeated variations of the conversation. "No one will know. We could practice a little each night after supper," Louise said.

"Nope," and the man wouldn't budge.

The Zints were almost to the outskirts of Bonetrail. Leo pulled the reins a little to slow the horses. "Should I look around for a pig? If we get two, then we would for sure have one to butcher later this fall."

Butchering was one of Louise's least favorite, but necessary, farm tasks. "I'll need to start buying canning jars on our town visits. Today, I'll buy some seed packets."

"If they don't have what you want, you could order from the Oscar Will catalog. What are you thinking for your garden?" Leo said.

"Tomatoes, onions, radishes, beets, lettuce, cabbage, cucumbers, potatoes, sweet corn, and so on, and some flowers." Louise recognized that Leo had used the word 'your' instead of 'our.' She shifted in her seat. "I noticed you called it my garden."

"I'll be busy in the fields with the crops and the cows. I'll leave the garden to you."

"Not too far down the road the soil will need to be turned so I can plant *my* garden. I'll let you do that part."

"Already on my work list, plus, digging you a bigger root cellar to store all of your garden harvest," Leo said.

"I'd rather you give me a night of music and dancing, but if we want to eat, we need a garden."

A happy laugh sprinted out of Leo. "I knew you would come around to this farm. We're going to make this place a success." Then he kissed Louise's cool cheek.

Louise gaped at her husband. She didn't have a choice.

Once in town, Leo dropped Louise at the grocery store, and he drove to the livestock sale barn. Louise bought only necessaries since she had purchased kitchen staples before they moved to the farmstead. The real pleasure was talking with the women who were also shopping. Louise already missed her friends, her co-workers, and café customers. She decided to stop by the cafe and say hello.

When Louise walked into the café, her small belly led the way. She heard customers call out, "Look who it is!"

"Hi there."

"Louise is here and wants her job back."

Clara came around the counter and hugged her

hard and firm, the kind of hug that a person is always a little reluctant to step back from.

"Sit at the counter and let me get you some coffee. Want anything to eat?" Clara called out as she reached for a metal coffee pot and ceramic-heavy ivory mug.

"Coffee and some pie would be nice."

"We have apple and peach today. Which one you want?"

"Apple, please."

The customers dropped questions on Louise: "Are you settled in? What's it like out there? When are you going to start planting? How many cows are you buying?"

In between sips and bites, Louise spent the hour answering questions and catching up on the news and gossip of the town. Since it had only been a few days, there wasn't much she didn't already know. It felt nice and right to be in their company. These were her friends.

Louise withdrew her coin purse. "I'd better get to the Schmidts'. We're making baby clothes."

Clara waved her hand at Louise. "On the house. Visit again soon."

Louise blushed. "Thank you."

After goodbyes and another hug from Clara, Louise exited the cafe. Standing on the other side of the door, she felt the separation from the restaurant. They, and she, had moved on.

Louise knocked and as she waited at Myra's door, Louise stared ahead so that she would not have to converse with Mother Shields should the woman appear. Myra swung the door full-open regardless of the brisk spring noon and pulled Louise inside and patted her on the back. "Hello, hello! Come in. Let's get you out of that coat and those gloves and hat. Sadie, come downstairs. Louise is here. Time to catch up and sew."

Sadie ran down the stairs. ""Hi! How's the farm?"

Louise hung up her coat. "Taking shape better than me."

Myra clucked. "Your belly is getting bigger. That's what we want to see. We have everything on the table to get going, but before we do, let's have luncheon. I made vegetable soup. I thought today would be a good soup day. Louise, sit down. Sadie, slice some bread and put it on the table."

"What can I do to help?" Louise asked.

"Let us do the work. You'll be running nonstop soon enough. Baby and summer are coming."

Louise did as she was told. Stacked on one end were folded up cotton fabric remnants, thread spools, needles, scissors, and other notions. Also included were flour sacks. Louise fingered a flour sack printed with red and blue butterflies.

Myra carried two bowls of soup and placed them on the table. She saw Louise touching the flour sack. "Some people think using flour sacks to make clothing means you're poor. Maybe it does, but that's good cloth. There's no sense in not using what you can. They make good diapers too."

"My mother would agree with you."

After lunch, it was an afternoon of measuring, pinning, cutting, Singer sewing, and talking. Myra was very proud of her tar-black Singer treadle sewing machine. Her hand cupped the balance wheel as one did with an infant's head. "See here. There's gold lettering and a chestnut wood cabinet with a side support table. Then two drawers on either side. The base is cast iron. No wind could blow this machine away."

Louise remembered when her mother had purchased a Singer sewing machine. The neighbor ladies had come to view the new household treasure. Her mother kept the machine in the parlor where it could be displayed. None of the children were allowed to touch the Singer without their mother being around. When Louise's mother used it, she was always happy during and afterward. Flowers and a sewing machine made that matriarch so happy.

The afternoon rolled quickly on the wheel of the Singer. The ladies had created several piles of baby, and even some toddler, clothing, and cloth diapers.

Myra bustled off to the kitchen to start supper. When Sadie saw her mother was out of earshot, she whispered, "Driscol asked me to marry him. He still has to ask father and mother, but I said yes."

"Congratulations. When?"

"We were thinking late May or even June. After planting. Would Leo play at the wedding?"

"Of course. I bet he could get a pickup band together with a few other musicians in the area."

Sadie clapped her hands in glee. "I can't wait to be married," and continued in a gush, "Have my man, my house, and our own farm."

Louise heard Sadie's words and looked down at the sewing project she held because the concern in Louise's eyes would prompt questions. Sadie, Louise wanted to say, be sure you know what direction Driscol is going before you make the vow. She couldn't say it or tell this newly engaged woman that her own marriage was not working out the way she had hoped. Louise loved Leo. He was her best friend, but the direction their lives had changed because of his new dream still pinched her.

Louise said, "After planting would be a good time." Before she realized the words were coming out of her mouth, she added, "I hope you get all you want."

After five o'clock the men arrived including Driscol, and Myra and Heinrich's two oldest boys. They shared a supper of spicy pork sausage fried in pork grease and seasoned with pepper, garlic, and brown sugar, cubed white potatoes and halved yellow onions, and cherry pie with pink, sweet filling running over the crust.

In a swig, Leo threw back the last sips of the homemade vodka. "Time for music."

Cheers chorused in response, and Leo unpacked his violin. After some adjusting of his instrument and seat, he played a fast-paced Irish jig that soon had everyone clapping in time. Louise reclined back in her chair and admired her husband. The lamp light reflected his shiny eyes. In the second song, Leo stood up and circled the room with a faster Romanian tune. They all laughed at Leo's showmanship and his gypsy music. It was during the fourth song that Myra stood up and began to clear the table.

Leo stopped playing. "Leaving so soon? I must be missing my notes and dropping my melodies."

Myra smirked. "My ears can hear in the kitchen just as well. It's not every day a woman has a live show in her home to do dishes by."

Louise noticed Sadie gave Driscol's hand a quick squeeze and then picked up dirty platters and followed her mother. Louise smiled. Gathering her load of dishware, she followed the Schmidt women.

In the kitchen, the ladies added shuffles, twirls, swings, and kicks to the cleaning chore. Louise couldn't have imagined washing dishes could be this much fun. She giggled as she and Sadie clasped hands and raised them high as Myra hoofed it underneath to put a clean pot on the stove. When the women returned to the dining room, Leo changed the mood with a church spiritual that a railroad hobo had taught him. Smiles settled into quiet expressions and heads started to nod in easy time with the reverent tempo. He ended in a peaceful crescendo that touched the gathered.

The ride back to the farm that night was encased in contentment. Louise felt a thimble-size of hope in her center.

"Home again, home again, jiggety-jig, jig," Leo said as they drove into the farmyard. "Why don't you take the lantern inside and light another one. Bring that one back so I can put away the horses. I'll start unloading the wagon. I want to get these chickens in the coop tonight yet."

"Alright. We'll soon find out what coyotes and foxes are around," Louise said.

"I was thinking we should get a dog. It would be good to have one around. Help keep an eye on things. I'm sure someone has a dog that needs a new home or is about to whelp."

Louise took Leo's hand as he helped her dismount from the wagon seat. "Are you asking what I think?"

"Yes."

"Me being pregnant is enough. We do not need a pregnant dog around here. Please get a male if you can."

Leo hugged Louise. "We agree." He then began moving crates, and the new chickens squawked their distress. "Be calm. You'll be in your new house soon enough."

Louise saw Leo's form merge into the night landscape. The northern wind came up making her shiver. She didn't move into the house but continued to breathe in the evening. To the west, she heard the low hoot of a field owl. Louise knew she should go inside the house. Leo would ask her if something was wrong. How could she describe her muddle of feelings? Louise didn't want this farm, and yet she had begun to make a life with Leo here. Why did Louise feel like she was betraying herself?

CHAPTER SEVENTEEN

Louise awoke in the morning dark needing to use the outhouse. She put on her shoes and left her coat behind. The stars were fading behind a light navy-blue sky, and a half circle of the moon shone. A warmer April breeze propelled her to extend her arms and spread her fingers so that it even touched the skin nestled between her fingers.

Closing her eyes, she widened her stance, and the wind ballooned her nightdress. There she stood in the dawn being cleansed by wind as if trying to blow disappointment away. An expansive peace spiraled a shiver up her spine. Opening her eyes, the landscape appeared the same, but she felt she had somehow made a mysterious pact with this land. Her bladder began to speak and eclipsed the moment.

After breakfast and milking the new Holstein

cows, Leo retrieved the two large bathtubs from their hanging hooks in the barn. Today was wash day. It was one of the tasks that Louise disliked. She put more wood in the stove to make the large tea kettle boil and steam in preparation for the bare hand-scrubbing and wringing of clothes in that rural kitchen. Later in the summer, the wash could be done outside in the sunshine.

As Louise washed the undergarments, socks, shirts, and pants, in that order, she thought about how Leo now walked and moved around the farm. When she had first met Leo, he walked with a big-city saunter. These days his carriage was different. The saunter had slipped into a determined stride as if he followed an invisible arrow with a clear trajectory.

Earlier that month, Leo told Louise, "Mr. Wheeler asked if I wanted to be one of his field hands again. It would be long days for a couple of months at least. We can milk the cows before sunrise and then I'll head to Wheeler's and return for evening milking and other chores. When planting starts, I'll plant our fields after supper. We can milk the cows when I get home. It will delay our fields by a few weeks, but Mr. Wheeler will let us borrow his tractor." He held back for a few beats and then asked, "What do you think?"

"You'll be away from the farm a lot. There'll be little to no rest for you," Louise said.

"The paychecks will help while we get our footing. Our baby and wheat growing side by side," Leo steamed on.

Louise stared into the blue-white sky and gave herself time to put the words together. "I know it's good for us that you take extra work where you can. You're young and strong. I'll miss having you around."

Leo swung his arm around Louise's shoulders and pulled her tight against his side. "We can do this. It will only be for a short while."

Louise slipped her arm around Leo's waist. "I'm glad we got to talk about this before things moved so quickly."

"Sweetheart, I told you: we're in this together."

Louise had kept a secret hope that when the daily to-do list and the forthcoming summer work were fully viewed and added up, Leo would announce that he wanted to trade this farm for a different course. With her arms submerged in dirty water up to her elbows, she crumpled the wish and let it drop and sink.

A week before moving to the farm, Louise had written to her family about the change in residence. Within the first month of being on the new place, two cardboard boxes arrived from her mother. Inside were a letter and the contents of Louise's hope chest she had accumulated all those years in Wheatville.

She waited to open the parcels until Leo went to work outside. The contents of the hope chest were a physical timeline of her mother's efforts to teach her to sew, stitch, collect, and prepare Louise for a life like hers. Included in one of the packages was an envelope with Louise's name written in her father's script and five dollars inside. She suspected he slipped it in without her mother knowing.

Louise touched each fabric, ceramic, wood, and paper and then read the letter that had accompanied the lot.

Dear Louise,

I hope this letter finds you and Leo well in your new home. Your father and I are relieved that you are settled. Nearby there are two farms for sale and several farms needing extra farmhands. Your father could recommend Leo if things don't work out in Bonetrail.

Enclosed are the contents of your hope chest. Now that you have a household of your own, these things can prove useful and be put to work. Your sisters, brother, and their families are all fine and say hello.

Keeping you in my prayers, Mother

Did her mother hope that Louise would return to her hometown?

In May, a small box had arrived from Wheatville. Inside was a crocheted lemon colored baby blanket, handmade baby clothes, cloth diapers, and another five dollars.

Seeing the blanket made Louise retrace her memory back to the evenings when her mother had knitted, embroidered, or sewed, her hands always in motion. Leo would have appreciated this about his mother-in-law. Absolute fatigue and being stuck in a field sometimes prevented his standing evening musical appointment. It was strange to consider that her mother and Leo were compelled to fill their free time with a pleasurable activity.

Her mother's sewing and garden were practical and necessary, but they also provided a personal expression, private space, beauty, and peace. Her mother would scoff at Louise's extravagant opinion. Louise would be forever a little different than the woman who had existed a few moments before, as she now understood a small part of her mother. Louise had not wanted to be like her mother, but in this instance, she envied those acts of creation. She loved Leo's music, but it was just that: Leo's music. What was Louise's pleasure?

In the late afternoon as the wash hung on the outside line, Louise moved a kitchen chair to the open doorway of the front door. "Baby, we're going to put our feet up."

She propped her feet onto a crate and sat in the sunshine. The combination of doing the laundry and her progressive pregnancy had pushed her in a state of exhaustion. Her water retention had swallowed her ankle bones and hidden them.

A tingling discomfort in her fingertips caused by pooling blood woke Louise. Before falling asleep, she had crossed her wrists and rested them at her pushed out belly but at some point, both had slipped off.

Easing from the chair, Louise walked several rotations in the front yard, working out the kinks. On the sixth circuit, she veered toward the barn for her tin cans. "It's time to start planting."

Louise dragged the bags to the dome of dirt that Leo created when he dug out more of the root cellar. Next, she retrieved the empty wood-slatted packing crates they had used for moving. After sorting the cans into three groups, Louise looked at the seeds she had purchased in town. "Baby, listen to these names: Hidatsa red beans, Mandan and Dakota white corn. They sound exotic. Wills Sugar Watermelon, now that's fancy. This land could use some fancy. With a name like Bison Tomatoes, they're sure to be good sized. We'll need to soak the peas overnight."

Using a kitchen spoon, Louise scooped dirt into a small can, then added a palm portion of bonemeal, dropped the seed, and covered the contents with dirt. Setting the finished can into a crate, she reached for another can and repeated the steps. When the illustrated seed packet was empty, and the crate was full, Louise attached the packet onto the crate. "Baby, we have one crate done and many more to start."

Louise planted her vegetable seeds into medium and large restaurant-sized cans with labels that read "Armstrong's Bird Brand Shortening," "Libby's

Tomato Juice," "M.J.B.'s Aladdin Coffee," and "Karo Syrup".

It was during the third and fourth crates she recognized that she was humming. The melodies were fragments of songs that Leo played and tunes from before this farm. At the twelfth crate, needles of pain began to poke at Louise's knees so placing a hand on the half-full crate she began to raise herself. Still hunched, a sharp arrow zoomed across her lower back. Bent in a semi-erect posture, she waited for the pain to dissipate and her breath to return.

"It's just time to stand up. You okay in there?" Louise waited for another surge. No more came.

"Now we water and then time to start supper." Using a tin ladle, she watered each crate of cans. Louise left her planting project scattered near the front door and went inside to begin cooking supper.

Leo strode into the house and went right to the pitcher and washbasin. "Hello!"

"Hello back."

"Smells good. I'm hungry. Got a lot done today." It was Louise's "oh?" that set Leo off recounting his day of chores and accomplishments. He was still chattering when they sat down for supper.

"I didn't get a chance to get the clothes in off the line. Can you bring them in and carry in my seed crates? I have more to do, but I have a start," Louise said.

Clothes and crates were brought in as the dishes were washed and dried.

Baby, time for our concert.

Louise wasn't sure, but she may have sighed out loud.

The laundry could wait. The clothes would be folded but not ironed. Her mother would disapprove about the proper way to clean clothes, but her mother was a thousand miles away. Clapping her hand down on the kitchen table, she closed off the matron's voice.

"Why don't we take our chairs outside. It's warmer out tonight," Leo said.

The light blue sky was the backdrop to a new spring setting sun and light jackets. Winter nudged into the pockets of winter coats stored in the back of the closet. The sunset hovered in the sky, not yet ready to leave the horizon.

Louise made herself comfortable in her chair with her feet propped up on a crate. Leo was going to serenade the land too.

The first set was eager and frisky, telling stories of adventure and heroics. It was a short skip to dancing in that dirt yard surrounded by growing crops and prairie grass. Louise, now a pregnant farmer's wife, was again being wooed by the man and his music. Her twenty-one-year-old self moved in a circle, and she lifted her skirt up as she twirled and sashayed one direction and then the other.

Leo plucked a solemn introduction, and then the

bow returned to position, and he began to play "Amazing Grace," its sweet sounds sailing across the prairie. The bright ball of the moon went behind the clouds, but as the clouds floated across the Northern Great Plains sky, they passed, releasing the white orb into sight, spotlighting the musician and a swaying pregnant woman.

The hymn ended and Louise stood still. She could not explain how, but she knew that entering into the house tonight crystallized a decision for the future and unseen roots would begin to grow and reach into her. Louise walked to Leo and held her palms open and up. He passed the violin to her, and then picked up the kitchen chairs.

Inside Louise took down a pie plate that hung from a nail on the wall. She dampened a kitchen towel, a gift from Myra, that was embroidered with roly-poly kittens and laid the towel in the pie plate so that half of the fabric hung off the edge. Into this damp nest, she poured pea seeds and covered them with the remaining cloth. Tomorrow she would plant more seeds.

Louise heated water on the cookstove and then poured half into the washbasin. She removed her daffodil colored day dress. In the dusky light, Louise stuck out her leg and peered at her toes, so swollen they had been forced to spread to the sides, attempting to make more room for each other. As she passed the soaked cloth across her skin, she made circles around where a tiny footprint appeared.

"There you are."

Louise finished her spit bath, slipped on her nightdress, and crawled into bed next to Leo. He settled in and his deep inhales and exhales of sleep moved the hair on the back of her neck. For Louise, that night's sleep was a combination of short deep naps and longer awake periods. She listened to the man beside her submerged in the fatigue of a laborer. Soon enough Leo would sleep even harder. The long nights performing would become faint memories exchanged for the body-weary days ahead.

Soon, Louise would return to Bonetrail to give birth. This meant an extended stay. She was ready and excited to meet the baby and be off the farm, to see her friends and begin to fill a hole of loneliness that farm living had created. There was a new whisper that wanted her to remain in her own house. This was an opportunity to stay in town. Her inability to sleep was causing her to slip into musings that made no sense.

She was awake when the sunrise birds began their vigorous chorus of squeaks and chirps. Louise looked out the kitchen window to see the sun rays streaking across the sky and cutting the dark blue fading night into ribbons. Today she'd wear the soft blue housedress that reminded her of blue flax blossoms. Her mother had liked blue flax because of the pale hue, and it also kept the deer away from her garden. That woman was stern and firm. For the first time, Louise questioned what kind of mother she'd be.

Louise craved something sweet for breakfast, so she made buckwheat pancakes with thicker-than-honey sorghum syrup and fried eggs. When she went into the root cellar for the buttermilk, she wished she had worn a sweater or jacket instead of just a house dress and apron. The small eight-by-eight-foot room had a trapped damp cold. Her hand curled around the shorter milk bottle, and she felt a shiver sprint up her arm. The action caused a deep intake of air. The earthy smell of the dugout spread across her lungs. She found the scent comforting.

Louise closed her eyes and sniffed again. She picked out the aromas of past burlap bags and long eaten vegetables. Then she imagined the room filled with her canned cherries, pickled beets, bags of apples and potatoes, jars of meats, hanging dried wild garlic, and other pantry foods. "Baby, we're going to have to fill this room."

At the end of April the soil had dried enough to start wheat planting. On Leo's first day working again with Mr. Wheeler, Louise awoke earlier that next morning. She pumped fresh water from the well and filled a jug for Leo to take with him. The underground water was so chilly that it would stay cold all day. The temperature could be a mean irritation in the winter, but on hot Dakota days, it would be sweetness and relief.

Louise set fried eggs next to bacon, pancakes, bread and, always, the coffee pot in front of Leo. As he finished breakfast, they heard Mr. Wheeler's pickup clank and growl into the yard. Leo pushed back his chair with a hard scrape of wood across wood. He grabbed his coat and field hat. "I'll see you tonight. Where's my lunch sack?"

Louise handed him his sack and the water jug. "Good luck today."

Leo took the items and looked towards the door into the stretch of his day. "I should be back for supper around six before I head back out to plant our fields. After you do the evening milking, just leave the milk cans inside the barn. The Creamery agreed to gather them from there."

"Today and the days ahead will be long," Louise noted.

Leo held his body in the cocksureness of the young and energetic. "I'm ready."

"I imagine you are. Supper will be on the table when you get home."

Louise stood in the front doorway and fixated on the departing men. The sun hugged the horizon and flared out gold and orange rays. The wind moved along the prairie from the northeast, pushing the night away and making room for the day.

She didn't want to close the door. Somehow,

closing the door would mean Leo went off without her. During the Musicale days, Louise was almost always with Leo. While living in Bonetrail, they had stretches of emotional distance, but he was never physically too far away. On this farm, Louise felt like Leo was leaving her behind.

In mid-May, Louise noticed her baby's position had lowered. It was still too early for her delivery date, but she decided that packing her travel-bruised suitcase would make her feel better, more reassured. Louise swept her hands across the cold, stiff, caramel brown leather. The scuffs and marks sent her on a Musicale memory trip to Spearfish, South Dakota; Duluth, Minnesota; and even a small farm outside of Madison, Wisconsin. She could hear the loud music, the staccato conversation, the smell of burning tobacco, and sometimes the dancing bodies' vinegary sweat.

Storing away those memories Louise packed several outfits for herself and the baby, diapers, and the baby blanket her mother had crocheted. She set the suitcase in the front room next to her germinating plant crates.

After breakfast, she baked several loaves of bread and began to line up shiny jars and canned goods on a wooden kitchen shelf for Leo to choose from during her maternity convalescence. Louise, being a betting woman, laid down imaginary money that her husband would wear the same pants he had on the day he took her to town to give birth until the day he came to retrieve her. The dirty pants would eventually stand up by themselves and could become her garden scarecrow.

"Time for my other babies," Louise said aloud.

Louise went to the crates of growing vegetables. Lifting one crate tagged "table beets" she heaved it outside to the front of the house where it would be the recipient of southern sunshine. All Seasons cabbage followed and then came the Mandan squash.

Leo turned up for supper. His gaze counted the crooked river of crates set in the front yard. "Your plants are growing well."

Louise grunted and hoisted a crate of bell peppers into Leo's waiting arms.

Leo grasped the crate. "Let me move them."

"Thank you," Louise huffed. "Maybe you can fiddle them into growing. When I'm in town be sure to water them each day and bring them inside at night."

Leo chortled. "I might just do that."

A few weeks later, just after five a.m., a discomfort across Louise's navel area metamorphosed into pain. At first, she thought it was heartburn or that she needed to use the bathroom. Inside the outhouse, Louise tried to sit down and felt her pelvis clamp down. She sucked in air. The sound amplified inside the tight walls.

Sitting on the seat, Louise concentrated on her

breathing as if she had never been given this task before. She spread her fingers to discern the baby adjusting its position within. Louise began sliding her hands along the sidewalls as leverage to gain her footing. Her new stance activated a sense of urgency.

Louise walked to the middle of the farmyard. "Leo! Leo!"

Leo came running from the barn.

"I'm in labor," Louise yelled.

"It's too early," Leo said before he sped to the corral.

Soon enough, mud kicked was up as the wheels turned, and hooves cantered the wagon and the two waiting parents into town.

Louise watched Leo's hands shake. "It's strange to be going into town knowing I'll be returning with an extra person."

"Yup, we're soon to be a trio," the father-to-be quipped.

"Make sure you water my plants and feed the chickens. Remember the plants."

"I hear you," Leo said, and he began singing a song from the Musicale days.

Close to town, the horses shied and skittered when automobiles passed. The Zints exchanged waves and nods as they made quick time to the two-story house turned hospital.

Once Louise was shepherded inside, Leo put his

newsboy cap back on and said, "I'm going to get Myra so you'll have some company."

When Leo was gone. Louise rubbed her belly. "Baby, I'm excited to meet you. Please be healthy."

It wasn't too long later that Myra arrived. "What have we here? About time. I was wondering when things would shake loose and get going." Myra's no-nonsense assessment aimed at Louise and she looked her over. "How are you feeling? Truthfully now. No keeping from Myra."

"Tired. A few days ago, I had back pain that almost toppled me. The baby dropped. I knew the time was getting closer."

"Good. Now we can catch up on all you've been doing these last weeks on the farm while we wait." Several hours later Myra said, "I need to go home and prepare supper. I'll be back shortly. Leo went home to milk the cows. Heinrich will drive out and get Leo after the baby arrives. Nap a little if you can. There's work ahead."

The baby boy arrived before midnight. Louise counted his fingers and toes several times, marveling at the tiniest Zint. Louise held her baby and studied his reddish-purple, swollen appearance. Louise questioned if he was supposed to look like that? Was he ill? The panic of the questions made Louise shift him closer to her chest. Maybe they're all like this at first? She couldn't recall any of her younger sisters looking like her child.

Myra sat down on the bed. "Welcome to the world, beautiful boy." She swept her knuckled fingers across the newborn's brow, and her large, calloused hand cradled his head.

After several beats, Louise blurted, "He's still so small, and red and swollen looking. Do you think there's something wrong?"

Myra patted Louise's forearm and said, "He'll be fine. He needs a little more time to get used to being out here."

Louise dropped her shoulders and pressed the pillow into the headboard. The headboard was solid. Myra was solid. The baby with blue veins showing like a map of creeks and rivers was fragile. His eyes closed and breath puffed out in a soft rhythm that matched the now softer beat of Louise's heart.

"I brought you a beer," Myra said.

"A beer? It's time to celebrate, but don't you think it's too soon for a beer?" Louise questioned.

"The hops will help bring your milk in faster. Now drink it all up."

There was a tentative knock on the half-open door. Leo stood at the threshold watching and waiting.

Louise called, "Come in and meet your son."

CHAPTER EIGHTEEN

Hours later Leo returned to the farm. Louise and the baby would stay in the hospital for two more days. Sadie, Clara, and several others paid calls and wished the new mother well. The most surprising was a visit from Mother Shields. Louise, still fatigued from delivery, was vexed at the sight of her former landlady. Concealing her irritation, she greeted the woman with, "Hello Mother Shields. Thank you for visiting us. Would you care to sit down?"

Mother Shields strode in as if she commanded the room. She sat, removed her black visiting gloves, and put them in her handbag. A practical day hat perched on her head and would not have dared dip to either side.

Sitting upright with her legs crossed at the ankles,

Mother Shields looked Louise over. "I see the delivery did you no harm. Do you intend to stay at the
hospital much longer?"

"We leave tomorrow. Leo will arrive after lunch
and drive us home."

"Make sure you keep the baby well covered. It
wouldn't do to make the baby cold because one
thought the day was warmer than it is," the veteran
mother reminded.

Louise wanted to divert the conversation and
asked, "Would you like to see Armstrong?" Her farm-
roughened hands picked up the baby lying next to
her on the bed. "Armstrong, this is Mother Shields."

The older woman reached over and took the baby
from Louise's cradling arms. The action left an aston-
ished Louise holding her hands in mid-air minus the
infant. She had not expected the other woman to
want to be too near, let alone touch, the child.

Mother Shields rubbed the infant's back. "He's
small but looks healthy. That's good. Out in the country, you need to be healthy and strong." She made the
last pronouncement a condemnation of sorts. Louise
blinked as her former landlady cradled Armstrong.

"He is healthy," Louise said.

"Make sure you feed him well and often. This
baby needs to be taken care of." The woman
somehow implied that once Louise returned home,
the baby would be set down on a chair and somehow

forgotten about like a month-old newspaper. "What kind of name is Armstrong? Sounds highfalutin."

Somewhat biting her tongue, Louise remarked with precise politeness, "He's named after the musician Louis Armstrong."

Mother Shields' frowned. There was no conversation for the next few minutes. Then Mother Shields began a monologue on the raising of children with more emphasis on discipline and chores. Louise thought of her mother. Both older women had crowned themselves the voice of guidance to those within reach, and even beyond if possible. When Louise had heard enough, she said, "I don't want to keep you from your errands. Thank you for the visit."

"I was not finished looking over the child. It would be best to feed him now. I'll leave you to it."

"I was going to do that too," Louise said.

"I should hope so. Take care of that baby."

"Of course, I will."

The same purposeful stride that brought Mother Shields into the room took her away.

The next day, Leo arrived to escort mother and baby home. Louise paid close attention to how she dressed and swaddled Armstrong for his ride to the farm.

Louise held Armstrong as Leo steered the team through Bonetrail and onto the county highway, too soon leaving pavement for the burnt-red scoria, rural road. The horses' hooves and the wagon wheels kicked up dust, creating a rusty cloud behind them.

She observed Leo's square shoulders, a smile that stayed on his lips and also rode shotgun with the tunes he whistled, and the happiness that showed on his face. Louise wanted to lean over and smell him. There would be a combination of fresh air, sweat, and lye soap. In a surreptitious whiff, Louise inhaled this man's scent. There was an addition. Leo smelled like prairie grass.

"It will be good to get you and Armstrong home," Leo said.

Louise shifted Armstrong in her arms. "Mmmmhmmm."

Then Leo kissed the top of her head. It felt subdued through her hat. "I missed you while you were in town."

"Missed you too."

"We haven't really been apart since we were courting." Leo filled the quiet and sang to his family, the horses, and the prairie. The lyrics moved through and around the missing that had begun creeping into the earlier conversation.

On the fence lines running parallel to them, meadowlarks, chickadees, and bluebirds flew from their perches and tipped their wingspans. They arced downward and settled further up the fence lines, almost like a game between the rumble and jangle of horse and wagon and the feathered fracas.

Prairie birds weren't the only creatures congregating at the fences. Herds of Holsteins and Herefords and other cattle stood eating the small clods of spring grasses in their pasture confinement.

"How are the cows doing?" Louise asked.

"The morning and evening milkings have been producing enough to fill all our milk canisters." Leo had had several choice remarks on the obstinacy of the herd. At his most frustrated, he had eyed several as potential candidates for winter butchering.

At their clattering arrival into the farmyard, a dog rounded the front of the house to stand barking with tail wagging.

"Did you get a dog?" Louise moved her head in an incredulous tilt.

"Yup." Leo walked around the rig to help his family down. Louise handed Armstrong into Leo's leathery hands, which held the baby as if holding a basket of breakable eggs, one didn't dare move too quickly or jostle about. He secured the infant in the crook of his arm and reached up to help Louise.

Leo inclined his head toward a canine muddle of dog. "Meet Hardy."

"You call the dog Hardy? After Laurel and Hardy or President Harding?"

"Neither. He looks hardy."

"It's a strange name for a dog," Louise said.

"We could call him Fiddle."

Fatigue made her crinkle her eyes and answered in a soft laugh. "I missed you."

Louise walked to the house and stopped before the doorway and stared at the plant starts scattered on the ground and in crates. The vegetables were sprouting. Some were a little worse for wear, but they seemed to be growing.

"I forgot to water them a few times, but they seem to like sitting out in the sun during the day," Leo said, carrying the baby inside.

Louise questioned if the plants had been left outside each night. She shook her head at Leo, who became excited at planting grain but could be so disinterested in the vegetables that would be on his plate this summer and in the root cellar come winter. Rolling her eyes, she followed her men through the doorway.

After taking off her coat and hat, Louise reached over for Armstrong and began unwrapping him from his swaddling layers. Mama and baby sat down while Leo unloaded groceries and other supplies. The late afternoon sunshine shone through the kitchen window in such a way that Louise could see floating dust motes. The quiet of the room eased Louise into a satisfied contentment that as an adult she was discovering was precious.

Louise looked at a small pile of dirty dishes. She guessed Leo had reused dishes to minimize kitchen cleanup. Coffee was still in the pot from the morning or maybe the day before. A few days had been long enough for dirt and dust to become roommates with her husband.

"Sorry about the mess. I was busy," Leo said.

Lightheartedness laced Louise's laughter. "I'll take care of this."

"Thanks. I'll put away the horses and wagon and be back real quick," Leo said and trotted outside.

Louise was surprised at how pleased she was to be home and in her kitchen.

During her stay in town, she had liked the company of Myra, Sadie, and the other women who had visited. Here she was, back on the farm, waiting and knowing that work would share her time far more often than anything or anyone else. Leo would have long days in the fields. She and Armstrong would largely be each other's company. One thought set in place and another laid on top until it was a figurative stone house of isolation that would be getting stronger over the days, the mortar colored with solitariness sealing in place. The loneliness of this life scared her.

When the house was habitable again, Louise went to examine the vegetable starts littered in a slapdash order in the front of the house. She ran her fingers along the tomato leaves. With a soft press, she coated her fingertips with its scent. Bringing her hand to her nostrils, she inhaled a smell of summer. Louise imagined a plate of scarlet Red River tomato slices.

She'd add salt and pepper and let the yellow seeds slide around her mouth.

Moving on from the young tomato plants, she scrutinized the shallow-rooted cucumbers and their inch-wide veined leaves and then the brittle stems of squash and peppers. "By the looks of things, Leo left you all outside at night."

Most of the vegetation was healthy enough. A handful would probably not make the spring. Gardening, like farming, was an optimist's game on the best of days but always involved risk of withering away. She heard Leo's footsteps.

"I have something to show you," Leo said.

"What's that?"

"It's in your garden."

Louise followed Leo to her garden. Surrounding half of the plot was a new fence using various sized boards. She was stunned.

Leo began, "I didn't fence it all. I thought the enclosed part could be for the vegetables that the rabbits would be more likely to go after. It's not pretty and won't keep out deer, but it will help."

"Thank you," tumbled out of Louise.

Leo eyed his project with pride.

Louise took Leo's hand, and they intertwined their fingers. After a quiet warming pause, she tugged Leo's hand. "Speaking of plants, help me move the plants and crates inside. There's still frost at night."

Armstrong's weak new baby cries called Louise's

attention. She went to their son while Leo finished bringing in the young plant life.

Later Leo watched his wife feed their child. Her husband had seen her naked, kissed her in her most intimate areas, but being observed nursing in the daylight produced an awkwardness that kept Louise's head lowered and her cheeks burning like lignite coal.

"Supper will be ready in an hour or so," Louise said while she closed buttons and straightened her yellow housedress.

Louise did not glance up until she heard Leo walk out into the yard.

Leo ate supper that night as if he hadn't had a meal that he liked in a long while. There was not much talking, but a continuous plunging into the food until it was gone. For dessert, Louise opened a can of pear halves and poured the juice into two glasses.

Leo raised his pear juice in a toast. "Welcome home." Smiling and toasting the glasses together, they drank the leftover canned sweetness. "I wish we had some whiskey to help celebrate. Tonight, we will have music."

When both instrument and musician were ready, with a slow caress of the bow, music eased into the kitchen. Magic followed right behind. Leo pulled the notes across the strings, not letting go until he was ready to move to the next. The frisky pulse proclaimed 'let the good times come' now and in all to-morrows. Louise felt happiness fly up and down her spine and the smallest Charleston step-tap as she moved around her kitchen cleaning up the supper. Armstrong slept through his first concert, but no matter because Leo's music was a firm promise of more to come.

CHAPTER NINETEEN

The next morning Louise considered her to-do list as she transported plants outside and settled them under spring sunlight and sheets of clouds. In a few days, she would be putting them into the ground. Farm life had become a balancing act between the repetitious, everyday tasks, the increased workload of the growing and harvesting seasons, and a baby. There would be more work than hours in the day. The firm constancy of burden that included bad weather, unwelcome insects, and low market prices stayed put on one's shoulders.

Chickens moved in a laggard high-step, pecking and bobbing at the ground, pebbles, and insects while they emitted soft clucks and squawks about the farm-yard. Leo must have let them out this morning. The dairy herd were standing beyond the barbed wire fence eating the prairie grass that appeared to be growing a half an inch a day and, of course, Louise felt the wind.

Today's wind was in the background, a quiet hovering that seemed to remind itself that it had a job and would bring along a moderate gust that choreographed the grasses and other living foliage before going still again. A hawk surged high on a thermal draft and then, with a slight tilt in its wingspan, made a smooth rotation in a new direction. That bird could fly anywhere, be it over the prairies to rolling hills or steel mountains.

With a sigh, Louise told herself that being envious of the hawk did not help her. It was like walking into a spider's web. The sticky silk clung to her as she went about her day.

Focus on Armstrong and the future. Leo will be home for supper.

Louise was amused at how, not so long ago she waited for baby Armstrong. She stood in the farmyard waiting for early evening and her husband to come home. Would she always be waiting on someone?

Stop thinking and get to work, Louise ordered herself.

She gathered the eggs and walked towards the coop's open door. The rooster had stationed himself near the entrance and oversaw his ladies as they took their turn around the yard. Louise's presence didn't so much as elicit a foul cry. As graceful as a belly dancer she had once seen perform, her own hands slipped in, around, and under, removing eggs and filling her apron pockets. She searched in the rafters, in corners, and any other places around the farm a hen might hide an egg. Next time she was in town, she'd have to ask the grocer if they would buy any of her extra eggs. Pleased with her kitchen bounty and future egg sales, she left the ladies and their sole gentleman to the rest of their day.

Louise walked back to the house and saw Hardy laying on his side napping next to the front door. When she was a few steps away from him, she said, "Shouldn't you be keeping a better eye on things around here? The rooster is doing a better job than you."

The dog opened his eyes half way, switched positions, and rested his head onto his front paws. Louise shook her head at the strange dog. Hardy was not what a person would call a well-appointed dog. He had mottled coloring where most of the black and brown were around his head and the orange, tan, and a few streaks of white were on the hind end. His long legs were attached to a thick belly of a body with a snub of a tail.

As the clock neared five, soon Leo would be back for supper. Louise checked on Armstrong, who slept on a milk-filled stomach, and then she visited the root cellar for an armful of last year's russet potatoes. The bag of potatoes had been a well-received gift from the Schmidts. The various neighbors had been very generous with their housewarming and congratulatory pints and quarts. This summer, Louise would can and stock from the entryway all the way to the far wall of her root cellar. Maybe she'd be able to buy a bushel of cherries to put up this summer to have something bright and sweet this winter.

Back in the kitchen, Louise thinly sliced the Midwest staples then fried them just shy of crisp; heated a can of corn and a can of chipped beef; and cut thick slices of bread. For dessert, she'd open a can of rounded peach halves and pour fresh cream and granulated sugar over the top. She made extra in case Driscol stayed for supper. Driscol was helping Leo plant hay in the last of the fields.

When Leo and Driscol arrived back at the farm, it was time for supper. The men washed up at the yard pump next to the windmill. Louise made a note to herself to leave a towel hanging near the pump or at least at the front door.

"How was your day?" Leo asked Louise as the dusty men sat down at the table in their rolled-up sleeves.

"Nothing new," Louise said as she pulled the warming plates out of the oven. Forks in hands, the men began to eat. Each appeared in good, but dirty, spirits. Field dust that Leo hadn't entirely cleaned off during his outdoors wash lined his eyebrows.

"Leo, where are your boots?" Louise asked.

"They were so dirty I left them outside the door."

Conversation ended while the three of them chewed and swallowed.

"More coffee?" Louise asked. The two farmers pushed their mugs towards her. "There's peaches and cream for dessert. Do you want a thermos of coffee? I'm going out to refill your water jugs while you both finish eating."

"A thermos would help. We were able to get in the field south of the Cannonball. Wheeler's got some water reservoir contraption rigged up so that his nearby fields will have water right away and throughout the summer," Leo said and then took a sip. "That area will probably get harvested first."

"That contraption was wasted money and work," Driscol said. "Rainfall has been good, and even when it's dry, with tractors these days a man can overplant and make up for a bad crop."

Louise admired her handsome husband talking business while he stretched and rotated the knots out of his muscles. There was determination working in that body. She added two refilled water jugs, slices of bread, a jar of thinned molasses, cookies, and the coffee thermos to the men's evening field supplies.

"Leo, do you want more food?" Louise asked.

"No, just what you have there. We need to get back in the field. The milking will be late. Those cows will be milk full and plenty ornery tonight." He spoke almost as if he was telling the farm his plan.

Driscol put on his straw hat. "Louise, thanks for supper. I'm headed to the outhouse. Meet you back at the truck."

Leo clasped Louise's elbow, targeted her lips and gave her a loud smacking kiss. Releasing her, he patted her bottom and started for the door.

Louise was now officially a spring planting widow. There was Armstrong to care for and evening chores. She still wasn't certain how to fill the hours. If Leo were here, he'd be playing his violin. She knew that she counted on the music he played. Some nights it was violin music, and other nights it was the fiddle. The violin tended to create the soulful and quiet music, where the fiddle brought out the passion and fire, sometimes a raucous mood. Tonight, she wanted the fiddle, loud and reverberating through the farmhouse, soothing the agitation racing up and down her nerves. Her body was fatigued from the day and still recovering from childbirth, but her mind wheeled around her chore list and the loneliness of the evening.

Squeezing her fists, she decided to lay down and rest while waiting for Leo to return for the evening milking. The bedroom was dusk-filled. Early evening light lingered in the room. The solitude was pervasive except for the breeze outside, a forever companion on the prairie. The rest of the landscape may have quieted down, but the wind was impervious to the human clock and the earth's daily rotation. It swung up, down, and to its own sense of timing.

Louise couldn't rest. Tonight, she craved her old life. Her wistfulness set into motion a talkie film of dancehalls, three-piece suit coats with red carnations, swishing flapper dresses, cigarette smoke-heavy air, fox trots, and heated-to-boiling music. Her left foot started to move side to side and then forward as if she was pressing a piano pedal. Bumm budda bum, budda bum bum bum bum. Her neck and torso swayed opposite directions on top of the bed quilt. Louise smiled in the dark. Hearing the imaginary soundtrack, she left the farm and reversed linear time and slipped back into her previous world.

In that different place, the atmosphere allowed people to leave their worlds for a short time and jump into music and laughter and touch a person only a few collapsible inches away. The dim lighting hid unfulfilled dreams, pain, dirt, and even poverty. The spirit of the liquor could help people momentarily forget responsibilities and burdens.

Little Armstrong gave a squawk. The fantasy vanished, and Louise was back on the farm. Her breathing stuttered. She opened her eyes and blinked until the raw plank ceiling came into focus.

Louise rolled over to Armstrong and murmured to him. Did he know she had gone away? Her mother would have scoffed at such a fanciful thought. She would have said, "The baby's hungry. Or needs a diaper change."

She picked up Armstrong and began to rock. She rubbed his small back, soothing him, but also herself. There was no music tonight with Leo gone, so instead, Louise hummed and rocked Armstrong, and herself, until the baby was asleep. She needed something more to distract her. Something pretty to look at.

The flower seeds had been a splurge buy during her vegetable seed buying. Each year her mother's large vegetable garden had also included hollyhocks, gladiolas, petunias, and roses, and there were also geranium flower pots placed near the front door of the house. So tonight, while Louise waited for Leo, for the first time without provocation or demand, she followed her mother's example and decided to plant geranium seeds. The flowers should have been started in November to be ready for spring, but instead, she would see valentine red and deep dark green at the end of summer.

Louise went into the barn and retrieved one of her sacks of cans. She brought a sack, a hammer, and one nail into the house and set them on the blue and white checkered oilcloth covered kitchen table. In each can, she made holes at the bottom for drainage. Placing the punctured cans in three neat rows, she began filling the empty cylinders from a burlap sack of soil. Her humming restarted. The tune was no identifiable song, but an amalgamation. The planting, melodies, and evening prairie opened a new space for thinking. Louise pondered if Leo ever missed life on the road, meeting new people and the comradery of the other musicians. Strange, she'd never asked him. He was not one to bring up the past. She missed that life too much to speak of it. Maybe when he decided his new direction he had let go? Maybe she should too?

Leo was now a one-man band of his land. Louise, in a way, still worked behind-the-scenes readying for the day, stepping in for the breaks with food and information, and helping to close down the show. This new show included a house, cows, a chicken coop, and even a baby. They had traded in the variety of acquaintanceships for the steadfast friendships in Bonetrail.

Dropping a seed into the soil chute, Louise felt a burst of angry longing vibrate within herself. Almost a year had passed. She still missed their wandering musical life. Her moving on was like one step forward and two steps back.

Louise looked out her kitchen window. The sun stuck in a small sector of the western horizon. The portion of orb hovered as if it intended to stay. Maybe it was deciding? Once it fell the rest of the way into the other side of the world, this day was over forever. She heard Driscol's truck crunch the scoria road that led to the farmhouse. Leo was home.

"I'm back." Leo's face showed tiredness and satisfaction. "I'm going to milk."

"Let me get Armstrong ready, and I'll be right out."

"Thanks. See you in the barn."

The rippled dirt barn floor swallowed the noise of Louise's steps and sent up puffs of dust and field debris that then drifted back down. The dairy cows' white marble teeth chewed last season's hay, and birds sheltered in the rafters ruffled their feathers and ignored the activity. Louise could smell breathing animals, newly broken hay and straw bales, excrement, and moist closed-up heat.

Armstrong slept heavy in his blanket-lined bushel basket. Leo settled cows in stalls, and they began to milk. Louise patted the cow's backside and with wariness approached, making sure the beast didn't kick her. She sat on the milking stool and began pulling the black spotted pink teats and sprayed milk into the galvanized bucket underneath. Leo dumped full buckets into tall two-handled silver metal creamery cans.

A tired Leo didn't speak, but he whistled. The high notes were tinged with a mellowness that Louise would say calmed cows and people. When an emptied cow was switched for a milk-full cow, the solo was interrupted. The intermission ended when Leo and his new milk machine were settled.

Towards the two-hour mark, Louise's fingers

cramped as she squeezed and pulled. Her forehead almost rested against the cow's coarse white and black hide. Louise panted and could taste the sourness of fresh manure. Instead of a barn dance, she was in a barn milking a cow. She used to wear pretty dresses and go to clubs. Her life was so different a year ago.

Milking was over. To be resumed at four o'clock the next morning. Louise rose and flattened her hand against the cow's rump. She lifted her chin, and her spine followed as she stood up. "All done?"

Leo gave a tired half smile. "Yup. I'll finish up. You head on in."

Later, when Louise laid her head on the bed's goose feather pillow sleep overrode all thoughts. She woke up in the deep well of night. The baby was hungry. Louise rose to attend to his need. Leo filled the room with his expansive snores. She woke again in the midnight blue dawn darkness. Some folks would have called it evening because the stars were still overhead, but the next day had begun.

Before either male could wake up, Louise went to the outhouse. There was an unruffled stillness in the yard. It was the gap between night and day where the nocturnal and diurnal creatures change shifts. She swung the outhouse door wide open and left it. Sitting down, she waited as her eyes adjusted to the revealing landscape. The barn began to have walls and a roofline. She could hear a swish, swish of prairie grass, but the fields stayed covered by night. To the right, she saw an animal lumber toward the outhouse. It took her several tight breaths and quick heartbeats to recognize Hardy. He must have wandered off and just now returned.

Louise spoke to the canine who had stopped at the weathered wood door, sat down on his haunches, and stared at her. "Did you enjoy yourself last night? You get to come and go as you please while I have to stay here."

Hardy stood and walked away.

CHAPTER TWENTY

At the end of May, the length of the daylight began to match the duration of the Zint's daily wakefulness. The nights were warmer and the farmers let go of their fear of frost. Today Louise would plant her garden.

She put Armstrong in his special bushel basket with a kitchen towel over the top to shade him and brought the infant to the vegetable plot. When Louise set the baby basket down, Hardy sprawled next to it and slept. When Armstrong was in tow, Hardy tended to watch Louise move around the farm while they waited for Leo's return. Leo wouldn't let the lovesick dog go with him to Wheeler's farm or the fields but allowed the canine to accompany him around the homesetead. During milking the dog was underfoot--close enough to watch Leo and the dairy activity but far enough away to not upset the bessies and avoid getting kicked. While Leo was in and out of the fields, Louise spent most of these days with a sleeping Armstrong, clucking chickens, and a silent Hardy.

Keeping her son safe while she worked was a priority. Insects, snakes, and other dangers came with the land, so Louise was hesitant to put the baby basket down. She needed to keep Armstrong off the ground. Louise decided she needed to build a wood platform next to the garden where she could keep him safe.

In the garden, she hoed and loosened the dirt into rows and began to situate Red River tomatoes, Sweet Siberian watermelons, and Arikara yellow bean starts and throw down Oxheart carrots seeds. As she moved along the rows, the soil became warmer in the afternoon sunshine of the blue sky. Louise padded barefooted between the rows, stems, and leaves.

As she worked the ground, Louise did the same to the land of her thoughts. She now understood that there had always been a farmer's soul deep within her husband, stored inside and out-of-sight, waiting to be resurrected in the future. In the absence of the Musicale, Leo listened to the music of the prairie. Louise had plodded to this farm; unlike the Musicale, they started this venture together. It was also during this inaugural spring that Louise and Leo began to grow their marriage into a truer partnership.

Much to her surprise, she liked this Leo who still had the quick smile, humor, and calluses that were now the cultivation of seeds, not strings. This farming dream may have been his, but Louise was beginning to understand and her accomplishments ripened as she took care of her family and responsibilities.

Louise considered if she dared to seed new hopes that this life might allow her a greater sense of choice and personal authority. Weather and the outer-world could damage and even destroy, or maybe they could strengthen all this newness. If these tender beginnings spent too long under her hot scrutiny would they wilt and die? What intangible bounty could she harvest? It was safe to wonder and consider here. No one was looking or listening to the woman wearing a housedress tending to her garden.

A few days later, Louise left a napping Armstrong on the bed between pillow barricades and went to the barn. Finding the wheelbarrow, she wheeled it over to the old woodpile of hodgepodge sizes, widths, and dirtiness. The warmth of the afternoon made her tie her sweater around her waist.

As she lifted a squat piece of wood, the daylight reflected off the gray-blue scales of a blue racer snake. The snake raised its head and hissed, its tail thumped a board, warning Louise. Fear tightened her neck and spine, and, holding her breath and the piece of wood like a bat, she tiptoed backward.

The supple blue racer posed stiffly and hissed

again, and then pushed off the wood and, in a serpentine motion, disappeared into the grass. When the snake was gone, Louise dropped her makeshift weapon and ran to the house. As she crossed the yard, she saw Hardy lying in the sunshine and yelled, "Where were you, you lazy dog?"

Hardy lifted his head and stared.

Louise slammed the screen door and pushed the interior door closed. She pressed her spine tight against the door and with a closed fist banged the wood. Thoughts crashed around her brain: *What am I doing on this lousy farm? Last year I went from a speakeasy to a party, not a garden to a barn.* Now she was hiding in her house and worrying about a baby, a man, and a farm. A snake lived in the woodpile.

Afraid she'd wake Armstrong, she stopped hitting the door. Louise wanted a gusty updraft to carry her, Armstrong, and Leo away from Bonetrail. Armstrong's crying interrupted the inner tirade circling her soul. She went to the bedroom and picked up the baby. Her hips began the instinctive sway of comfort. She rubbed the little boy's back in slow circles. When an hour had passed, Louise knew she had to go back to the woodpile. She nestled Armstrong into his basket and left the baby on the kitchen table. Wearing gloves and taking the broom, she went outside. Louise called Hardy to her. The canine stretched his back legs, and with a perturbed eye, he raised his other half and ambled to Louise.

"Hardy, for once you are going to help me."

Before the animal could lie down again Louise said, "come," and they headed back to the woodpile. When they were ten feet away, she began singing a loud scramble of lyrics. Standing near the woodpile but far enough away to jump back, she hit the boards with the broom. Wood against wood clattered and bounced in response. She stopped the satisfying noise making after several minutes. Louise looked around for Hardy and saw that the dog had shimmied underneath the shade of the wheelbarrow.

Again she moved planks and culled out shorter, cleaner boards that she loaded onto the wheelbarrow. When Louise lifted the load, Hardy wiggled out from underneath, but it wouldn't roll. Swinging her fisted arms in the air, she yelled all her frustration to the prairie, and then stomped the ground.

"This darn thing is gonna move." Regripping the handles and adding a grunt and body thrust that rose from the balls of her feet, Louise lifted the wheelbarrow. The wheel made a slow rotation.

When Louise reached the garden, she was sweaty and breathing so hard that her head was bobbing up and down attempting to suck in more air. She sat down on one of the handles and swiped her forearm across her forehead and caught the sweat before it could drip into her eyes.

Louise didn't have time to rest, she had a platform to build. The platform would be Armstrong's elevated haven while she weeded, watered, and picked their food.

Looking around for Hardy, Louise saw him lying near the house.

"You good-for-nothing mutt. I don't know why we have you on the farm. You lay around and eat. You go off in the evenings and come back in the morning. How are you supposed to protect the farm or run off an intruder if you're not here? The only person you're interested in is Leo, and he doesn't have time for you, either. This wasn't supposed to be my life."

With the upsurge in work demands, there had been little violin music in the evenings. Leo's exhaustion was such that the fiddle tunes were often being stored away for another day. The fields had sprouted, and watching weather had begun. The worries of needed rain, not enough warm sunshine, too much rain, a surprise frost, and if it hailed--the season was over, settled on Louise's shoulders and squeezed her heart before she could protest.

The risks of farming were making her hold her breath throughout the day. She'd realize what she was doing and force quiet and controlled releases of air exchange. Worry with the Musicale was always short-lived. There had been the kerfuffle in Colorado and a few times when there were longish gaps between jobs, but these breaks sometimes became vacations or a holiday.

For Louise, that was all part of the adventure. She recalled that Cleone had said a dame had to have moxie. Louise questioned if she still did.

The next day Louise decided she needed to go somewhere, escape the farmwork. While Leo was in the fields, she would scout the land and ditches looking for wild onions or chamomile and any distractions that would interrupt her daily routine.

After mixing and setting the day's bread dough to rise underneath a fruit-decorated kitchen towel, Louise looped a small blanket around her shoulders and torso making a nest so that she could hands-free carry Armstrong. Leaving behind her hat, she and Armstrong left the small, tight kitchen for open land. Today the temperatures were sure to reach the eighties, but a light breeze zipped over the plains.

Louise began walking west toward lilac bushes that may have been someone's idea of a decorative shelterbelt. There she investigated the short, exposed branches sparsely covered with petite lavender-colored blossoms; the shrubs looked stunted and weary. Her mother would have had these blooming. Louise bent down for an inhale of the flower's perfume.

"Armstrong, can you smell the perfume too? We'll come back this way. I'll cut off some of the branches and take them into the house. We'll have something pretty to look at."

Moving past the lilacs, Louise discovered the slender, rounded haphazard branches of chokecherry bushes and nearby the silver-green oval leaves of buffalo berry trees.

"Looks like we'll be berry picking and jam making this year. It will be nice having something bright to eat in the middle of winter." What would it be like stuck out here this winter?" Louise didn't like the feel of the question. She'd worry about that later.

The sky was a tender blue that invited daydreaming. Louise accepted the invitation. The breeze and minutes of the day sent the spread of clouds above floating over the next county like white kite tails. Further northeast, Louise saw early-season wildflowers scattered among swaying native grass. There was no churchyard fencing here. Her feet followed the path of the prairie beauty her eyes located.

Louise stood among the flowers. Her imagination added a disorderly mix of later summer wild sunflowers: upright, frosted sage; purple cornflowers of Echinacea; and of course, yellow blossom fingers of sweet clover and low-bush prairie roses that rooted where they wished.

"Armstrong, you and I will have to make a trip back here to see the summer flowers."

Next Louise traipsed around a plowed field and across the rust-colored scoria rock road into a ditch on the opposite side. She recalled seeing some wild onions over this way. The combination of the sun overhead and Armstrong's small but robust body heat made Louise sweat and moistened the fabrics that separated them. The breeze felt good on her bare legs. She liked the faint whap, whap sounds that her skirt made.

Louise probably should have worn a pair of Leo's old trousers. The grass wasn't too tall, and the sticker weeds had not yet matured. Overhead, two red-tailed hawks flew high.

She walked in a zigzag pattern until she found a cluster of low, bushy chamomile plants. Louise raked her fingers through the white daisy-like cluster flowers beheading the lot. It didn't take long to fill the flour bag she brought. A Western Meadowlark whistled and ticked.

"Armstrong, where do you think the garlic and onions are hiding?" The baby continued to sleep.

Louise wasn't finding either. Since it was early in the season and the grass was shorter, the wild onions should have been easier to locate. Armstrong began to root for food. It was time to turn for home. Instead of backtracking for lilacs, she walked along grain fields and up and out of ditches.

Louise rubbed Armstrong's back and told her child, "I decided when I was young, that farm life was not for me. Before coming here, your Dad and I lived in Bonetrail. It's a small town like most small towns. You were born there. Before Bonetrail, there was the Musicale. The Musicale was wonderful! Your Dad played violin in the Musicale. You should have heard the music. I miss the music, new places, traveling, and the work was fun. Farm work is work. But I'll say this: the prairie has its own beauty."

Louise looked down at her son and patted his bottom. "We need to get home and start supper."

The growth in the fields became the unofficial timetable. Driscol and Sadie's wedding was scheduled for the last Saturday in June. Louise looked forward to the celebration and offered to help with the food and Leo with the music. They all deserved a party after the spring planting.

CHAPTER TWENTY-ONE

Days before the wedding, Leo began practicing many of the wedding song favorites from the Musicale days. The music lifted the atmosphere in the house.

On one of those evenings, as Louise did the dishes, Leo pulled out his violin. After a rousing rendition of 'Camptown Races,' the music was silent for too long.

Louise glanced at Leo and saw him staring into space. It was the look of someone swimming in deep thinking waters. After several minutes he spoke. "I don't miss touring with the Musicale so much as I miss the music and the guys. Wonder what horseplay Erik is up to?"

Louise wiped dry a jelly jar. "I am sure Erik is doing what he's always done. There're a few musicians around here you could play with. I miss the excitement of new places and people and the anticipation in the hour before the show started. Do you miss anything else?"

Leo set his bow on the table. "I miss whipping the crowd up with the music. I miss hearing the latest songs."

Louise reached for another dish. "Maybe we could buy a battery-operated radio. It would help get through this winter."

She wasn't sure how she was going to stay steady this winter on the farm. They could use the second five dollars her father had sent. Leo knew about the first five dollars but not the latter money. Louise knew she should have told Leo but she had attached a sense of security to that cash and kept it hidden for a day they'd need it.

"Do you have any song requests for the wedding party?" Leo asked.

"Just play some more. Drown out the sound of the wind outside."

On Driscol and Sadie's wedding day the Zints arrived at the Schmidt's and found Myra reprimanding her adult sons in the yard. "Do not be late for your sister's wedding!" The young men waved to the Zints and jostled each other in the opposite direction of their mother.

Myra focused on Armstrong. "Hello! Let me see that sweet baby. Hand him over," the happy matriarch said. "Hi, sweet boy. It's a big day for my little girl." Myra turned to Louise. "Thanks for coming early to help. You look very pretty in your yellow dress. That band of satin at the top is so elegant."

"Thank you. This is a dress from my Musicale days," Louise said. Then she held up a dark brown stoneware bean pot for Myra's inspection. "I brought baked beans, rhubarb cake, and fresh butter for the wedding supper."

"Delicious! We'll be feeding everyone right."

Out of the corner of her eye, Louise saw Mother Shields standing on her porch steps watching them. *Hello you old bat* Louise thought and nodded to her former landlady. Courtesies complete Louise followed Myra, who was carrying Armstrong, while Leo held open the Schmidt's front door.

"I see you've arrived early for Sadie's wedding," Mother Shields called out.

Louise stopped walking. "Hello, Mother Shields. Will you be attending also?"

"Of course. The Schmidts are my neighbors."

"I wouldn't expect anything less from you," Louise said.

Mother Shields jacked her chin higher. "Why wouldn't I come? Being a good neighbor is part of living in Bonetrail."

"I understand small town rules. Everyone knows what is expected and how to behave. It's all very dependable," Louise said.

"You make it sound like it's a bad situation.

When everyone knows the rules, there is order and dependability."

Louise sighed. "But then not much ever changes. There's a big world out there moving around. Most of the change around here starts in the ground and follows the seasons. Planting, waiting, harvesting, waiting, and then it all begins again. It's very reliable."

Mother Shields' eyes narrowed in tight. "If you don't like farming or small towns, why are you here?"

"Because my husband wants to farm in Bonetrail."

Louise saw Mother Shields' intense focused eyes retract. "Well, you chose to marry the man. If you wanted a different life, why would you choose a farmer?"

Mother Shields had trespassed too far into Louise's life. She glared a blizzard at the former landlady who stirred up the residue of the anger, hurt, and helplessness Louise had lugged to Bonetrail. "I chose a musician. I didn't think my husband would wander back to the farm."

This woman Louise so disliked had laid bare the quandary that she tried to move around and kept bumping into.

"Excuse me. I'm needed inside," Louise said.

Before Mother Shields could speak more, Louise strode into the Schmidts' house out of Mother Shields' sight. Why was that harridan stirring up Louise's feelings, especially today so near her own wedding anniversary? Louise was beginning to like the friendships and community ties she and Leo were creating, and at times even the life they were building, but it was coming along in small steps, and pushing questions from Mother Shields was not helping Louise along the path.

She was happy at her friend's marriage. Sadie wanted to marry her Driscol and stay in Bonetrail. Their future was already written. The bride and groom were content with the narrative. However Louise felt about her situation, she would not let it draw storm clouds over the day. It was time to celebrate. That thought accompanied her into the parlor. A double-stacked white wedding cake sat on the dining table. The sweet linger of baking bread and cake frosting wafted in the air.

"Where's the bride?" Louise asked.

Myra bustled around the dining table. "Thank you for helping with the food. You can set your dishes on the table. Sadie and the girls are upstairs finishing getting dressed. I have a few things down here to get ready. You go up. I'll be up shortly."

Louise followed the trail of tumbling feminine chatter to Sadie's bedroom door. Inside was Sadie in an ivory dress and four other teenage girls dressed in floral summer dresses. "Congratulations, Sadie."

Sadie whirled and the matching heeled shoe in her hand swung. "Hi, Louise! Come in."

"You look lovely."

"Thank you. What did you wear on your wedding day?" Sadie asked.

Louise sat on a quilt of pastel blocked flowers that covered the bed. "Leo and I married quickly, so my wedding dress was my best summer dress and I added a matching ribbon to my hat." She was surprised by the attention of the young women. How much should Louise tell? It would be easy to speak of the exciting parts of her wedding day.

"We were married in my parents' yard next to my mother's large flower garden. We had the ceremony, lunch, and then Leo and his band played. My favorite part was when Leo played a song just for me. The afternoon was lovely, but I wanted to fly through it and get on the road."

Louise realized she had slipped into the memory and viewed the day's speed like when a person holds a book and pulls back the pages, and let's go. In several eye blinks, all the pages are on the other side.

Sadie waltzed in a tight circle. "My wedding day will go into the evening. We're going to kick up our dancing heels. To help celebrate, Driscol has been homebrewing beer for the wedding. He got a hold of some Redeye. Don't tell my mother. The beer is acceptable, but not the hard liquor."

The last announcement resulted in squeals, gasps, and a "There's going to be some sore heads tomorrow!"

Myra appeared in the bedroom doorway. "Girls,

it's almost time. Heinrich needs to change, then we'll leave for the church. If we're late, I'm sure Mother Shields will remark upon it."

Sadie propped a hand on her hip. "When I was young, Mother Shields was a nice lady. But in the last few years, she's become so cantankerous. Louise, however did you live in that woman's house for as long as you did? I bet that old fussbudget doesn't even like music."

"Leo and I needed a place to live, and she rents rooms. Leo never played around her. She once told me being a musician wasn't a real job."

"She didn't! That woman. To say that Leo is a ne'er-do-well, how rude," multiple more responses followed.

Louise stood up. "I've never told Leo about her comment. He would have tried to prove her wrong, and she doesn't deserve to hear him play just for her," Louise said.

"Are you ready up there?" Heinrich yelled upstairs.

"Almost!" Myra yelled down. "Sadie, let me look at you. Pretty, so pretty. Oh, goodness, all this and that going on, and we forgot to make the bridal bouquet." Myra put her hand on her forehead.

"Rats!" Sadie said. "Who says I have to have a bouquet to marry Driscol? He'll marry me with or without a bouquet."

Louise touched Myra's arm. "Why don't I leave

now for the church? There are plenty of wildflowers near there. I can pick enough for a bouquet. Just give me some ribbon to wrap the stems together."

"Wonderful," Myra breathed out.

Sadie opened a round wicker sewing basket on her dresser. "I have some leftover ribbons. Mostly blues, a few ivory, and plain white."

"Give me those and that yellow hatband too. Do you have a pair of scissors I can take with?"

"Oh, Louise, thank you so much for helping. A bride should have a bouquet on her wedding day," Myra said.

The ribbons is Louise's hand fluttered like a kite's tail. "My mother would agree with you. Can you bring Armstrong to the church with you?"

"Yes. We'll take care of him."

With scissors and ribbons in hand and a lilac-colored cloche on her head, Louise walked to the churchyard she had visited on her first day in Bonetrail. The neighborhood streets were quiet. People were finishing up chores before the wedding. She was excited to hear Leo play for the guests. He hadn't really played a gig since the Schmidt Christmas.

Louise walked the path to the small cemetery. Someone had cut the grass earlier in the spring. There were no roses like the storybook blooms her mother grew and groomed. She found the low, broad shrub of the sturdy five-petaled pink prairie roses with their sunshine button centers growing along the bottom of the black fence. The prairie roses would droop but if she placed them in the middle they would be propped up by other wildflowers.

She added velvet blue and yellow prairie violets, pink and tangerine wild columbine with its dangling blossom heads of wings and spires, and purple fluttering flag blossoms of American vetch. Last, Louise threaded tiny white petals of Hood's phlox threaded throughout. The bouquet's colorful and exuberant blossoms and petals sprung out of the top and floated higgledy-piggledy out the sides while colored ribbons wrapped the stems and their tails draped down the front.

Her errand completed, she closed her eyes. The absence of wind gave the cemetery a weighty peace. She found herself returning to her conversation with Mother Shields. Very little would have stopped Louise from marrying Leo, and again she pored over what would have happened if she had put her foot down on leaving the Musicale? Or fought for a city instead of a farm? Why didn't she resist harder? Secretly, Louise hoped it wouldn't have come this far or even for this long. But her choices would have been too socially extreme if she hadn't come with Leo. How big a loss was her marrying gamble? Would she have risked it if she had known Bonetrail was in her future?

Louise, carrying the wedding bouquet, left the noisy quiet and the graves. She had walked half a block and turned at the hullabaloo of a wheezy Model T horn and its passengers. The vehicle stopped alongside her. Driscol and Leo sat in the front, and the Schmidt sons and other assorted Bonetrail young men occupied wherever else a body could fit, standing on the running boards and bumper or sitting on the hood.

"Running the streets, I see," Louise said.

The men laughed.

Leo got out of the vehicle. "More tearing up the roads. I'll walk back with you."

"Zint, I have a bride waiting for me. We'll see you two there," Driscol said, and with a grind and clatter, the car shifted into gear and bucked toward the church.

Leo brushed a finger over a rose petal. "You make this?"

"I did. Myra realized at the last minute that they had forgotten to make the bridal bouquet, so I offered to go get some flowers and put one together."

"Where'd you get the flowers?"

"A cemetery."

Leo's laughter echoed in the empty street. He swiped at the tears that had sprinted from his eyes.

"Let's keep my picking spot a secret. They might not like where I gathered the flowers," Louise said.

"I won't mention it."

"What were you and the boys up to?"

Leo slipped his arm through Louise's arm. "Mischief. How much can we get into here? Plus, Driscol won't be missing his wedding. Says once he and Sadie are married, we can start getting together like married folks."

Louise titled her head into Leo's shoulder. "It would be fun to have people over or to go somewhere. It gets quiet at the farm."

"Quiet! The wind blows most of the time. Plus, all the songbirds and such about the place, me, and my violin."

"You know what I mean. The sounds of people, of living. Even cars. Bonetrail is small, but at least there is some town noise."

"I don't miss the city noise, and all the other things that go with it," Leo said.

Louise held back. She weighed how much to say. If she told him that she didn't like living so isolated on the farm, Leo would feel bad, but she wanted him to know.

"I've wanted a life that wasn't ordinary for as long as I can remember. Marrying you and traveling with the Musicale was extraordinary and I still miss it. I didn't know I'd be standing here next to you in Bonetrail, North Dakota, carrying wildflowers to our friends' wedding, but there's not another man I want taking me there." Halfway through her reply, she stopped walking. "Only you. This land will either give to us or release us."

Leo caressed Louise's chin with the back of his

hand. "I know this isn't exactly the life you always wanted. We're making it work together."

Louise began to walk. "I know you are moving toward what you think is the good life. The destination looks so different than what I imagined."

Before more could be said, they arrived at the church. Townspeople clustered in small groups and several children chased each other in the side yard.

Heinrich called out, "Oh, good. You're here now. Myra has been fretting about the flowers. I told her they were only flowers. A gal doesn't need flowers to get hitched. Just a groom and minister."

Louise saw Myra holding Armstrong and beckoning them into the church. As they came to the top step, Myra traded Armstrong for the bouquet. "Thank you so much for helping. How wonderful! Heinrich, get everyone inside. It's time to start."

The guests and the wedding party took their places. The Zints small family settled into a back pew, and as the ceremony started, Leo picked up Louise's hand. Louise felt the warmth and strength packed into her husband's hold. His callused and sun-darkened hand was similar to hers. During the Musicale days, her hands had softened and been without a hint of suntan.

When Sadie and Driscol said their vows, Louise could feel the sweetness of the promises they made to each other. She decided to let that tenderness soften this day and enjoy the celebration.

Heinrich stood before the congregation. "Now, we're all headed back to the house for a late lunch, and then we'll start the music and dancing. Leo, you and the other musicians, get yourselves ready because we have celebrating to do."

Louise was pleased at how Heinrich and the others were excited to hear Leo play. Some of them had heard him play last Christmas, so they knew that this day's music was something to anticipate.

Leo spoke low in her ear. "We'll be seeing the bottoms of these people's shoes tonight."

It didn't take long for the wedding to reassemble in the Schmidts' yard. Louise asked one of the grandmas to tend to Armstrong while she helped bring the food dishes and bowls to the outside table. As she sat a crockery bowl of potato salad out, she was reminded of her family in Wheatville. Louise wondered about them all. She hadn't written since Armstrong's birth. Her sisters had written their excitement for the baby's arrival and included well wishes from their parents.

"Louise, can you bring out more serving spoons?"

It took a few eye blinks to register that Myra was speaking to her. "Okay."

Serving spoon retrieved, Louise crossed the kitchen but stopped in front of the window and gazed at the nuptial celebration in the yard. People were happy. Louise liked the view of it all. The only person not sharing in the mood was Mother Shields.

She sat near the Schmidts' porch step on a kitchen chair and held a glass of water in her hand.

The 'Bonetrail Band' looked different from the Musicale, but the old excitement of a show about to start was beginning to vibrate within her. *I want to be at this party.* The thought accompanied Louise over to the new trio. Hand on her hip she said, "You better eat well because this crowd is waiting to be entertained."

Leo gave a firm nod. "We'll be ready."

Heinrich clapped his hands. "Everyone, please let's toast to the new married couple. Mother, put that plate down. We hope blessings of happiness, children, long lives, and good crops for the newlyweds," and with that, Heinrich raised his mug of beer into the air.

The gathered mirrored the action. Then the crowd yelled, "Here, here," accompanied by a few long whistles.

Driscol, with one hand raising his glass of beer and the other settled on Sadie's hip said, "Sadie and I want to thank everyone for coming. Let's celebrate. Leo and the boys are playing for us today and tonight."

The music started, and the official lovebirds three-stepped one direction and then the other making circles in the grass. Halfway through the song, other couples joined, even Heinrich and Myra.

The big father was quick and graceful on his feet. Louise gently swayed with Armstrong in her arms.

Louise admired Leo. He held his back straight and stretched into one direction and then switched to the other as the vibrations and soul of the music claimed his body. His chin was thrust down, his right foot tapped out the rhythm, but the left kept his body stabilized. The new band synced the harmonies and the beat intensified. By the fifth song, Louise shuffled and spun with her toothless dance partner.

A Bonetrail grandmother offered, "Let me hold Armstrong for you. You go dance."

"Louise, are you dancing?" a cousin of Sadie's asked.

"I'm ready," and before she could say more, the young man partnered her across a trampled grass floor. Spinning, dipping, and kicking carried the town into early evening.

The entertainment stopped for evening milking. Groups and pairs of farmers left to attend to their livestock and the women stayed behind to prepare supper. Several women sat on wooden kitchen chairs or on colorful homemade quilts, or moved about carrying dishes. All the while chatter continued to skip as they spoke about the spring, forecasted the summer, and waited for the men to return.

"It's been warmer than usual so far this year," a guest said. "My lettuce is going gangbusters."

"My cucumber plants are doing well too. I'm having to water more," another added.

As the men returned, Myra issued orders and directions as the guests waited in loose circles around the food tables. "Heinrich, go get the lanterns before it gets dark. Leo, you and the other musicians eat first. Everyone, start lining up over there."

Later when bright lines of orange, gold, and pink stitched to the horizon and the sun began to set, Leo returned to his post and the music began calling and captivating the guests. Driscol and Sadie danced like a couple in love does with a powerful sense of vigor and anticipation, locking arms and private gazes.

The men played the opening chords of Bishop's 'Home Sweet Home,' and the dancers stopped. The gathered began to sing along. The lyrics spoke of pleasures and palaces discovered by the roamers, but still, there is no place like home, sweet home.

Louise regarded the guests. There were expressions of open-faced contentment, appreciation, and even a bittersweet undertone. Most everyone had come from somewhere else, across acres of ocean, and settled on these flat northern plains. Survival and community meant creating relationships with people who claimed a cultural legacy, sometimes different from one's original. In Louise's visual sweep of this human landscape, she saw Mother Shields standing on her porch. There she stood, arms crossed, her hands holding either shoulder and head tilted as if she received the song like a blessing.

As the liquid purple, heavy blue, and black of nighttime took over recasting the yard, into a close and cozy atmosphere, the music chased after this new direction and the dancers followed. In the dimness of lantern light, it was harder for Louise to see where violin and Leo came together and separated.

In the next set, the Bonetrail band slowed the music for cuddled-up close heart-to-heart swaying. Leo improvised and added in some jazz riffs with long-noted mellow harmonies and hot, cool, fast, and slow grooves that balanced between popular and improper. The other musicians tried and almost caught up with that spontaneous mastery.

That's when Louise noticed that Mother Shields was not there. The woman might have heard the borderline risqué music and gone home. Though living next door, Mother Shields would hear it all until the end. Maybe the old gal stuffed handkerchiefs in her ears. Or as Louise's imagination jumped and flew, the woman was in her house dancing in the dark where no one could see her. Somehow the music had absorbed into her shoes, ran her veins and arteries, been able to pass through her heart and then onto her soul that had to dance. Maybe Mother Shields had an invisible dance partner who bowed to her curtsy and swung them around the room or threw up their arms and heads in abandon and beat.

Shortly thereafter, Leo put down his violin and asked Louise's dance partner to move aside. She stepped into Leo's arms.

"I think the way you all started with ragtime, slid into jazz, and came back around to old country music was brilliant," Louise said. "I haven't seen Mother Shields for hours, so those stern eyes weren't around to stop you."

"Stop me. Not likely. Where's Armstrong?"

"He's been sleeping inside the house for a few hours."

"It's been good playing for a big audience again. I know you and Armstrong are appreciative, but it's good to see others dancing and even doing a little chair swaying. I saw you took a few turns," Leo said.

"The men of Bonetrail made themselves available."

"As I keep seeing."

"It's a tough place to be in when you're with the band and you want to dance with your girl," Louise said.

Leo rested his forehead on Louise's forehead. "Always has been when it comes to you."

The guitar slowed to almost mournful chords as if the song was a calling to a missed love or an unmet dream that was still felt on the outer edges, far away and unable to cleave to it. This moment under a partial crescent moon, Louise felt content letting the music pull without caring where it would take them.

The timbre changed, and Louise knew their one dance was almost done. She smelled Leo's soap and sweat, hoping to imprint this moment.

When the wedding was over, the Zints strolled down the street to where Leo had left the horses and wagon. It was dark. The blackness hadn't yet been invaded by the calico blue of early morning. Sunrise was only a few hours away.

"'Home Sweet Home' was an excellent song choice this evening," Louise said.

Leo's head rose up from re-harnessing the horses and his teeth glowed in the lantern light. "It felt right to play."

"Does the music ever stop for you?" Louise asked.

"No, but sometimes it does have to wait."

CHAPTER TWENTY-TWO

Those first summer months of 1929 dissolved in high heat and filled long work hours. The prairie sunrise started before six o'clock and sunset settled in after eight o'clock. The Zints were generally playing catch up with time.

Louise was setting the supper table with rabbit, garden fresh corn-on-the-cob, fried zucchini, tomato slices, and always bread and butter as Leo ambled into the house and sat down at the table.

Leo dripped water droplets onto the table that he hadn't completely shaken off while washing up outside. "Not too far off we'll be harvesting our first crops."

Louise felt her concern expand. "Between working for Mr. Wheeler and our own fields, your workdays are already nonstop. Harvesting will add to the load. Will Mr. Wheeler let us borrow his equipment? Do you think you can do all the fieldwork on your own? We don't have the money to hire more hands."

Leo buttered a slice of bread. "I know what's ahead for me. I'll trade my labor for equipment and help with the other farmers. I'll work on the other farms in exchange for their help on our own. You'll be there too. You worked for the Musicale, why wouldn't you be there for the harvesting? Do you think you could drive the horses to cut the wheat?" Leo asked.

"I drove the Musicale's car. I can manage to steer a few horses."

That evening Leo played for his audience as if they were not two people sitting at a kitchen table, but a whole club of listeners. It didn't occur to Louise that Armstrong would be frightened by the louder music. When she looked down at her son, he was staring at his father with only the faintest blinks. When a song jumped high and full, the boy kicked his legs as if he was trying to touch it. A swing tune had Louise dancing her version of the promenade with Armstrong. Louise looked from her son to her husband and laughed with the joy that was pumping through her.

After an hour of the private concert, she glanced down at Armstrong. His eyes were low but not closed. She touched Leo's knee and said, "Play something soft."

Leo stopped in a mid-upward swoop and stared at his wife and then his boy. He began playing a gypsy folk song whose tone and touch would have partnered well with a campfire as people, animals, and land let go of the day, readying for slumber. Louise rocked side to side and could feel her child drop deeper against her body. They stayed in this Madonna and child pose until Leo finished playing.

With a tender deftness, Leo put his violin and bow back into their case. Louise left the room and put Armstrong to bed. She heard the front door close and knew that Leo was doing a last check around the farm. Louise walked back into the kitchen and readied the coffee for the next morning. In this moment, her home felt right, as if it slipped into a state of rest.

On the first day of wheat harvesting, Leo herded cows into the barn for morning milking. He saw his wife strut inside. "I like the look of those trousers on you."

"Thank you. They're an old pair of yours I hemmed. They came together well," Louise said.

"It's nice to see a woman's legs, but those dresses don't protect much when you're in the field."

As the young family arrived at the wheat field, the pink sun rays pushed into the indigo morning. Prairie music greeted their arrival as if led by a southeast wind conductor making the wheat heads circular motion rattle the kernels, and the beard strains float in the air. The dry chaff twirled and sang. The soft rasp was like sandpaper rubbing against each other.

"I have to tie Armstrong onto my chest," Louise said.

"Need help? I brought you a hat."

Louise began fastening a small blanket to her torso creating a pouch in front to carry Armstrong in. "It's cool out. I don't need a hat."

"You will," Leo said.

"Hats make my head sweat."

"Sweating is better than heatstroke. Plus, you won't be doing a whole lot of good if you faint."

Louise knotted the blanket ends near her hip. "I'm not going to faint."

"Drink water throughout the day too."

"Leo, I have worked outside before."

"I know, but this heat is strong and doesn't seem to be letting up. Plus, it's so dry. You've seen some of the crops. With the high temperatures and little rain we've gotten, things are looking a little worse for wear. I suspect much of the moisture from last winter's heavy snow pack was used up real quick."

The last sentence distracted Louise from what she was doing. Why hadn't Leo mentioned his crop concerns before. "Is the harvest in trouble?" Louise asked.

"No, not in trouble, just not as strong as I would

like it to be. The high price of wheat will help offset a smaller yield, but with the amount of wheat on the market, that has me a little concerned."

Leo had Louise's full attention. "Is the market still oversupplied?"

"Yup."

"Can we hold over more of the grain this winter and sell later?" Louise asked.

"A little, but we'll still owe rent."

Louise placed Armstrong in the fabric carrier. "There's some money left in our savings."

Leo set a straw hat on Louise's head. "Let's wait and see what tomorrow brings. Better get started. When it gets too hot, you stop, and I'll take over."

Leo showed Louise where he wanted her to steer the horses that were now pulling the newly attached, borrowed grain binder. The binder cut and bundled the grain into shocks. She knew Leo was judging her ability as she cut broad swaths. When he yelled, "Looks good," Louise sat up taller in her seat. It wasn't until her third pass that she noticed that Leo had begun to gather the shocks placing them into small tipi structures that would allow the grain dry out.

Louise admired the tall wheat stalks in the dim field as the peony pink, orange, and light blue sky cast over the bucolic scene. Armstrong was warm against her chest. He felt good nestled next to her. Even in the early morning warmth, it wasn't uncomfortable.

The horses and she had found a gentle rumble rhythm that moved them well together. She was surprised that she enjoyed the snap and crunch of horse hooves on cut dry wheat, creaking wood, and rubbing metal as the team moved up and down the field.

The early hours and the repeated pattern lulled her into a contemplation. Louise's relatives were probably harvesting right now too. She knew they would be curious about the outcome of the Zint's first farm season, Armstrong's growth, and the general goings-on. Her Minnesota family had stayed put and never ventured too far from home. An orphaned Leo had been sent to live with relatives, and as soon as he could, the teenage Leo had lit out. Louise left with Leo when the opportunity came. Each of their feelings about home had propelled them to make choices.

When she thought of her mother, she didn't feel the rigid childhood angst anymore. The distance of time, geography, and motherhood had begun to transform her and how she regarded her memories. Louise knew her mother and she were different women. The ditch between them was shrinking. They were both farmwives, mothers, and even gardeners.

Leo's traveling feet had planted them here. Louise had not wanted Bonetrail and farming. Nonetheless, she had followed. Now Louise and Leo created a home together in both attitude and address.

The horse's steps, combined with light winds, created a fence of small dust clouds around the team.

They worked the field until 10:30, when everything stopped for a light lunch.

"Louise, breaktime," Leo yelled from a few yards away. She could see he held one of the lunch crates they had loaded onto the wagon before leaving the farm that morning.

Louise patted a fussing Armstrong. "It's a good time to take a break. Help me untie the blanket so I can lay him on the ground. I did pretty good driving the binder."

Leo untied the blanket knot. "You did a fine job. With the hot sun, Armstrong needs a hat or bonnet. What's in the food crate?"

"I have something to shade Armstrong. There are peanut butter and honey sandwiches, apples, and oatmeal cookies."

Leo lifted Armstrong out of his carrier. "Wouldn't mind a beer."

"A batch should be ready. I'll check the root cellar when I get home."

Leo handed Louise the water jug. "With all the work to do, there'll be no music tonight. This evening I'll come back out and put together more shocks. Tonight's going to be another late night."

"Aren't they all until harvesting is over?"

Leo laughed. "You have a point there. All those late nights with the Musicale trained me well."

Louise handed Leo a sandwich from the crate. "Next year, maybe we can bring on a girl to help

with Armstrong. Then I can be in the field more."
Louise looked at the half-cut field. "It is dry out
here. Even with the heat and dryness, my garden
should produce enough for beyond winter and push
us into spring. We'll be finishing last year's canned
jars as I start harvesting the new season's
vegetables."

"My lady farmer."

Louise's eyes widened underneath her hat. The
jarring of this alternate identity left her mute.

"Do you think you can finish the field you're
working in before we break for lunch?" Leo asked.

"I think so. You're right about the soil. The high
temperatures have been having their way with the
land. We could use more rain."

Leo reached for a cookie. "Eventually the clouds
have to let loose some moisture."

Louise scrutinized Leo as he scanned the big
white cotton clouds fastened to the light blue sky,
peering into them for any sign of rain. "It'll come in
its time," said the farmer in him.

The Zints returned to work and stopped again for
lunch. While eating, Driscol pulled up. When lunch
was over, Leo said to Louise, "Driscol's going to drop
you and Armstrong off at the house. He and I will
work until around five and then come home for
supper before going back out into Driscol's fields."

"The food will be ready."

"Looking forward to it," Leo said and then turned

to Driscol. "Louise and Armstrong are ready to head home."

They hurried back to the farm. Driscol spoke proudly the entire ride about the harvesting and how he and Sadie had settled into married life. Louise listened with half an ear to the nuances of the man's speech so she could make the appropriate mms and hmms sounds. She removed her hat. The truck created a continuous breeze that blew over the sweat-wet hair that stuck to her forehead and began to dry her neck and torso. Louise was content being chauffeured home in an automobile; a breeze, warm or not, moved across her heated body.

Driscol turned the truck onto the driveway to the Zints' farmstead. "You're home."

"Thanks," Louise said.

"You bet. Bye," Driscol shifted gears and rolled and skittered out of the farmyard causing the chickens wandering about to cluck and scatter. Hardy crossed towards them in a quiet amble. He passed Louise and laid in the shade of the roof overhang. All looked in its place.

"Dog, you look hot. Let's get you some water. Then some for the garden." Louise turned to Armstrong. "I need to feed you and get you down for a nap."

Holding the screen door open with her foot, she swung the front door wide open calling in the outside air. A faint thwap closed the screen door behind her.

Two steps in and the hot heaviness of the house labored her breathing. If they had electricity, they could buy a fan, but there was no point in dreaming about something that was unlikely to happen.

"Armstrong, I think it's best to put you in the front room. The air is a little cooler." She removed any unnecessary clothing, fed, and then laid the sleeping baby in his bigger blanket lined apple box. Rubbing his belly in small circles, she whispered, "Stay here until I return."

Louise watered Hardy and moved onto her garden. The back and forth between the windmill well and garden allowed her to survey the rows of vegetables. She saw limp plants and curling leaves. These poor things are taking a beating in this heat. She sidestepped along the rows and watered the thirsty plants and added on several more hours of watering and weeding. Each time a bucket was near empty, her arms and back felt a pleasurable release and relief and she would begin again.

During weeding, Louise mused again about her life. She had returned to the farm. If someone like the Watkins salesman came along peddling household goods, all he would see is another farm wife and not the Musicale's assistant manager. Albeit, this one wore trousers instead of a house dress. If her mother, or even Mother Shields, could see Louise stride about the place like a man, they would have apoplexy. The thought made her smile and she began to hum.

Her Golden Queen tomatoes needed to be picked, along with the long and squat emerald green cucumbers. The idea of canning in this heat depressed her. The work of the day would push canning into the evening. The night would be hot, but she wouldn't have to contend with direct sunshine making the kitchen an even hotter oven. Louise might have to ask Leo to help her set up an outside summer kitchen.

Her Fancy Rag gourds were growing well in the heat. The Great Northern beans were coming along well, too, and soon enough would be yanked out of the soil soon and hung up to finish drying. She inspected the rows and inventoried what was ready to harvest, pull, and wait.

It was quiet with no one around to talk to. After an hour Louise returned to the house to retrieve Armstrong.

Louise told the baby, "You need a hat before going outside, little fellow. Now I sound like my mother and Leo. We won't be mentioning that to either of them."

Later in the garden after several hours, Louise stood up and stretched her back and rolled one shoulder, then the other. When the apple-sized discomfort in her middle back released, she canvassed the area. She saw Hardy had wandered into the Mandan sweet corn stalks and was napping in their shade. "Hardy, you find napping spots anywhere." Once

Leo got home, Hardy would ignore Louise and follow Leo about the farm.

The Golden Queen tomatoes again drew her admiration. They were grand in size and shone like small suns on the vines. Louise liked the name of the tomato, too. It was dignified. This vegetable did not hide, unlike her green, oblong neighbors found by pulling and pushing aside the sandpaper leaves. Her hand cupped a tomato, and the smooth, warm outer skin caressed her calluses. With a quick yank, the tomato broke away from the stem.

The cucumber plants prickled, plate-sized leaves swept across Louise's ankles and scratched her as she tiptoed among and around the plants, searching for the hidden small pickling cucumbers. Louise enjoyed the satisfying snap that broke the undercover cucumbers off the vines.

The work in the garden lasted longer than she had planned. The plants were drinking up the water as soon as it fell around their bases, which meant she had to make more trips to the well for refills. Once watered, the plants stood firmer and taller.

"Hardy, Armstrong, and I are going into the house." She waited for the dog to demonstrate some manner of attentiveness. Nothing happened. "Once again, I'm complimented by your attentive companionship."

As Louise walked into the house Armstrong gurgled.

"Armstrong are you talking to me? Time to start supper. Good thing I baked bread yesterday." Louise chatted to the staring baby as she moved about the kitchen. It felt good to talk to someone, even if her companion had no words and teeth. She felt lonely out on this farm. At her parents' farm, there had been people about and the only time a person had privacy was in the outhouse, and even then, someone could be standing on the other side of the door yelling to hurry up. On the road, there had been people about, and if she and Leo weren't with the band, they were together. There were times at Mother Shields' when Louise detested being around the woman, but at least there was another person around and Myra was next door.

"We're having sausage and peppers, baked potatoes, leaf lettuce salad with cream sauce, and pickles? We'll have chicken for tomorrow's supper. I should have made a pie. Cookies and cake will have to do. Better make sure I have enough coffee ground up. Those men will probably drink a gallon each."

Some days there were long stretches of hours of only Armstrong, Hardy, and Louise on the farmstead, not counting the farm animals. At supper, she and Leo would speak about how they had each filled their days. During the milking, the time together tended to be cocooned in the barn's walls. Louise was chomping at the bit for Saturdays because that was the day the Zints went to town. Town meant supplies and other people.

"I'm going out to the root cellar to get the potatoes. You stay put, Armstrong." The baby gummed a smile in response.

In the root cellar, Louise stood motionless and let the cooler air settle on her arms and lift her short hairs, drift between her damp collarbones, around her neck, and underneath her grown out bob haircut causing the skin on her scalp to tighten. She inhaled deep lung fills and pushed out from her belly. She tasted chilled air, dark earth, and waiting vegetables. In the pitch dark, she felt protected and allayed. Louise knew minutes had evaporated because the skin on her arms began to bump. She rubbed her toughened hands along her forearms. Louise opened a potato sack nearest to the entrance and withdrew a handful of potatoes which she transferred to her makeshift apron bowl.

Back in the kitchen, Louise told Armstrong, "Potatoes are in the oven. Everything else is ready to finish off when your Dad and Driscol arrive. I suspect they will roll in closer to 6. Might as well harvest some more of the garden."

When Hardy saw Louise place the bonneted Armstrong and his crate on the garden platform, he yawned then lifted his backside and stretched his front legs. When his canine kinks had been relieved, he trotted over to Armstrong's platform and reclined.

The sun had moved to the west, lessening its heat. Louise removed her shoes and socks and turned up the pant legs to her knees. When her feet stepped on the soil, earth erupted between her toes.

"Dog, you do have a comfortable life. It would help if you could keep the rabbits and deer out of my garden. How'd the rabbits get through my fence?" Her Tendersweet carrot, kohlrabi, and table beet tops displayed chewed leaves. While she picked vegetables, Louise sang to the two nearby males. She started with "Buffalo Gals," picked beets, green beans, tomatoes and a bushel basket of mixed vegetables and finished with "Wall Street Baby."

"Gentlemen, I will be carrying all this over to the well for washing. I will come back for you two when I'm done."

When she returned to Armstrong and Hardy, she found both napping. The baby curled and flexed his fingers while he slept. Maybe Armstrong was dreaming? Louise hoped whatever adventure was playing in her son's head, it was exciting.

She picked up the apple crate that cradled Armstrong and whispered, "Back to the house."

Louise guessed that the men would be arriving soon. She opened a jar of pork sausages and poured them into a cast iron pan. In minutes, the fat and peppercorns snapped and jumped in the crackle and hiss. Next came cut up garden-fresh globe onions, colored peppers, and purple cabbage. She settled the lid on the stuffed mixed pot of pork and rainbow vegetables. The Golden Queen tomatoes were sliced and lined up on two plates with a salt shaker nearby.

Hardy barked before Louise heard Driscol's truck. She stared out the window and watched the men stride across the front yard. They removed their hats and beat them against their legs to shake out the field dust.

"Hello Louise," Driscol called out. "You ready for hungry men?"

"Supper is on the table."

Without further words, Leo and Driscol sat down to eat. Louise poured coffee as fork tines shoveled into food.

When each man had a half-empty plate, Louise asked, "How did it go this afternoon?"

Leo spoke around bites. "We got most of what we wanted done today. That heat was something else. The only shade to be found was underneath the wagon. I wonder if it will be this hot at threshing time."

"Will you need me in the morning?"

"Yes. It will be another long morning, but your help will get it done faster. What are you doing this evening?"

"Hold onto your hat, oh wait you made me wear it, but the kitchen is going to get hot tonight."

A chuckle rolled out of Leo. "How's that?"

"Canning vegetables. Might as well do it when the evening's cooler."

"We could set your canning operation up outside."

"Maybe next year."

His eyebrow lifted in response. "Can do."

Louise thought over what she had said and what it meant. She had said next year like she was planning for her future. Not knowing what else to say, Louise shrugged her shoulders.

The men left the yard with a refilled food crate and water canteens. Louise walked out to the yard and watched a dust cloud trail after the departing farmers. The sight reminded Louise of when Leo and the Musicale had left Wheatville for the first time. The destination of the fields was so different from the band's stages.

This life on the land had become her daily routine, and now it was integrating with her psyche. She could feel invisible roots going deep. She did not have a hoe to break them, nor the desire to step away. The feelings unsettled Louise. Her heels stepped heavy on the ground as she reentered the house. She bit her lower lip. Something Louise could not name swung inside toward a new North.

CHAPTER TWENTY-THREE

Harvesting finished, and the collective farmers exhaled the unconscious breath they held since early spring. The Zints spent the remaining fall days preparing fields for the next planting cycle and season, repairing equipment, making a to-do list for next year, and storing food for the upcoming months. Having the hot summer sun move towards the other side of the world helped lessen the heat in the kitchen and on the northern prairie. Doors and windows remained open and small holes in the screens allowed a few mosquitos and flies to seek out the lantern light.

Tonight, Louise wished for the music. Her hair, which hung past her shoulders developed waves as she hovered over the steamy stovetop canner. The notes of sugar, tangy vinegar, crisp garlic, sharp white onions, and grassy dill replaced harmonies, trebles, and crescendos. Instead of perfume, Louise smelled of pickled eggs, canned watermelon, chokecherry jelly, and vegetable soups. Someone had once told her that dill was used in love potions and spells for protection. The scents could lead Leo to Louise, but the strength of their odor combined with her sweat could well keep them apart.

Her forearm swiped her forehead to catch the rolling sweat, and in the next movement she moved, filled, and sealed jars around the kitchen until neat lines of rounded Mason quart jars lined up on the table. The pop, pop, pop of the sealing lids and the poof, poof of air from a sleeping Armstrong was tonight's percussion and tempo.

It was another late night. Leo would come back from working at Wheeler's and then depart for the barn. The impatient cows waited for their evening milking. Louise stepped from the hot coal heat and walked across the room to the dried branches of faded chamomile flowers, black licorice anise, and crackled northern beans that hung and decorated the dim makeshift parlor. On a bench sat potted blooming red lipstick geraniums, brighter in color than Louise had hoped, and on the other end were languishing tomato plants. The moon's rays bounced off the metal food cans and shone from between twigs, branches, and leaves and created a shadowed starry constellation on the walls and floor.

Louise ran her hand along the hanging shrinking vegetation. The contact let loose brittle noises and a waft of scents. It was not a distinct smell but an aromatic jumble of spring, summer, and fall. Louise closed her eyes seeking the memory of the lilacs. She turned in a circle following its trail. The rough boards underneath her shoes creaked. Louise opened her eyes and saw the autumn moonlight touch her legs. When Leo returned home, they went out to the barn for the evening milking. Afterward, a drooping Leo said, "I'll button up everything; you go on inside."

Later, as Leo walked into the house, he took off his hat. With a tired toss, it landed on a hook next to his coat. "It's still warm out. I hope this winter's snow waters the prairie."

From a pitcher, Louise poured washing water into the basin for Leo. "All my body knows lately is how to sweat. My garden is harvested and my canning is almost done."

Water splashed and dripped on the floor as Leo dipped and wrung the rag in and out of the washing bowl while he cleaned himself. " I could let the pigs eat what's left in the garden. I hope we get some good snow this winter. It would help put some water back into the ground."

Louise drooped inside. "Winter. Stuck in the house."

Leo considered Louise before he hung his head over the bowl and rinsed his hair with the water pitcher. The man pulled the towel over his head and started to rub dry. "Stuck?" he asked.

"The snow and cold makes it hard to get into town. It's not like we can just go next door to catch up with the neighbors, or to the café."

"True. It's only bad for a few months. Are you worried about the coming winter?" Leo asked.

"This is our first winter on the farm. I'm nervous being so far from town."

"Sweetheart, we'll be fine. There'll be snow and cold, but we'll be warm and safe in our house. Leave the worrying to me." Then Leo pulled her into his arms. Standing in the weak light of the kerosene lantern, the couple rested in each other. A sweaty forehead pressed into a washed dry one. One over-heated body touched the other. A second touch so slow that it was almost imperceptible. A new diversion carried the couple through the night and when one and then the other gasped, they settled into deep sleep.

October saw the leaves drop from the few trees on the western North Dakota prairie. The garden pumpkins were stored underneath the Zints' bed. The few remaining watermelons were placed in the grain bin with held over bushels of wheat. Armstrong had mastered rolling over both directions. The screen door was pushed back against the house, and the front door kept closed.

Louise had canned, preserved, stocked, stacked,

hung, and stored the garden and other foodstuffs found in the field, ditch, and grocery store. Pints, quarts, and gallons filled from belly to neck, bushel baskets of apples, yellow and white onions, and burlap sacks of potatoes shared space in the root cellar. This buried food safe was tangible evidence of Louise's first year on the farm. She was proud of her harvest, and it would see her family through the winter and spring.

On a November Saturday morning in the kitchen, Louise heard a mumbled, "Morning" and felt Leo hug her from behind. "Coffee ready?"

"Yes. Bread's on the table. I opened a jar of rhubarb jelly. Eggs are almost done."

Louise could smell the cooler air and hay that stuck to Leo. "Did you milk the cows?"

"Milked them and fed the other livestock. Could use some breakfast myself. I'll separate out the cream after I'm done eating," Leo said.

"Sit down. I'll dish up.' Leo didn't move. He pressed into Louise. She moved the frying pan to a cold burner and reclined back and shared touch and warmth.

Louise closed her eyes. "Tonight, let's have music."

"Already on my mind."

Louise whipped around to look Leo in the eyes. "How about a party? Driscol, Sadie, Myra, Heinrich, the Hochhalters, the Hubers down the road, maybe a few others. We could use some celebrating after the season. Could you build an extra table from wood scraps? We'll need to ask them to bring extra chairs. If the evening stays warm enough, we could go outside for a short time. The first freeze took care of the mosquitos."

Leo waltzed Louise in a circle. "Sounds like we're having a party tonight."

"Yes, and I won't have to sell drinks."

Leo patted her bottom and then sat at the table. ""No police, either. I'll get the cream ready. Then we can go to town. We'll pull into the Hochhalter's place on the way. Do you want to stop by the grocery store before or after Myra's?"

"The store first. I have more eggs to sell."

Plans were made, changed, and set again, and the chore list was reviewed and divided over breakfast. The party plan put a buoyancy into Louise's spirit and step.

"Armstrong, we're having a party," Louise sang as she dressed the baby in his navy coat and matching homemade knitted hat and mittens that had been sent by Louise's mother. The fall days were warm enough, but the mornings were gathering and holding onto the crispness of cooler evenings.

The Zints made their stops and when they arrived at the Schmidts', the trio traipsed to the back door. Louise glanced at Mother Shields' house hoping not to see their former landlady.

After knocking on the door, they heard Myra ring out, "Come on in."

Leo opened the door and stepped back to let Louise in first. "Morning."

Myra wearing a bright red apron said, "Look who we have here. Plus, you brought one of my favorite little men."

"I hope you mean my son?" Leo teased.

"Oh, you. Let me see that baby." Myra held Armstrong. The little boy chortled and then nested into her voluptuous bosom. "Coffee is on. There are fresh doughnuts. Help yourself," Myra said and then squeezed Louise's shoulder and patted Leo on the back.

Leo reached for a doughnut. "I'll take one for the road. I have to get over to the hardware store. Do you and Heinrich have plans tonight?"

"No. Why?"

"How about coming out to the farm for a party? Cards and music. The pleasure of your company."

Myra hooted. "Son, it's clearer and clearer how you were able to convince Louise to marry you."

Leo reached for another doughnut. "That, and my fine, good looks helped."

Myra found a paper sack and began filling it with doughnuts. "What time? I'll let Sadie and Driscol know. I don't know if my boys can come with all their working. We might bring a couple along."

"Come around 6. We'll share a meal before cards.

I have to get over to the store. Be back in an hour. We'll need to get home earlier to get the cows milked," Leo said.

Myra handed Leo the sack. "Take these with you. Heinrich's around town, so you'll more than likely run into him. He's probably at the hardware store keeping a chair from flying away. Since you men will be shooting the bull with all your tall tales, we'll be catching up over coffee."

After Leo left, the ladies settled in at the table and caught up on their own family news and town gossip. Soon enough, the Zints were back in the wagon headed for home. Cleaning and preparation for the evening festivities commandeered the remaining afternoon hours. Close to five o'clock, Leo called Louise for help moving a jerry-rigged wood-scrap table into the parlor.

Louise laid a light blue tablecloth with embroidered songbirds she had made as a young girl over the top then said to Leo, "I'm heating water for a quick wash. You want one too?"

"Might as well have a quick rinse. Before I do that..." Louise watched Leo pick up Armstrong. "How's my boy?!"

Armstrong giggled and waved his chubby arms. Leo raised Armstrong into the air like a bird in flight and the child's musical laughter and baby drool fell around them.

When the father and son play slowed, Louise

asked, "After you're done washing up, will you get the extra lantern from the root cellar? My grease is almost hot enough to start frying the chicken. Also, we need to fill the coal shed."

Leo laid a quilt and Armstrong on the parlor floor, and then stepped up to the wash basin. "While in town I asked Gleason to bring by a load of coal. He said he'd be here in a day or two."

"How much did the coal cost?" Louise asked.

With water dripping down Leo's face, he said, "We have the money to pay for the coal. While I was at the store, I asked about buying a radio."

"You did?"

"Mmhmmm."

"What's available? How much are they?" Louise rushed out.

"The hardware store didn't have one on hand. One can be ordered in or we can look at the Montgomery Wards' catalog. We'll also need to buy a few extra battery packs for it."

"Thank you," Louise said.

"You're welcome."

Louise began to add uncooked chicken to the hot grease sizzling on the stovetop. "We can listen to the music programs, the news, and even the weather report. We'd know more about what's going on out east with that Wall Street crash business."

Leo wiped dry his face and neck. "I can tell you

the weather report by looking at the sky and the feel in my bones."

"You're too young to feel it in your bones."

"Maybe, but I know things."

Louise added more chicken to the frying pan. "So, if you know things, what's the summer of 1930 going to be like?"

Leo stalled for a moment then smiled ear-to-ear. "Why, it's going to be a harvest of milk and honey."

"We already have milk. I'm interested in wheat turning into money."

Leo's laughter bounced around the kitchen. "I think every farmer is. I'd better spiffy up and change my clothes for tonight's party."

Louise was happy as she sliced fluffy buns and white cheese, and retrieved the dill-dashed potato salad from outside the front door, and checked on the apple pie waiting on the window sill.

Leo stood in the parlor. He asked, "Are you going to leave these twigs and branches hanging up all winter? Maybe they should go into the root cellar with the others?" The suggestion included a hopeful inflection.

"Some are already down there, but these I'm keeping up here. It will help remind us of spring when we're deep into winter. Be careful moving them to the side."

"I'm taking care. I should get my fiddle tuned before they all get here."

Leo sat down and what followed were plucks, pings, and thrums, but the out-of-order resonance began to take shape. The sun had started to set in the west. The daytime wrens and nuthatches quieted. The barn owls and red foxes stalked the land. Even the autumn air transformed in anticipation of a prairie party.

Hardy woofed each time Driscol and Sadie, the Schmidts, the Hochhalters, and several other neighbors arrived by vehicle or horses and wagon.

"Welcome! Come on in," Leo called as each rig pulled into the farmyard.

When people strode into the house Louise said, "Hi, let's put coats on the bed. If you're hungry, there's food already laid out. You can put whatever food you brought on the kitchen table. Here come Leo and Driscol with extra chairs. What homebrew is that? Smells like raspberry wine. Leo, get the beer and root beer out of the root cellar. The 'shine is already on the table."

Added to the kitchen table were chewy whole wheat bread, odorous headcheese, pickled eggs, cut carrots, fried potato slices covered in cream, peach kuchen, and cocoa fudge. People broke bread and settled into conversation, laughter, and glasses of contentment. A smaller group of men, including Heinrich, discussed the recent Wall Street stock market crash. "What were those fancy people thinking when they lost all that money?" Heinrich asked.

Another voice said, "From what I read in the paper, that wasn't even real money."

"Oh, the money was real, but how's it going to affect us, farmers?"

"We're states away from those old boys--it won't affect us."

"I don't know about that. Grain is a commodity stock that's sold on Wall Street."

"People need to eat, so farmers will always be needed. It's Mother Nature we have to watch out for."

"Crops have been good sized. The weather's been fine, a little too warm this summer."

Louise murmured to Leo, "Do you hear the talk about the market crash?"

Leo moved his hand like he was swatting at a fly. "People like to talk. It helps that each of them has been drinking."

"Have you enjoyed Driscol's still special?"

"Maybe a sip or two."

Louise snorted. "A sip? I suspect a whole glass."

Not even the darker conversation could dull the evening's festiveness. After the supper was over, most of the party settled in for pinochle and canasta except for Louise and Sadie, who cleaned up.

Louise asked Sadie, "How's life on your farm?"

"I love being in charge of my own home."

"That's good. Do you ever get, you know, lonely by yourself? Especially when Driscol's out in the field?"

"Sometimes. But, on the long days, my Mother and Dad have come out to help."

Louise placed clean plates on the food table. "If I want to see Leo, I have to go find him in the field or wait for him to come home."

"Don't you work in the fields with Leo? Plus, you have Armstrong. Look over there. Armstrong keeps trying to grab my Dad's cards. I can't wait to have a baby."

Louise glanced at Heinrich and Armstrong. "Sometimes, I'm in the fields with Leo. There are stretches of time when it's me, Armstrong, and the dog. Not a whole lot of talking going on. It can be so quiet that all I hear is the wind."

Sadie nodded her head. "On those days, I'm especially glad we have the radio. Listening to my afternoon programs makes the day move faster. Will Leo be playing music later?"

"Try and stop that man," Louise said.

Heinrich whooped. "I think my son-in-law tried to steal my trick. Sadie, Louise come switch out Driscol. If I'm going to lose, I'd prefer it be to a pretty face."

Around ten o'clock, Driscol asked, "Leo, when are you going to play that violin of yours?"

Leo rose from his chair. "How about now?!"

Heinrich put down his cards. "Let's move the tables to the side so people have more room to dance. Mother, do you have your dancing shoes on?"

"I do, Mr. Schmidt. Will all the noise and whatnot wake Armstrong?"

"Armstrong is a dependable sleeper with or without music," Louise said.

"I won't take offense from that comment," Leo called out.

Chuckles and guffaws followed. Leo moved a chair to the east wall and took the measure of the group. For a little extra show, he strummed and vibrated the strings. The big, bright new moon high in the coal black sky illuminated the turning pegs and scroll carving as Leo notched the violin between his cheek and shoulder, lifted the bow, tapped his right foot three times, and then let loose a song into the room. The listeners and dancers were pulled into a closed world created inside that small farmhouse on those Great Plains.

At midnight Myra announced, "Would you look at the time!"

The farmers didn't tarry and assembled their belongings and left the yard like a tired caravan. They called out: "Time for home. Thanks again for inviting us over. Don't get to hear music like that often enough. Let's do this again. Thanks, Leo. Thanks, Louise."

The front car lit the road and the horses and

wagons with their swaying lanterns brought up the rear. Louise and Leo each encircled an arm around the other's waist and with their free hands waved and said, "Thanks for coming. Get home safe."

Leo, holding a lantern, said, "I'm going to make sure everything is closed up."

Louise moved to stand in the front doorway. Her eyes followed the tiny, disparate light flickers of their departing friends. She continued to absorb the evening's merriment that had dripped like blossom honey and filled the holes and cracks of the farmhouse walls. An invisible glow coated the weathered, coarse planks and the muscle and tissue of the hearts of the dwellers.

Later, as they settled into bed, Louise said, "That was fun. Reminded me of the early morning jam sessions after all the customers went home and the band and staff played."

Leo stroked her arm with his thumb. "It was like our harvest celebration."

"For a farmer that's very poetic," Louise said.

"Being a musician and farmer, or a poet for that matter, isn't so different. We're all trying to grow and harvest something. Notes, seeds, or words."

CHAPTER TWENTY-FOUR

Winter had left its calling card of light snow on the ground. Louise looked out her foggy kitchen window. She saw Leo's silhouette standing in the farmyard. With a dishtowel embroidered with purple pansies, Louise wiped the window, making a circle so she could see her husband staring at the prairie underneath a stone-white sky. There was a stillness in his absorption that made Louise throw on a coat over her apron.

When Louise stood next to Leo, she asked, "What are you looking at?"

"Just thinking about the harvest."

"How'd we really do this year?" Louise asked.

"Not as well as I hoped, but next year will be better. More rain would have helped the yield. It's the first year on the farm." Leo paused, then added, "We're getting our feet under us."

Leo's speaking break prompted Louise to turn away from the horizon and stare at him full on. "If wheat prices are low next year that doesn't forecast well for us."

"It's not that bad. Next year will be better."

Concern made Louise's stomach clench. "Do you think all that Wall Street shouting could leave a mark on us somehow?

"Maybe. According to the Farm Bureau, there's plenty of wheat available to sell, so the supply is still high."

"What if we have trouble selling our grain next year?" Louise asked.

"Sweetheart, you're jumping to something that's not going to happen."

"But it can happen."

"We're in a good place. We're coming along fine. I have some work to do in the barn."

Louise didn't like the tone of the conversation. She and Leo were doing okay, but there was much riding on next year's harvest. Over the summer, her husband worked like a dog and was happy about it. She mused if it was the satisfaction of being in charge of his farm and days that overrode the stresses of the rent contract, the risk of bad prices, and crop failure. Lately, there were times Louise thought Leo went

somewhere else when he played his violin, resur-
facing when the song was over.

She went back into the house. Armstrong was sitting on the parlor floor on top of a patchwork geometric quilt Myra had created. He stretched his neck
like he was one of the little turtles down at the creek.
The creek water was beginning to ice over, and the
land was hardening as winter crept in. Louise regarded the coming winter with mixed feelings. She
liked that the workload lessened, and Leo was nearby,
but it was also a time of isolation as it kept her from
their friends, and the house was a shelter that could
eventually make her feel like a hostage.

Snow landed on the plains, burying all evidence
of grass and crops. The tall, encompassing drifts
made it harder for animals and humans to move
about and stay warm. Unbroken sheets of white went
past the horizon and made it more difficult to orient
without visible landmarks.

Each day the cows were milked, stove coal ash
was dumped outside and blackened the snow, and
the chickens' egg production slowed. Armstrong
began to crawl, and Louise applauded his achieve-
ments. During their hibernation, Louise thought
about the summer every day. In her mind, she escaped into Bonetrail, into the landscape of tall grass
and wildflowers, and occasionally into Musicale
memories.

Louise contemplated how she would do her

summer work with an active Armstrong. She prayed
for an early defrost. The coming winter was made
more bearable with Thanksgiving at the Schmidts'
and the purchase of a new radio. The little family listened to the music and story programs, the weather,
farm reports, and the country's worrisome economic
news. One of the saving graces that kept Louise paci-
fied was the increased hours that she and Leo were
together. She broached him about learning to read.
His "no" remained, and he used some of his winter-
time to carve a small chair for Armstrong.

When winter solstice was days away, Louise's un-
ease with the shortening daylight and the near-zero
temperatures intensified. Leo had gone alone on his
last three trips into town.

That afternoon, as Louise heated water for coffee,
the impulse to run out of the house raced within her.
She repeated to herself, stay put, breathe. Then the
door opened, and Leo said, "Coffee ready? It's getting
colder again."

Louise swallowed, and in a higher octave than
usual, she replied, "Almost."

After they finished their coffee break, Leo returned to his work in the barn. Louise stayed at the
table. She went back to the moments just before Leo
had walked into the house. The feeling of being out
of control had been strong, and it scared her. What if
it happened again? *Be reasonable and get to work,* she
told herself. That's what her mother would say. The

amount of summer work and accompanying fatigue
had kept some of Louise's concern about the forthcoming winter loneliness, and even panic, at bay. She
stared down at her hands and saw them shake. With
deliberate action, Louise wrapped her hands around
her coffee mug and held tight until the shakes went
away.

Again, the Zints were invited to the Schmidts for
Christmas. Driscol drove out to the farm and picked
them up, and then brought them home hours later.
Louise had stitched small silver bells to Armstrong's
shirt which he kept trying to chew on. The Christmas
celebration was similar to the year before though no
piano was abducted as the Congregational minister
had remained in Bonetrail. New Year's Eve was
spent listening to the radio as Leo played along with
the songs and gave several solo performances.

On a late-January morning, the below-zero wind
chill tried to push in and replace the stove heat.
Louise felt the boxed-in feeling bang loud in her
head. She could smell the bread in the oven burning.
Minutes passed and smoke emitted from inside the
stove. Louise knew she needed to take the bread out,
but she couldn't make herself do it. Smoke inhalation
made her cough, and it was the contractions of her
lungs that released her from immobility. She was able
to remove the loaves from the oven.

The kitchen was smoky. Louise went to the front
door. She didn't want to open it. On the other side

was a hard-hued white that could make one snow blind. Louise heard Armstrong cry. The baby needed fresh air. Louise opened the door a crack but stared at the floor.

Armstrong's cries grew stronger. She knew she should go to him. Louise stayed by the door. She was unaware of the time. Armstrong's crying had stopped. The room temperature rivaled the outdoors. Louise shivered, and again her body's involuntary movement triggered a release. She shut the door and walked to the table.

Louise didn't know what to do. Her eyes darted from the table, to a shelf with dishes, to a butter churn, and on and stopped at the pocket calendar with the days above and a pouch below for bills, lists, and other papers. The picture on the calendar was a bright red barn nestled in its New England winter landscape. The image's mood was calm and settled. Louise stared at that barn until her panic receded.

For the rest of the season and the earliest of spring, whenever Louise felt the winter nerves, she'd grip a coffee mug, or the back of a chair, a spoon in each hand, or whatever else was nearby until the overwhelm and agitation ebbed enough for her to move again. Leo was unaware, and she said nothing about her episodes. When Leo was within talking distance, Louise felt safe and tethered. Spring couldn't come soon enough. The announcing honks from the flocks of returning Canadian Geese and extended hours of daylight helped to move Louise further and further away from her winter spells.

The previous year's spring farm schedule began to repeat itself. Louise stood in the near-empty root cellar and recollected how she had stocked it. A mental pantry contracted and expanded as she considered her new season garden choices. Cauliflower would not be planted and a second smaller garden of potatoes was added.

For the next three years, the farming routine mostly resembled the first year on the farm. Louise's winter panics did not return. She surmised it was because she had too many other worries. Insufficient rain and dust storms made the land dryer, scarce grain yields, and low wheat prices meant little money. Across the United States, and in many countries, the Great Depression, and now the Dust Bowl, was bottoming out people's lives.

Each time a dust storm picked up and stole turned over, exposed nutrient-rich topsoil, it flung and scattered the wrecked soil around the county and beyond. Louise had to scrub the windows and woodwork; wash the towels, curtains, clothing, and bedding; beat the rugs and cushions, wipe out cupboards and closets, and brush off anything else. Turning her dishware upside down hadn't done enough, so now there was paper perpetually laid over the lot.

The black and white Musicale dress that helped Louise transform from a young girl to a lady had yellowed and began to disintegrate. One fall morning, after Leo had left for the field and Armstrong napped, Louise went to her garbage burn barrel. She tossed the dress in and lit a match. Its brittle fabric burned quickly. Tears cascaded down her cheeks. She heard Armstrong call her name. Louise swiped at her wet face and turned away from the pyre of the old Louise.

The word "drought" stuck and stayed on the farmers' cotton-mouthed tongues. America had temporarily become a little wetter on December 5, 1933, as prohibition was repealed.

At the end of the 1935 summer, the strong, gusty winds stole any moisture and chaffed the thin and brittle remaining topsoil. The dairy cows were hungry and had eaten what grass they could scavenge from pastures and ditches. If one could make hay, it was put up in the morning because the afternoon heat could dehydrate and even kill the horses.

One night after supper, Louise asked Leo, "The little we can harvest will not even cover our summer's expenses. How are we going to feed the animals this winter? We'll only have a hundred dollars left in the bank to get us through into next spring."

"I know what the problems are," Leo said.

"It's never been this bad before. The land has become hardscrabble."

"I know. I'm trying to figure out a solution."

"Stop saying, 'I know,'" Louise said.

"What do you want me to say? The drought has us by the tail. The country's falling apart. I keep trying to take care of my family and my farm, but things are getting worse. I know how to do two things: play music and farm and either barely keeps a roof over our heads."

Louise's frustration and fear wanted to yell, I knew farming wasn't any good for us. Instead, she said, "We'll figure something out."

Leo raked field and ditch brush, Russian thistle, and any dried grass he could find and bailed it with the remaining hay to feed the herd. The cows didn't like the new feed, but it was better than starving. The pheasants, deer, and other prairie roamers were leaner, and their populations shrunk. The rabbits were surviving though, and to Louise's displeasure using her garden to supplement their diets. Much of the water that would have been used on her garden was diverted to the livestock and to prevent the well from going dry.

Armstrong had grown into a little boy, and an unplanned sibling was on its way.

"Armstrong, put away your toys. We're going to eat supper soon." With a low bass grunt, Louise stretched and pulled the bunched muscles in her back. She carried this baby differently. Myra said that meant this one would be a girl. Girl or boy, Louise was ready to give birth and move about with ease. Adding another mouth to feed did worry her.

"Santa's coming again this year, isn't he?" Armstrong asked.

"If you keep being a good boy, I imagine he'll bring you a toy and a sweet treat."

Armstrong focused on Louise's rounded belly, "The baby comes after Santa?"

"Yes. Sometime next month. Remember how we talked about how after Christmas, you and I were going to stay at Myra and Heinrich's so we'll be in town when the baby comes?"

Louise reminded herself not to burn all the newspaper so she could wrap Armstrong's new toy truck. This year again, she and Leo would not exchange gifts. Louise had been able to use her egg money for fabric to sew Leo a new button-up shirt that he could wear when he played at the school's Christmas pageant. She needed to remind Leo to buy several oranges and some candy for Armstrong's Christmas stocking. The extreme cold and continuous wind chill limited the trips into town.

Last week she and Leo had spoken about readying for the baby's delivery. To save money they previously decided that Leo would get the doctor to come out to the farm instead of paying for a stay at the town house hospital.

"This cold has me worried about getting the doctor out here when I go into labor. What if there's a storm or it's so cold, and he can't get here?" Louise asked.

"There's no need to worry. When you go into labor, I'll go into town and bring back the doctor. I've birthed livestock. If something comes up, I can help with the delivery."

Louise rubbed her hands. "It's so cold. I can barely get water out of the well. I've resorted to melting ice and snow on the stove. Maybe Armstrong and I should go into Bonetrail early? We can ask Myra and Heinrich if Armstrong and I can stay with them."

Leo looked down. "That's an idea."

"Could you ask Myra and Heinrich on Saturday when you're in town?"

Leo didn't reply but stayed quiet. Louise could tell he was surprised, but her intuition told her there was something more intertwined in Leo's response.

"It will be quiet with you and Armstrong gone," Leo said.

The word 'gone' activated a guess and Louise followed it. "This is not like when your family was split up, and everyone went different directions. We'll be in town. You'll come for supplies and to see us. When the baby comes, I'll ask Heinrich to come get you."

"That would work. I guess this time you're heading out," Leo said.

Louise grasped Leo's hand. "I'm going down the road. Not even leaving the county. Hardy will keep you company. There's always the cows."

"Neither are big talkers," Leo said.

"When we return; you'll give the three of us a big welcome home show."

Leo squeezed Louise's hand. "That I can do."

Bacon grease jumped and singed Louise's wrist, and the sharpness of the burn made her step back to the present.

Armstrong didn't notice and asked, "Why can't Dad come with us?"

"Someone needs to stay and milk and take care of the chickens. Hardy too." Louise said a silent thank you for the cream checks. They were getting by, but each consecutive year it was less and leaner. Her garden had increased in size each year, paralleling the diminished grain profits, but the plants were struggling to produce. Food was harder to grow, and scarcity was directing their family's consumption and potatoes became a food mainstay.

Louise's 1935 Christmas wishes were "please, please, please, let this baby be healthy and do not let 1936 do us in."

CHAPTER TWENTY-FIVE

On Christmas Eve, the Zints stayed home because of a sudden blizzard. The wind sucked fire up the chimneys, increasing the likelihood of house fires. The outside conditions were whiteout and farmers tied clothesline and ropes between house and barn to go back and forth. Several people froze to death.

Three weeks later into the beginning of 1936, Louise and Armstrong made a temporary move into Bonetrail for the new baby's birth. Earlier that month, another blizzard had pummeled the state with average temperatures between ten and thirty below zero with windchill. Some snow drifts were almost eighteen feet high. As cumbersome as the snow was, it would help the land come spring.

Louise's covered belly bump stuck out as the three

wrapped and layered individuals rode the wagon and horses into town. She was thankful that the day's January wind had dropped to a shiver breeze. Leo had become even quieter this last year. The timbre of his music had become less energized and at times sorrowful.

Every new year, Louise had asked him his upcoming farming forecast.

Last year Leo said, "We'll get by. Mother Nature is resetting. Things will change." There was less ambition and more numbness. This year when Louise asked Leo all he said was, "I don't know." This added to her pile of concerns.

The Zints pulled up to the Schmidts' house. Leo helped Louise and then Armstrong off the wagon. The young boy tore up the walkway and stopped when he saw Mother Shields shoveling.

"Hello, Mother Shields! I'm going to be a big brother. We're in town until the baby comes. Ma doesn't know when that is. We have to wait. Santa brought me a toy truck, two oranges, and candy. What did Santa bring you?"

"Hello, Armstrong. Stand still when you're speaking to adults and don't yell."

"Okay," the wiggling little boy half-yelled.

"I had a quiet Christmas here at the house. Santa does not stop," Mother Shields said.

"Why not? Maybe he forgot, and will come tomorrow? Did you get a present?" Armstrong asked.

"I'm too old for Santa. Each of my children sent a card."

"No present! Golly. My grandparents in Minnesota sent a present and a card."

"Hello, and Happy New Year," Myra said to the Zints.

Armstrong waved and smiled big to the greeting, waved goodbye to Mother Shields, and dashed up Myra's steps.

"Hello, Mother Shields," Louise said.

Leo showered Mother Shields with a "Happy New Year, ma'am. Would you like me to finish shoveling your walkway?"

"No thank you. I'm almost done. It appears another Zint is soon to make its way into the state."

"Yup. I told Louise that when the barometric pressure drops my pregnant cows go into labor, so maybe she should keep that in mind."

"Leo, your wife is not a cow."

"No, ma'am. Not at all. I was pointing out a strategy that may help," Leo said.

"A baby comes when it's ready."

"Yes ma'am, sure does."

"It's cold out; you both had better get inside and warm up," Mother Shields said.

The couple started to walk Armstrong's course when Louise turned to Mother Shields and said, "Happy new year. I hope the year treats you well."

A deft nod preceded a "Thank you."

Leo spent most of the day at the Schmidts. They ate beef vegetable stew thick with last summer's carrots, onions, turnips, and potatoes. The group played pinochle into the late afternoon.

"Too bad you didn't bring your fiddle. Music would be good to hear," Heinrich said.

"Too cold for the instrument to ride in the wagon. Next time," Leo said and he played a black spade that trumped the trick.

It occurred to Louise that this was the first social visit into Bonetrail that Leo hadn't brought his violin. They could have wrapped the violin well and kept it safe from the cold. The realization unnerved her. Leo always made the most of his opportunities to play for their Bonetrail friends and neighbors.

To distract herself, Louise asked, "How are Sadie and Driscol? We haven't seen or talked to them in a long while. The last time may have been after harvest."

Myra and Heinrich stared at each other, silent-speaking in that private way couples do. Myra cleared her throat. "The last few years farming's been real tough. For all of us. They're doing what they can to keep things going. Like everyone around here is doing."

"This drought has to let up," Heinrich declared.

Louise snuck a look at Leo. He didn't look up and stayed focused on his playing cards.

Myra cleared her throat. "A few families started getting the commodity boxes."

Louise turned her full attention to Myra. "I saw in the Farm Bureau's newsletter that they're available for people who qualify."

Heinrich slapped down a king of diamonds. "A person should be able to feed their family. The land's supposed to feed and take care of the people."

Myra reached over and laid her hand on his forearm. "A person's got to feed their family. It may not be comfortable standing in line to get the box but at least its food to eat. Things will turn around. This summer will be better."

Everyone was quiet as a spade trumped a king. As the feelings were repacked, the conversation picked up. The talk was about anything other than farming and weather. When Myra's German cuckoo clock trilled four o'clock, Leo said, "I'd better head for home. It will be dark soon."

Myra rushed into the kitchen. "Let me put together some supper for you to take with."

Heinrich stood up. "I'll get your horses ready while you say goodbye to your Mrs. and Armstrong."

Then the expectant parents were alone. Leo picked up Louise's hand and threaded his fingers through hers.

Louise tried to clear the lump in her throat. "I'll miss you."

"You'll enjoy being off the farm and in town for a while with company around," Leo said.

Louise didn't disagree. This stay in town was different. Things on the farm had hardened. She sensed Leo had moved from her not in a geographic distance but an emotional separation that she was stumbling to follow.

"You'll be coming into town each week, right? Louise asked.

"I'll be in town. When the baby's born, I'll come get you all and bring you home."

"Leo, times are hard. It has to change."

"Will it pass before we're flat broke and we don't have a pot to piss in?"

It wasn't just the vulgarity of the phrase that made Louise wince but also the despair and pain they wore. She had never heard Leo speak in defeat. The man brushed aside criticism and naysayers with a turn of the head and flick of the hand. This was a different Leo. All this time on the farm, Louise had seen her husband walking his fields, cupping different soils in his hand, scrutinizing the clumps and particles, and in the last few years, this task became a land check duty that was quieting his hope. His music had become prayers to Mother Nature asking, clamoring, and even begging for fecund rains, reduced heat, and cooling and sweet breezes that comforted.

"Maybe it's best that Armstrong and I come

home with you? When I go into labor, we can come back into town."

"No. Things will be fine at the farm. No worse, anyway. You and Armstrong stay here. I can get by."

"Here you are," Myra called ahead, and then after delayed seconds, she entered the room. "I have a nice supper and even lunch for tomorrow. Did I hear you mention washing? When you come into town next, bring your dirty clothes. I'll wash them."

"You don't need to," Leo said.

"I know, but if I'm doing the washing, what's another shirt or pair of overalls?"

Louise passed a silent glance of "thank you" to Myra.

Heinrich brought the January cold inside. "Horses are ready."

Leo stood and shook Heinrich's hand. "Thanks. I'll go say goodbye to Armstrong and be on my way."

No one said anything. Each person felt the strong feelings that infused the dining room. Louise hugged Leo hard before he exited the house. She didn't want to let go. This goodbye was a mix of resolve and sadness. Louise wondered who would return to collect them: the hopeful or the despairing farmer or a hybrid in-between.

On the front porch, she shivered and brooded as Leo tucked his chin into his coat, and the rig rolled down the street. When it was out of sight, a movement swung her attention to Mother Shields' house.

Louise's former landlady stood at her window with a full view to also watch Leo's leaving. Louise was too weary to acknowledge or become annoyed at the woman's nosey interest."

As concerned as Louise was about her husband, the state of the farm's finances and longevity, the Great Depression, and a thermometer that stayed below zero, she enjoyed her stay at the Schmidts'. She and Myra cooked, sewed, and talked. Louise was compelled to spend as much time as she could in this intimate sisterhood. As warm as the conversation was in the house, the cold outside punished the prairie. At the end of January, on one of the coldest, crystal blue days, a little girl Zint was born.

Heinrich went to the farm to get Leo. He returned alone. Leo had told Heinrich that he couldn't leave the animals and would come into town the following week to bring home his family. Louise was disappointed, but a bigger apprehension regarding Leo's well-being burned away the hurt. Louise suspected her husband was in his own great depression.

A week later, Louise sat at the kitchen table feeding the baby while Myra moved the rolling pin back and forth across pie crust dough. The soft knock was almost too quiet to be heard because of the chatter and baking hoopla inside the kitchen. Then the knocking started again.

"Is that knocking?" Louise asked.

The pause allowed them to hear the sound of glove on wood.

"Goodness, it is," Myra said and went to the backdoor. "Leo, come in, come in! Why didn't you walk in? It is so cold out there that it makes one's teeth hurt. Here, let me take your things."

Leo removed his outer clothing layers while Armstrong jumped up and down next to him and recited his few weeks in town. "Dad, we went to the movies, I got candy at the store, there's a boy down the street who came over to play, we went to church. It's harder to sit still there than the movies. How's Hardy? Does he miss me?"

Louise's eyes searched Leo as he listened to the jumping little boy and then patted the small shoulder and said, "I'm glad you've been enjoying yourself." Then Leo turned to his wife and the small yellow quilt-wrapped baby she held. "Hello, there, So this is the newest one."

"Meet your daughter, Geraldine."

A large winter-cracked finger pushed aside the blanket that Louise's mother had sent and caressed the brand new velvet soft cheek. "Now, we have one of each."

Armstrong rushed over to the group and poked his head between his parents like a curious goose. "Was I that little too?" Then, letting out a big groan for a little boy, "She cries a lot. You'll have to play louder so we can hear the music."

All the adults in the room laughed at the young instruction.

"I can do that. You been helping your Mom and Myra?" Leo asked.

Armstrong puffed out his chest. "I'm Myra's helper. And Heinrich's. Heinrich lets me fill the coal pail. Myra showed me how to peel potatoes."

Louise ruffled her son's hair. "You've been a good helper. You're getting better at saying please and thank you."

"Yup. I'm strong. Dad, did you have to feed the cows in the cold?"

"Yes, son. Have to feed all the animals every day."

Myra, who held a carrot and vegetable peeler in her hand said, "Armstrong I need help with these carrots."

Armstrong moved in a fast streak with an accompanying yell, "I can help."

The Zints watched their son join Myra and then held their contented gaze with each other. Louise saw the fatigue on Leo's face. It matched the burden he carried.

"You look tired," Louise said.

"I'm all right. The cold takes something out of a person."

"How are things at the farm?" Louise asked.

"The cows are hungry and trying to stay warm. Pretty much like the rest of us. I brought Hardy inside."

"Good." Leo bringing the dog inside the house from the barn brought a quiet relief to Louise's concerned heart. The motivation may have been to keep the dog alive, but she knew the companionship helped Leo.

Leo gazed at his new daughter. "You ready to come home? Or do you want to stay in town a while longer?"

Surprise at the second question bucked up Louise's chin. "Stay in town?" Louise asked.

"There are more people around if something comes up."

Consideration sparked inside Louise. It was true that if she stayed it would be more comfortable and there'd be people about, but the thought and ache of no Leo blew away the consideration.

Louise focused on the man who sat across from her. Leo looked older, as if his aging had accelerated with the twins of tough farming and a poor economic situation. Her stomach rippled like a fish on the line. She grasped his hand and began a gentle rub of her thumb across the bumps of his knuckles. "It's time to go home."

Leo's exhale tripped on his words. "I'm going to ask Heinrich if he'll drive you and the children home in the car. I'll follow in the wagon."

With Myra's help, the young family packed and readied. Louise buttoned her coat halfway and placed the swaddled Geraldine inside.

Armstrong danced in place. "Can I ride in the wagon with Dad?"

"No, it's too cold. You'll ride in Heinrich's car," Louise said.

"But I want to ride in the wagon."

"You heard the answer. Please go get into Heinrich's car now. It's time to get going."

Myra frowned at the hoarfrost-covered raspberry bushes in her yard. "Louise, you ready? Heinrich has the car out front. Leo looks so cold in the wagon. Even riding back at noon with the sun shining isn't helping much with the wind chill. Seeing him all hunched up on that wagon seat makes my back ache."

"We're ready. Thank you again for everything," Louise said.

"Glad to help. It's nice to have young people around. With all the children gone and settled, my house is too quiet."

Armstrong's scarf muffled his yell as he ran to Heinrich's car. "Bye, Myra,"

The horn tooted as they headed to the farm. Heinrich filled the drive time telling stories about neighbors and what building or house was there before the present one. Louise knew some of these tales and was even included in a few of them but what drew her attention most was how every fourth sentence or so Heinrich would say, "Things will get better." He did not use the word drought. It was as if saying the word out loud would bruise him further. Today, she imagined Leo wished for a hot day instead of this frozen landscape.

Because of the extreme cold, Heinrich stayed long enough to see them enter the house and with a farewell horn, he reversed out of the farmyard. Once Louise and the children were inside, she caught a new scent inside the house. She sniffed hard. It smelled strong like burnt grass.

Louise stacked quilts on a cranky Armstrong in the bedroom and told him to stay covered up while she got the fire going in the kitchen stove. Geraldine remained tucked inside Louise's coat. Next to the stove, Louise looked at her pail of fire starter-dried cow patties and a nearly empty coal bucket.

When Leo returned from the barn, Louise had coffee ready along with the pound cake Myra had sent.

"Coffee's ready. Get some heat in you," Louise said.

"Thanks. That wagon ride was cold. It took thirty minutes working in the barn for me to warm up."

"How are the cows doing?"

"I'm keeping them in the corrals huddled together. The barn overhang is helping break the wind some, but then it switches direction, and they're directly in it. I've been going out in the middle of the night a couple of times to check on them, bringing them into the barn and then switching them out after a while. We have a couple that don't look so good." He waited. "We might lose one."

"I see."

"If we lose the cow, we can butcher it," Leo said.

Keeping a neutral face that did not show the distress running in her veins, Louise said, "That will cut into the cream checks."

Leo rubbed his face with his hands. "I can't make an animal magically well. We'll have to do what we can and see what happens."

Louise wanted to lay her forehead on the kitchen table. That's what they had been doing every year on this farm and look where they were. She asked, "Are we almost out of coal?"

Her husband wrapped both hands around his mug. "Close to it. I'm trying to make what coal we have last. I've been mostly burning cow patties. I'm glad I gathered a pile of them last fall."

"Armstrong can start gathering them this spring. He'll probably enjoy throwing them around," Louise said.

Leo cocked his head and regarded his wife. "Probably so."

Louise reached across the table and threaded her fingers through his. "We're in this together."

They sat like that until Armstrong heavy footed it into the kitchen and announced, "I'm hungry."

CHAPTER TWENTY-SIX

Bonetrail's consistent below-zero temperatures and frequent blizzards pushed livestock and people into tighter circles. The Zints burned coal and cow patties to keep the house from becoming an icebox. By mid-March, the snow began to melt and diminish winter.

On March 26, Leo came in for lunch. "You and the childern stay inside today as much as possible. Melt extra ice and snow for water. I'll take care of the milking after lunch, feed the chickens, and make sure the horses are settled. The wind is picking up something fierce. It's going to be a bad night."

Louise set a mug of coffee in front of Leo. "I'll get supper going and will make sure there's enough fuel for the stove. We can eat whenever you want."

Leo scraped ice off the kitchen window. He scanned the clouds and the prairie, reading the weather. "Send Armstrong out to the coal shed to fill extra bags of cow patties. They burn fast, but it will help slow down our coal use. Tell him no fooling around and get back inside as soon as he can."

"I'll add another layer on him and send him right now. He can take Hardy with."

Leo opened the door and yelled over the wind. "Hardy, come."

The dog ran inside and Leo walked outside pulling the door shut behind him.

Louise grabbed Leo's summer field jacket. "Armstrong!"

The little boy came into the kitchen from the back bedroom. "Go and fill the burlap bags with cow patties. Put Dad's jacket over your coat and pull your scarf over your mouth and nose. Take Hardy with you and no dawdling. There's a storm coming. I'll be along to get the coal, so let's get to it."

Armstrong took the bags and ran out of the house with Hardy on his heels. Leaving Geraldine nested in her newly lined apple crate near the kitchen stove, Louise added a second sweater before putting on her winter coat. Her scarf was double looped around her neck and then tied on top of her stocking hat so the hat wouldn't be blown away. She joined Armstrong in the shed and filled her coal pails and galvanized washing tubs. She set the extra lignite rocks in the parlor.

The kitchen stove was having trouble heating the

front room. Tonight, maybe they should sleep in the kitchen. It'd be warmer. The pipe that ran from the back of the stove through the wall to the bedroom warmed somewhat on ordinary winter nights. It would be insufficient tonight.

Louise checked on Geraldine. "You've come just in time for some excitement."

The comment made Louise reflect on when all she desired was excitement. Hot music, flashy shows, and new places that were so opposite of her current life. Those memories were precious. Standing in this cold farmhouse made her heart desire a mundane stability.

She headed outside to help Armstrong. The partial storm had accelerated and the temperature had dropped.

When the bags were filled Louise twisted them closed. "Let's get back into the house. Race you."

Armstrong's short legs cycled fast and he led his mother back inside the house.

Louise huffed out, "Armstrong, leave your coat and hat on until you've warmed up."

"Okay. Where'd Hardy go?"

Louise rubbed Armstrong's arms and legs trying to warm her son. "Once we were inside, he ran over to the barn to find Dad."

"It's cold outside. He should be in the house too," Armstrong pleaded.

"When Dad's finished, they'll both come in."

It would be several more hours before Leo and Hardy returned to the house. The dog laid next to the fire just far enough away not to singe his fur.

Louise had turned on the radio earlier for the weather report and companion noise. The announcer reported that temperatures in the negatives were expected to continue. The weather service recommended that people stay in their homes and be prepared for a long blizzard.

"Leo, sit, here's some coffee and a bowl of soup. The sausage is almost ready. The potatoes are still frying. Did you get everything buttoned up?"

"I put as many cows as I could in the barn. It's tight. Maybe we won't lose the whole herd."

The words 'no, no, no that can't happen spun' in Louise's mind making her dizzy.

Leo unfurled his back from the rounded position over the bean and vegetable soup. "We'll ride out the storm and hope for the best."

All Louise could do was nod her agreement. She turned to the stove so Leo wouldn't see her fright. Fear tightened her muscles. She pushed the potato slices across the sizzling cast iron skillet. The snapping lard competed with the buzzing in her ears. If they lost the cattle, the farm was over. Would they be forced to leave? Where would they go? She had dragged her feet to this farm, and the possibility of losing their home because of dead cows scraped sharp across her heart.

"Did you listen to the radio?" Leo's voice seemed to come from a longer distance than the five feet that separated them.

"Yes, um, the announcer said that it would stay cold tonight and to keep indoors." Leo didn't ask for the exact temperature, and Louise didn't tell. "I was thinking we should move the bed into the kitchen for the night. It'll be warmer."

Leo refilled his coffee cup. "Good idea. I don't know how much sleep I'll get tonight. I'll need to check on the livestock every hour or so if I can."

"Then you'll be closer to the door. Potatoes are ready. Armstrong, put away your toys. It's time to eat."

After supper was cleared and washed, the Zints moved their household around. They placed the bed in the kitchen and the kitchen table went into the parlor. Every blanket in the house except for three that Louise had tacked over the windows and the front door were on the bed. She kept the coffee hot, and using the last two teaspoons of cocoa powder, she made a treat for Armstrong. Her family was sitting on a scrap fabric quilt on the bed gathered all together. Leo rocked a sleeping Geraldine, and Armstrong and Louise played checkers.

After the sixth game Louise said, "That's it. No more, you little shyster. Leo, play us some music."

"Play," Armstrong echoed.

Leo handed Geraldine to Louise and crossed to the other side of the room. He returned to the bed with the violin case. A click sounded, and then the mahogany gloss of the violin gleamed in the lantern light. He tuned and tightened and then settled his strong back against the chipped, white metal bed frame.

The melodies glided and tumbled into the room, danced and drafted up and down, soared and landed. For a few hours, that evening music buoyed a family who did not know what change came with the sunrise.

The blizzard lasted three days. Record negative temperatures were reported in North Dakota. The Zints lost two milking cows and won smaller creamery checks. They canned and preserved what they could and then began to eat from the frozen animals that now hung in their grain bin.

The spring weather system begrudged the farming timeline. In chilly April, Louise asked Leo about planting season. "What are your crop plans this year?"

She had waited until after the evening's violin music, and the children were sleeping in their parents' bed to ask the question. It had been a good night. Leo had taught Armstrong new songs. She had watched her son rock side to side while his father entertained them. Leo tapped his fingers on the closed violin case resting on the kitchen table before he answered. "Try again this year. I'll start with the less muddy acres."

"How are we going to pay for the seed? There isn't enough in savings. We can't use credit," Louise said.

"We'll plant less and use up what we have."

"How will we buy groceries? There's some food in the root cellar, but we still need sugar, coffee, and the like."

"Maybe I can pick up some extra work at Wheeler's or around town."

Louise's squared head and torso made a straight, strong line. "I think we should sign up for the commodity boxes. Now don't get cross. There's nothing wrong with getting some help when a person needs it."

Leo's eyes narrowed, showing a storm of upset. "It's tight. We're getting by. We need some time to let this turnaround."

"I'm not saying you haven't or can't, but who's to say this year will be different from the last five years? Last year the prairie was like a tinderbox. It could be that way again this summer."

Leo stiffened. "I can feed my family. The commodity boxes are a government handout."

The heat of her anger added force to her next words. "We pay taxes, and some help would help us.

Plus, those commodity boxes are food, and we need to eat."

Leo stood up and looked out the window into the deep blue night. "You don't think I know this? That's what I'm trying to do, raise wheat and milk cows to feed my family and other people's families. If you want those commodity boxes, then you can go into town and pick them up yourself. I want nothing to do with it."

Hurt made Louise stride to the front door wanting any breeze to help cool her. "Fine. I will do what I think needs to be done. I'm going into town on Friday instead of Saturday to sign up."

"Do what you want."

Louise whirled around so each of her next words would be hurled at Leo. "You think I want this? What I want is for our lives to be different. I want this whole, big country to be different. You don't think I see those lost souls hopping on and off the rail-cars searching for food, a job, something better? The desperation of our neighbors whose farms have been foreclosed? Our town is dying and becoming a bone-yard of worn-out carcasses, and I'm not just talking cows. I understand why people have let go and given up or moved West. Because it's too much."

"I see it too. We've worked hard to make this our home. Let's hang on a little longer. It has to get better. It just has to."

Louise crossed her arms. "We need help. The commodity boxes will make things a little better."

No more words were said, but a silent acceptance of the two sides anchored into place. When Louise readied the wagon on Friday, Leo came over and finished hitching the horses. "Thank you," Louise said to Leo's back.

"You're welcome," Leo said, without turning to her. "I thought I'd come too and see what this is all about. Plus, we need supplies."

"I'm glad you're coming."

The ride into town would have been quiet except for Armstrong's chatter. Armstrong's parents listened and didn't listen. They looked at the landscape both natural and financial as their wagon rolled towards Bonetrail. The prairie was warming up from the ice block winter.

The Zints were almost to town when Leo said, "Why don't we ask Myra to watch the kids while we take care of business?"

"That's a good idea." The foursome headed to the Schmidts'. Bonetrail was quieter. The town was supported by and supportive of farming. The losses and grief were transmitted and shared.

At the Schmidts' they knocked on the front door, but no one answered.

"That's strange," Louise said.

"I guess we'll take the children with us."

As they walked back to the horses, Leo called out, "Morning, Mother Shields."

"Good morning. If you're looking for Myra, she and Heinrich went to Sadie and Driscol's farm. I don't know when they'll be back."

"Thank you."

"It's Friday. You usually come to town on Saturday. Is it the Works Progress Administration goings-on at the county office?" Mother Shields asked.

Louise stiffened at Mother Shield's presumptive inquiry, "We have some business in town and thought the children could stay with Myra while we attend to it."

"I can watch them."

The couple stood struck dumb. Armstrong began to walk into Mother Shields' yard. "Myra always gives me a slice of bread with jelly. Do you have jelly? I like chokecherry."

"I have buffalo berry jelly, and I made bread yesterday," Mother Shields said.

Louise looked at Leo and he back at her. All their past and recent burdens converged along with the weight of their next task. The tired farmers acquiesced and accepted their former landlady's offer.

"You sure it won't be a bother?" Louise asked.

"I've raised my own children. I'm certainly capable of watching your two."

"Of course. I just meant that we didn't want to impose."

"I wouldn't have made the offer if I wasn't sure."

"Uh, uh, thank you, Mother Shields," Leo said and took Geraldine from Louise. "We appreciate the offer. Our errands should only take a few hours. Armstrong, you do as Mother Shields says." Then he placed Geraldine in Mother Shields' arms. "We'd better get the day moving along."

Louise said nothing more and set the children's supplies on Mother Shields' front steps.

"Thanks again. We'll be back soon," Leo said as he hooked his arm through Louise's arm. They headed to the county office. Louise fumed while Leo clicked the horses into motion. "Having Mother Shields watch the children was the cleanest answer. The woman is as honest and dependable as the day is long."

"She'd better treat my children well," Louise said.

"Armstrong's a friendly boy. He'll get along with her and Geraldine will nap."

Louise neither agreed nor disagreed but kept silent. They pulled up in front of the office. She undid the pants underneath her skirt and pulled them off. "I'll go in. You take care of the horses. Maybe, I'll be done before you're finished."

Leo straightened his battered fedora. "I may not like being here, but I'm not going to hide either. We'll go in together."

Inside the office, there were several area farm

wives in line at a table covered with papers. They all knew each other. Louise stood tall and approached the group. She channeled the strength of her mother's no-nonsense personality. When it was her turn, she said, "I'd like to sign up for the commodity boxes." She could feel and hear Leo breathing right next to her.

The clerk looked up and handed her several forms. "Fill these out. If you qualify, your first box will be here next week. Pick up day is Wednesday. There shouldn't be any problems. Most folks around here qualify even if they don't want to. Here's a pen."

Louise wiped her right hand on her navy skirt and then reached for the papers that would recast her family as the drought and depression's working wounded. Leo pointed to two empty chairs, and they sat down.

He said nothing and nodded to the other women in the room as Louise began to read. She knew he was nervous when he began to turn his hat in loops. Louise reached over and stilled the motion. Before she let go, she squeezed his hand. Comfort flowed from her to him and back. A few minutes later, the forms were completed, and then she and Leo signed their names.

In a quiet voice meant only for Leo, Louise said, "It's done," and returned to the clerk. No goodbye greetings were said to the other waiting women. Slow head nods with unfocused eyes were exchanged. To be grouped in this situation was strange, and it carried an element of silent shame. Outside the entrance, Louise and Leo gulped and exhaled spring air.

"We need to stop for supplies before getting the kids and heading home," Leo said.

At the store, both she and Leo playacted busy around the other customers is an attempt to subdue the feeling stirred up in the WPA office. Back at Mother Shields', Leo stayed in the wagon and did not come inside. Mother Shields asked, "Did you complete your errands?"

"Yes. Did the children behave?"

"I was very good, Ma," Armstrong chirped.

"Armstrong, your mother asked me the question. Let me answer. Then you may speak."

"I forget," Armstrong said.

"You will learn," and for once Louise glimpsed a kind regard from the older woman to the little boy. "The children behaved well. Geraldine will need to be fed immediately."

"Then we'd better get going. Thank you for watching the children."

"You're welcome. Feed that baby soon."

Once outside, Louise saw Heinrich speaking to Leo. The expressions on the men's faces were upset, and she couldn't hear what they were saying. When the men saw her and the children approach, they stopped speaking.

"Hello, Louise," Heinrich said.

"Hi Heinrich. How are you?"

"I've had better days, but you know, getting by."

"Is everything ok?" Louise asked.

"That's a matter of where you stand, I guess. Have to get going. Good seeing you all." The older man went inside his house.

"Leo, is everything okay with Heinrich and Myra?"

Leo shook his head. "Sadie told Heinrich and Myra that Driscol has been acting strange. He's not getting his farm work done. Plus, he's been drinking more," then Leo pointed his head at Armstrong to indicate small ears listened.

The rest of the ride home would have been silent if not for Armstrong's stories about the surprise crumb cake he had eaten at Mother Shields' and his observations about the songbirds and clouds trailing the little family.

Louise knew the visit to sign up for the commodity box had been hard on Leo. She was embarrassed at having to ask for help, but the Great Depression and Dust Bowl had taken a toll on their farm, finances, and lives. Now, something was going on in the Schmidt family. If there was one, the saving grace was that most everyone in the town was in the soup too. The soup had simmered, and it had reached boiling. Some Bonetrail residents had already jumped out of the pot.

She silently pleaded to the wind, *please, let this season be better. It doesn't have to be big. An ordinary, dependable harvest would help a lot.* Her desperation wanted the wind that grew colder as they were closer to home to take that prayer to whatever god would listen and help. She didn't care if it was Lutheran, Catholic, or pagan.

By June, the sun had hardened the land, making it parched and scabbed. Weeds had trouble rooting in the soil. The fields were wrung out and too unnourished to grow anything. The animals looked raw and boney. Louise felt the same.

One afternoon, while Louise and Armstrong gathered cow patties, the little boy said, "I'm tired of picking up cow poop."

"It's better than picking up rocks, so don't complain," Louise said.

"I heard Dad say we get a cream check. Why can't we use that to buy more coal?"

"We need the checks to buy groceries and supplies."

"Can't we grow more food in the garden?" Armstrong asked.

"I'm trying the best I can," Louise said but wanted to whimper.

"Those darn grasshoppers like our garden too," Armstrong said.

"Don't say 'darn.'"

"Sorry," the little boy mumbled.

The grasshoppers that showed up as black-winged untrustworthy clouds on a more regular basis added to the farmer's problems. Louise's mother had always said troubles come in threes, and between the depression, drought, and the now grasshoppers, they and everyone around them had seen their three.

CHAPTER TWENTY-SEVEN

At breakfast Louise reminded Leo, "Today is the commodity box pick up."

"I remember," Leo said.

"You don't have to go with if you don't want to. Lots of husbands are letting their wives get the box or pick it up later."

Leo set his fork on his plate. "I'm not happy about the commodity boxes, but I won't make my wife be the only one people see or slink over after dark."

Louise picked up his dirty plate. "Why don't we stop by Myra's and see if she'll watch the children while we pick up the box and buy a few other groceries?"

In Bonetrail, Louise noted that the streets were empty. "Sure is quiet. Wonder where the people are?" Louise asked.

"Maybe the hot day is sending people to seek shade. With so many moving out West, it's leaving a bigger mark on this town."

Louise agreed with her silence. Not only did the town have fewer people, but their vitality was ebbing and spirits breaking. Eyes searched the horizons for rain, but they only found more heartache. People's bodies were shrinking in relation to the water table. Their clothing matched their machinery. Both farmer and farm claimed a resigned attitude to keep what one still had and make it last with patches and repairs.

"Now, Armstrong, at Myra's, you behave and do as she tells you," came the maternal direction.

"Yes, Mama. If Myra's not home, will I go to Mother Shields' house?"

"We'll see if Myra is home first and ask if you and your sister can stay while your Dad and I do our business."

The family stood on the Schmidts' back steps and knocked.

Louise looked over at Mother Shields and saw her windows open. In the past when they knocked Myra's voice sang out a welcome "I'm coming" followed by a generous "Hello," but today the door opened slowly. Myra looked at them in with a still regard. "Morning."

Leo cleared his throat. "Morning, Myra."

The exchange was so unusual that the Zints waited for Myra to initiate the next part.

Armstrong, oblivious to the adults' cautious behavior, sang out, "Morning, Mrs. Myra. Did you miss me?"

Myra gave a bittersweet smile to Armstrong.

Louise brushed Armstrong's hair with her fingers. "Myra, did something come up?"

"Come in. The coffee is ready." Myra turned away, and Armstrong followed.

Louise adjusted Geraldine in her arms. Her knowing expression mirrored Leo's. They both understood the news coming wouldn't be good. Armstrong settled in a corner with wood blocks. The Zints balanced on kitchen chairs while Myra sagged in hers. Ivory coffee cups full to the rim steamed into the air, but conversation didn't follow right away. Myra sat with her hands folded prayer-like in her lap. Leo turned the mug around in circles but hadn't taken a sip. Louise rocked a sleeping Geraldine.

Myra shifted in her chair. "You know, Sadie and Driscol have been having a tough time of it out on the farm." A sharp laugh started and stalled in Myra's throat, but she continued. "Much like everyone in this town. In the state. They've worked hard on that farm. They improved the buildings, worked the land, and made that house theirs. They were making a future. Well, that land didn't appreciate them back. Mother Nature was a witch who couldn't be bothered to let them get a solid start and ride the lean years. Farming in North Dakota is a lost cause." She sniffed hard and looked down. "Driscol bolted."

Louise felt shoved from center. She touched the oak table with her fingertips and pressed hard. She wanted to feel an object that wouldn't blow away.

In a low octave, Leo rumbled, "Bolted? What do you mean?"

"Got in his and left town. No note, nothing. Heinrich's at the farm now, helping Sadie." Myra's voice had tripped on the word 'farm.' "Sadie won't come into town."

Louise pitched forward and then back in her chair. "When did he leave?"

"About a month ago."

"Oh, Myra, how could he? Poor Sadie!"

Leo shook his head, trying to make the shock make sense. "Driscol? Just left?"

The little group sat around the table, watching the steam disappear as their coffee cooled.

Armstrong tromped over to the table. "Myra, can I have a glass of water? Please."

"Yes. It's so nice to have a bit of your sunshine back in my day."

"I'm not sunshine. I'm a boy."

"You are both," Myra said.

Louise cleared her throat. "Would you mind watching the children while Leo and I complete some business around town? It will only take a few hours."

"That, I can do. Be nice to have these little ones underfoot. Pass over that baby girl."

The Zints didn't linger but left the Schmidt house in sober companionship and went to the county welfare office. While they waited in line with the other wives, each Zint thought about Driscol's fleeing and abandonment. A federal official wearing a wearied brown suit approached Leo.

The man took off his brushed clean fedora. "Hello. My name is Richard Wattly. I work for the Civil Conservation Corps. The CCC employs men to work on civil projects around the country..."

Leo cut him off. "I've heard of the CCC."

Wattly waved his hat in front of his chest. "Good. We're looking for some more men. If you're interested in work, we might be able to help you." Leo said nothing. "Don't mean to pry but we have an age limit. Are you younger than twenty-eight?"

"Yes."

"That's good. It's manual labor, but you look strong. We pay $30 a month, including food, housing, and clothing. $25 goes back to the Mrs. You'd be sent somewhere around the Midwest. You being here in North Dakota, you might work with one of the crews up north building roads or in South Dakota. Maybe even Montana. Would you like to see more of the country? Something outside this town? You interested?"

"Is the CCC still working on the Mount Rushmore project?" Leo asked.

"Yes. Projects are going on all over the country. If you're interested, I'll be in town until next Wednesday. I'm lodging at some old gal's place by the name of Mother Shields. Ma'am," and with a downward tip of his chin, the official put on his hat and left.

Neither Louise nor Leo said anything after the man's departure. Louise knew Leo was chewing over Driscol and the encounter with the CCC man just as she was. Why did Driscol run away? Why didn't he and Sadie leave together? Head to Washington State and pick the fruit fields or something else, anything else, like the CCC?

She and Leo could let the farm go. Pack what they could and go somewhere. Maybe even a big city or bigger town? Leo could start playing music for extra money. Louise rubbed one hand over the other and created a heat that had nothing to do with the day's temperatures and instead the imagined moving plans.

Then she felt a dry, cracked hand cover her hands and still the movements. Leo pointed to their commodity box with his free hand. "I need to stop by the hardware store. When we get the wagon, look inside the box. We can get any other supplies at the grocery store before getting the kids."

"Okay," Louise said.

Their stop at Myra's to retrieve the children was quick and the conversation of the necessary kind that didn't travel into the personal. Armstrong chatted about his day until he fell asleep in the wagon bed. Neither of the adults said much.

"Do you want to stop in at Driscol and Sadie's before home?" Leo asked.

Louise stopped gazing at a dried out fallow field. "You mean Sadie's farm. Why'd Driscol do it? Just cut and run. He left behind his wife, home, friends, everything."

"I don't know. Maybe something in him broke. The drought and Depression are grinding people down. A man can barely stand or walk upright. A man doesn't want to fail his family or himself. Sometimes quitting seems like the best answer. Start over. Let a man breathe again," Leo said.

"Is it quitting or just knowing when to cut one's losses and move on?"

"Maybe a little of both."

Louise rubbed her forehead. "Do you think we should move on?"

"No." Leo watched a hawk catch an updraft and glide on the invisible current. "Maybe? Do you want to go?" Leo asked.

This was an opportunity Louise had buried so deep in her inner hope chest that it had laid unexamined and almost forgotten. It could be the moment when this mad escapade was over and they moved on. The "yes" didn't burst out as she had imagined. It went limp and unsaid. The confusion at this lack of immediate agreement had her mind spinning.

What is happening? This is it. The moment. Say yes. It was then that Louise acknowledged her metamorphosis. She had thought she kept one foot set on the prairie and the other pointed to a different future. The farm had begun to rotate the second foot at such a slow, almost unconscious speed, that it was now inches from its mate.

"It's best to keep that as an idea. Who knows, maybe if things don't get any better, it will be out of our hands. We still have a choice. Let's see what this season does," Louise said.

Leo whistled relief. "Okay."

The wagon drove into Driscol and Sadie's tidy farmyard. Chickens wandered about, the dairy cows were in the adjacent field, and a hidden havoc was having its way with the property. Heinrich strode out of the barn and half-waved to the Zints. When Heinrich saw their expressions, he said, "So you heard the news."

Leo set the wagon brake. "We saw Myra this morning."

"I would have stopped by to tell you in person, but there was so much to be done around here," Heinrich explained. His body and the weary volume of his words seemed to slump. "I figured telling people would have to wait."

"Is Sadie in the house?" Louise asked.

"Yes."

Louise left the sleeping children in the wagon and went to the house's front door and knocked. "Sadie?"

Through the screen door, Louise saw Sadie move into her line of sight. Sadie's faded housedress hung loosely, and her braid had more hair out than in. Louise waited. Sadie did not open the door or call her in.

"Can I come in?" Louise asked.

Sadie fluttered her hand in response.

Louise stepped inside. "How are you?"

"I've been better," Sadie said.

"Is there anything we can do to help?"

"No. My parents and brothers have been helping."

"I wish this was different," Louise said.

"Me too. It was supposed to be different. Driscol and I were ready to farm. The rain stopped coming, the wheat didn't grow, and the dust kept flying into our faces. Ruining everything."

Louise moved closer to Sadie in the way a person approaches a wild rabbit. "This drought seems to want to bury us all."

"Driscol started saying, 'Let's move West.' I told him Bonetrail is our home and the rains will come. I grew up in Bonetrail. I know this country. I thought I did. I thought I knew Driscol too."

Louise studied the disheveled woman and then the used plates stacked on the kitchen table. Soiled laundry was piled near the wall. She was unable to view the prairie through the grubby windows. "Maybe once he's had some thinking time, he'll come home."

"I don't know if I want him to. It would have been easier if he had died. A widow gets sympathy and a new life. A left-behind woman is pitied and is stuck to a man she may never see again. This farm is bone dry. Maybe it's time to just let it all go," Sadie said.

"We're all struggling to survive."

"Struggling? We're busted."

The teeth of Sadie's words nipped Louise. Louise didn't know how to reply, so she said, "I'm sorry for your pain."

Sadie walked across the parlor. When she sat on a padded chair, a small dust cloud puffed out. "I'm sorry that my parents now also carry my shame and embarrassment."

Louise didn't know what to say, and stayed quiet. She heard a western meadowlark whistle. The background sound of ordinary life during extraordinary times. Then each woman reached for an unspoken truce.

Leo spoke from the other side of the screen door, "Hello, Sadie. I'm sorry about all that has happened."

Sadie's face contorted into a grimace. "Thank you."

Leo stepped into the house. "You're strong. You'll get through this."

Sadie turned her head and stared at the wall. Louise noted a vacant expression had slipped over Sadie's face and knew an invisible barrier had been erected between the Zints and the betrayed woman.

"You both better get going. Chores are waiting," Sadie said.

"If you need anything, let us know," Leo said and paused as if deciding whether to continue before saying, "Take care."

Neither Leo nor Louise spoke much on the way home. Each turned inward to their private well of thoughts about Driscol, Sadie, and all the other lives in and beyond Bonetrail that had been fractured or ground down by the friction of the bad times. Another brother had gone out of Leo's life. Their friends' lives were changed forever. Louise was glad Sadie had her family helping her.

The evening music provided evidence of Leo's distraction. He forced out upbeat tunes but the songs had tempo missteps of upset. Even the children's normal cheerful behavior was swatted into irritability by these unseen energies. When everyone was in bed, the evening's collective songs gathered together and floated around the house reaching for somewhere to root.

On Saturday evening, the family went to a card party four farms over. The night included conversation about the upcoming planting season, news about the neighbors, simple food with many potato and macaroni dishes, enough to feed everyone, and, of course, cards and Leo's music. No one spoke about Driscol and Sadie. Goodbyes were said under a cream-colored full moon. The children slept as the wagon rolled across the prairie roads. Coyotes sang in the distance.

Louise looked up at the stars. "That was enjoyable. Strange not to have Driscol and Sadie there. Guess we'll get used to that."

"I guess," Leo said.

"You played well."

Leo saluted. "Thank you, ma'am."

"It was good to have a party night before we're all so busy in the fields."

"Speaking of busy, I've been thinking," Leo said.

Louise knew. She'd been watching Leo since all that had transpired the day before. "About what?" Louise asked.

"You remember that fellow from the CCC who was talking about jobs?"

"I remember."

It was dark, but Leo stared into Louise's eyes. "Do you think I should take one of those jobs?"

"It means you have to leave and go elsewhere to work. What about the farm?" She didn't say out loud, what about us?

"If I joined the CCC, we could hire a man part-time to help while I'm gone. Those CCC checks would pay for that, and they would be extra money."

"The money would help. I'd be overseeing the farm by myself," Louise said.

It was Leo's turn to look up at the stars. "A job with a paycheck is hard to pass up. Last year was tough. We barely got through it. We don't know when this drought will end. It's looking like this summer will be just as bad?"

Louise understood the dilemma. "Are you asking me what you should do?"

"Yes," Leo said.

The moon's illumination and the sounds of the prairie's nightlife followed the Zints back to the farm. Louise put the children to bed and then turned in herself. Leo took longer than usual to check the farm before coming to bed. Louise knew this was on purpose. She obliged his action with her own and pretended to be asleep when he laid on the bed. Deep, bass snores escaped the man. Rest could not overtake her brain.

Could Louise run this farm by herself? She had more than enough of her own chores, much less adding the hours of Leo's work to her list. Louise had never been on her own before. Could she do this?

Not seeing Leo and sharing every day, no tender touches or the nearness of the other person, and no violin music. Even in these hard last years, Louise could rely on Leo being there.

Tears followed that last thought and flowed down the pillowcase onto the sheets. Louise was scared. The crying stopped after sleep overwhelmed the momentum.

CHAPTER TWENTY-EIGHT

The next morning Louise woke up alone to Geraldine's hunger and wet wails. Armstrong continued to sleep in the deep rest of the young, and Leo was busy in the barn with the morning milking. After attending to the baby's needs, Louise lit the kitchen stove and made coffee. She sat at the table and again thought about her choices. The last time when such a life-altering decision affected their lives, they had moved to Bonetrail to farm. Leo had decided for them. This time he was seeking her consent. She knew the additional paychecks would help, but asking her to take care of the farm by herself was a bigger request. She didn't know if she wanted to, much less if she even could.

During her third cup, Leo entered the house. He

didn't let the screen door slam behind and instead guided it closed. "Morning."

Louise raised her mug in response. Leo retrieved his cup, poured himself a coffee and then sat down across from her. She studied this man who, as a young girl, Louise had married in two parts heavy infatuation and the promise of an exciting life. Those feelings grew into a deep love and partnership. She didn't know what the future held. Louise knew where she was, and in that clarity, she made her decision.

"Take the job," Louise said.

"Are you sure?"

"No. I don't know what the right decision is. I don't know what our future holds, but this job will help us."

"I'll go into town today and sign on."

"Do you want me to go with you in case there are papers to read?" Louise asked.

"They'll take me or they won't. The man said they were looking for strong backs." Leo pushed the cup left, then right, then back to center. "You know, you and the children could move into town while I'm away."

For long seconds, Louise considered cutting loose the farm and moving into Bonetrail. "That's an idea, but we'll stay here. I better get to my work."

When Leo returned home from town, he quietly announced, "I'm hired; I leave next week."

"Next week! There's too much to do yet," Louise said.

"I stopped by Mr. Wheeler's, and he said he'd help. If there's no pasture grass left for the cattle, cut the wild grass and thistles again to mix in with any remaining feed hay and possibly some grain, if we can afford it. Mr. Wheeler said he'll help with the cutting. Just let him know. I'll get as much taken care of before I leave."

"Where are they sending you?" Louise asked.

"Around the state. I'll start with a road crew in the northwestern part. As we complete those projects, we move onto other areas."

"Where do they house you?"

"A combination of tents and some type of barracks," Leo said.

"You'll be living on the road again."

"Now a crew instead of a band."

"Are you taking your violin?" Louise asked.

"I can't. Each man is allowed one bag." He stared at the far wall and then looked back. "It's for the best. Wouldn't want it to get damaged."

"I'll keep it safe for when you come home," Louise said.

"Never doubted that."

Louise coughed back the tears in her throat. She put the seasoned cast-iron skillet on the stovetop and then Leo's hand planted on her waist. His chest cradled her back, and her spine supported his body. Leo kissed Louise's neck and stepped away.

The Zints made more plans for when Leo was away working for the CCC, completed the tasks they could, and quickly it was the night before Leo's morning departure. Louise decided she would make Myra's strudels and two vanilla cakes for their last meal together. The second cake she'd send with Leo.

As Louise rolled and stretched the white pancakes of dough into big white ropes and then cut them into domino size tiles, she thought about life with and without Leo. She had traveled with him and the Musicale around the Midwest, and then moved to Bonetrail and this farm. He was going off without her. Louise reminded herself that Leo wasn't running away. He'd be back.

Armstrong was in the front yard throwing rocks at the dirt and grass-patched ground. Hardy sat nearby watching. Armstrong and Hardy were going to miss Leo too.

Telling Armstrong had been difficult. It occurred after breakfast a few days ago.

"What do you mean, you're going away to work?" the little boy asked.

"Son, I need to make money, so I'm going to go build roads."

"Like for cars?" Armstrong asked.

"Yup, like for Heinrich and Myra's car. I'm helping build up the country."

"Are you coming back?"

Louise's breath had caught. She'd looked at Leo and saw sadness curtain his face. She guessed he was thinking back to when his father had left him behind.

Leo cleared his throat. "Yes. I'll find a way to send you letters and let you know what I'm doing."

"Okay. When are you coming home?" Armstrong asked.

"Not real sure. Maybe at threshing time if I can swing it."

The little boy cocked his head trying hard to make sense of what the news meant.

"The night before I go, how about I play all your favorite songs?" Leo asked.

Then Armstrong wrinkled his forehead, gazed at the rough plank floor and then back at his father. "Okay. Will you say goodbye to me before you go?"

Louise almost sat on a kitchen chair and wept all her sadness right there. Instead she grabbed a chair back and squeezed white-knuckle tight.

Leo stuttered out, "Yes. I'll say goodbye and give you a hug."

"Hardy will miss you, but I'll take care of him," Armstrong said.

"Thanks. I'd appreciate that. I have a few chores to take care of in the barn. Why don't you come help me?"

At their last supper together, for however long, Louise placed a green glass plate piled high with strudels in the center of the table surrounded by a ceramic bowl of cubed soft potatoes, a platter of fried chicken, a wooden bowl of pickled carrot sticks and white onions slices, a dish of warmed squishy stewed tomatoes, and the goodbye vanilla cake. Louise would have liked to have served Leo's favorite bread and butter pickles, but they were eaten two months ago.

"Armstrong, go outside and get your Dad. Tell him supper is on the table, please."

The boy sprinted out the door. A "Dad" echoed behind him.

"Geraldine, let's get you closer to the table so you can be part of supper too." The baby girl drooled and threw out her arms and kicked her legs to accompany the occasional gurgles, babbles, and spits she produced.

"Dad said to tell you he's washing up in the yard and will be right in," Armstrong said.

"What's he doing that for? I have warm water and a clean towel right here for him."

Armstrong shrugged at his Mom's question. Louise had enjoyed preparing the water and towel.

"Smells good," Leo said as he knocked the dust off his boots before entering the house. "We haven't eaten anything this special in a very long time."

Armstrong jumped in. "We eat potatoes all the time."

"Potatoes are good for you," Louise said, then grimaced. Potatoes had been their inexpensive staple.

The drought made it harder to grow vegetables, but the potatoes continued to produce enough food. The radio news reported many people in the cities had little to nothing to eat. "Food's ready, so sit down. Armstrong, wash your hands."

"I did at the pump with Dad."

A loving, tender smile hung on Louise's face. "Thank you."

Leo and Armstrong did most of the talking through dinner. They spoke about chores, strange livestock behaviors, and knowing how to read the weather.

"Dad, should I turn on the radio so we can hear the programs?"

"Not tonight. Remember, I promised to play your favorite songs." Winking at Louise, he added, "Even a few of your Mom's favorites."

"I'll get your violin," Armstrong said.

Leo pushed his chair back. "Louise, leave the dishes for tomorrow. They're not going anywhere."

"Let me get the worst of it. Plus, I like listening to you play while I clean up."

"Any special requests?" Leo asked.

"No. Just play for us until we can't keep our eyes open."

That evening Leo played more than strings and wood. He was a musical alchemist, transforming vibrating melody and harmony into feeling and story. It was an intersection of man, music, and muse. Armstrong cheered and danced in his clamoring joy. Geraldine kicked her legs and waved her arms. Music infused the atoms in each of those people lucky enough to be in that small prairie kitchen.

When Armstrong tired, he went slack with sleep against his mother. Louise combed her fingers through the youngster's fine hair and picked out a small twig that had attached at some point in the day. Leo stopped playing. Louise looked up.

"Now, just for you," Leo said.

The invisible tether of love and friendship vibrated between them. The love song he played rippled in waves one direction, then the other. When the serenade was over, a peace deposited itself.

Louise's heart was full, though the ache of missing Leo was already beginning to make itself known.

CHAPTER TWENTY-NINE

For Louise and Leo, a shared contentment was found in walking across the yard to begin the morning milking. When done, they returned to the house for breakfast and to find the children awake. Leo held Geraldine while he ate, and Armstrong sat as close as he could to his Dad. A little after eight, a truck revved and jostled into the yard.

"The CCC is here," Leo said.

Louise wiped her hands on her apron. "Do you have everything?"

"Yes."

Louise followed Leo outside to the waiting truck. "I put a loaf of bread, a jar of beets, and canned chicken in your suitcase in case there isn't enough food at the camp."

"There'll be plenty," Leo said, then laid one hand

on Armstrong's shoulder and ruffled the boy's hair with the other. "Son, see you down the road. Do what your Mom tells you."

"I will."

Then Leo stepped so close to Louise. They inhaled each other's exhales. "Take care," he whispered. A hard kiss punctuated his sentence. The quick goodbye finished, Leo carrying his old Musicale suitcase, climbed into the truck. Hand waves escorted the dust cloud, truck, and Leo out onto the county road. The remaining Zints moved when there was nothing left to see.

Louise eyed her son's bare foot as he toed the dirt. "He'll be back before we know it. You'll see. Go collect the chicken eggs."

"Yes, Mama."

Louise filled the day with chores. It was after an early children's bedtime that she sat in the kitchen playing solitaire. Her body was exhausted, and her mind was not.

She wondered if Leo had met the rest of the crew? Maybe he'll know someone? What were the barracks like? Louise pondered how Leo would write to them and tell them about his new job, and in part, his new life. There was no telephone service out here. The thought depressed Louise, and she turned the direction of her thinking to her garden.

The plants were surviving in the heat. Louise had been able to harvest a few vegetables for the ta-

ble. Thank goodness, soon there would be more vegetables ready to begin canning and preserving for the
upcoming winter. Please, let it not be as hot as last
summer. Let the vegetable and grain crops have a
fighting chance to come to fruition. Louise sent out a
hope that her family and Bonetrail would hang on in
the upcoming months. Armstrong needs new shoes.
With the CCC checks, there'll be money for them.
Should she leave Geraldine with Armstrong for the
morning milking and bring the children into the barn
for the evening milking?

A sound outside interrupted her ruminating.
Louise held a playing card in mid-air and listened
again. Her hearing intensified; she went to the screen
door and looked out into the night. She had to wait
minutes before her eyes adjusted to the darkness.
Then Louise saw the movements. A small herd of
deer bounded across the east fields. Only deer. She
scanned the yard again, making sure all was in its
place. Moos from the dairy cows were caught on the
wind and flew to her. They sounded like low-pitched
kazoos with either a hint of dismay or question.

Louise closed and locked the front door. She
pulled the knob back to reaffirm it was bolted. Then
she unlocked it.

"Hardy, come."

The dog didn't come. Dang dog.

"Hardy, come!"

A dark four-legged shadow ambled towards the

house.

"Inside," Louise ordered.

The dog trotted in, walked to the stove, and lay down. Louise repeated the steps of securing the door. "Goodnight, Hardy," Louise said and went to bed.

The first few nights, Louise slept uneasily in the vulnerability and closed windows hothouse stuffiness of their new sleeping situation. She decided to keep the shotgun on the floor next to the bed with strict instructions to Armstrong to never touch it. At bedtime, Hardy began turning up to lay in front of the screen door. It was as if the dog knew the household needed his sentry guarding.

Louise, the children, and the farm established a new routine without Leo. All the work took longer and was harder. In addition, she had to keep an eye on the children, so they did not injure themselves by accident or by mad scheme. All the demands made Louise dizzy with fatigue, and she relished it. It helped keep worry, fear, and loneliness tucked inside her apron pocket. The tiredness meant early bedtimes and no need to fill her nights. She and the children would listen to the radio for a bit each evening. The music made her pine for Leo.

Mr. Wheeler and a few hired men helped Louise care for the farmstead. Heinrich drove Myra out to the farm several times to watch the children while Louise was in the fields.

At the end of June, Myra delivered a letter from

Leo. Shock and excitement made Louise's hand shake as she took the envelope. She placed the letter in a kitchen cabinet and would read it when Myra left for home, and the workday was complete.

Throughout the day, Louise thirsted for the contents of Leo's letter. The hours moved slowly. She straddled frustration and annoyance by the time she returned to the farmhouse. After a rushed goodbye to Myra, Louise served Armstrong buttered bread and applesauce and began to give Geraldine spoonfuls of the mashed fruit while silently reading Leo's letter.

Dear Louise, Armstrong, and Geraldine,

I hope you are well on the farm. I'm helping build a road near the Canadian border. The days are long and look the same. How are the crops and cattle? How's the garden growing? Has there been good weather? Any rain come?

The other men on the crew are mostly from North Dakota. Several men are from Eastern Montana. I stood next to a John Ziegler in the lineup on the first day. We've become friends. He's the one writing this letter.

Our crew will be working on a dam project in the center of the state. We'll be camping in tents for several weeks. Because of work, you won't hear from me for a while.

Armstrong, keep helping your Mom like the good boy you are. Louise, give Geraldine a squeeze. I miss you all and will be home when I can.

Love, Leo

P.S. How's Hardy?

Louise didn't know whether to smile or cheer first. Leo's working for the CCC was going fine. And even if it wasn't, Louise doubted Leo would tell her, much less include it in a letter. Work was work, and there was nothing to be done, but do it.

"Is the letter from Minnesota?" Armstrong asked.

"No. It's from your Dad. I'll read it to you."

The farm's demands and workload began to overwhelm Louise. She was trying to keep herself, the children, and the herd alive. The fields were left in Mother Nature's hands. Louise hoped that the 'other mother' would eventually take pity on Louise's family and the rest of the farmers and bring rain for the 1937 crops.

The prairie looked sore and fragile. The acres of grasses that had been plowed under to create grain fields now couldn't hold the minimal moisture to protect the land. The topsoil was thin or missing, and what remained baked and burned and loosened enough to be picked up by the winds. The drought continued to punish them all.

The prairie wildlife habitat was also eroding. It was becoming rare for Louise to see glimpses and evidence of deer, pheasant, or other manner of prairie roamers. She suspected the animals were moving to whatever plentiful feeding grounds they could find.

On July 3rd, Louise realized they had run out of

clean clothes. They would be going into town to-morrow for Bonetrail's 4th of July picnic and would need to be dressed up for the holiday. With the uptick in her workload, certain chores had become less attended to, and others had dropped off the list. She couldn't put off the laundry any longer. She pumped water and readied the basins to scrub and pummel the clothes, and set up the wringer to twist the water out. She saved the dirty laundry water to give to her garden.

Armstrong was barefoot, playing in the dirt with sticks and rocks, while Geraldine crawled after her big brother. Hardy was nearby, watching the children.

Louise looked into the sky and judged if she dared put the clothes on the line or needed to hang dry the clothing in the house. The sudden dust storms covered and seeped into the house and their noses, but at least the laundry would take less of a beating if dried inside. Putting the clothes on the line outside might be asking for trouble. If a dust storm whipped up, all her work would be for nothing.

The day was hot as all the summer days had become, and the clothes would double-quick dry. They'd smell like good sunshine and happier summer days.

Louise decided to chance it and, after wiping down the line, hung up the trousers she had started to wear daily. She also added underclothing, Armstrong's other set of overalls, the flour sack dresses and diapers for Geraldine, and Louise's day dresses. She wore the dresses into town for the sake of propriety.

The day moved on. Louise forgot about the clothing on the clothesline until around nine in the evening. The children were in bed, and the animals were taken care of for the day.

Louise tramped outside with her basket. She yanked up wooden clothespins and dropped the dried clothing and pins into the basket. When the lines were clear, Louise stretched her back. It was then she saw the horizon. It was bright pink, gold, orange, and lemon-yellow melding layer into layer. She gulped at the splendor and richness of beauty. It was so grand that the desperate landscape disappeared for a short time.

Her vision would not stop feasting on the sunset she hadn't witnessed for weeks. Louise realized she had forgotten such views existed. That wearied her, but she was seeing it now.

When the inky dusk extinguished the sunset, Louise took the full basket into the house.

On July 6, the day began hot and continued burning through the morning into mid-afternoon. Louise questioned if she shouldn't take the children into the root cellar to escape the high heat. She went down into the darkened room to investigate the possibility. Even in that hole in the ground, it was warm, and bugs and ground creatures had sought refuge already. Louise was exhausted, hot, and angry. The anger made her swelter more. In absolute frustration, she raised her fists to the ceiling and roared her despair. Vanished was the sense of escape and peace that this room had provided. It became a private cell to unleash her anger, fear, and heartache. When her voice was hoarse, and her feelings went below a simmer, she returned to above ground. The record temperature for that day was 121 degrees Fahrenheit.

As the summer moved along, the heat continued to grow faster than any of the crops. Between watering the cows and her gardens, Louise's optimism for a better summer was drying out, along with every living thing in the county. Two gentle, sunny triumphs were Armstrong's learning to read and Geraldine's new spoken words.

They received two more letters from Leo that were examples of brevity and matched the first letter. The CCC crew finished a small dam, moved onto a road project, and were slated to start building cabins and shelter in a new state park.

Louise wanted to tell Leo about her days on the farm. She imagined the letters she'd write.

Dear Leo,

We're doing okay. There is much to do. I'm trying to water livestock and plants without running the well dry. It's hotter than last year. I've gotten good at getting the gasoline pump motor started for the cows' water tank. Those animals can't wait to get to the tank

*in the evening after coming out of the pasture all day.
Their tails are whipping nonstop at the flies and heat.*

*We've received the CCC money. I've paid the
extra help, several of our outstanding bills, and saved a
few dollars. The pastures don't have much grass in
them. More thistle and stubble than anything else.
Should I buy extra feed if it's available? We're still in
this Dmust Bowl, and the drought's not letting up.* ·

*The children and I miss you. Come home as soon
as you can. Write to me.*

Love, Louise

With the hired help, Louise followed Leo's
feeding suggestions, but by August, she had rationed
the feed to keep the cows just above starvation. Between the lack of food, the heat, and the increased
dust storms, they were all hungry and parched. The
checks from the creamery had dwindled again.

All summer, Louise's garden limped. Now the
scorched plants stood on fragile stems and leaves
curled into themselves. The vegetables sometimes
baked in the sun before they could reach maturity.
The plants were a spectrum of speckled, striped, dot-
ted, and marred orange, yellow, and brown colors
with very little healthy plant green. The wheat and
hay fields were more dirt clumps than crops. The
heat and wind from the previous years were the fore-
runner to this season of continued blowing and eroding. The dust dervishes kicked up sudden and fierce.
Louise started to keep the children inside or close to

the house or the barn to escape the biting dust storms. The prairie wind threw the dirt into the air with a velocity that pinged skin and labored breathing.

Last summer and again this year, Louise kept the house closed up when she could, but more than once, she had left the windows open to release the summer heat, and a dust storm blew through and covered everything.

A closed-up house didn't stop the dust from finding the cracks, holes, and gaps. She and Armstrong took turns sweeping, dusting, and shaking out. She rubbed Vaseline into the children's and her noses to help keep out the dust and covered their faces when storms occurred.

Armstrong had developed the habit of every few days asking when Leo would return. In the beginning, Louise would say, "When the job's done." After several weeks, she began responding, "Maybe at the end of summer." By mid-August, she said, "I don't know."

On a morning a few days before the start of wheat threshing of what had survived the summer, Louise came in from the morning milking and heard a rattling cough come from Armstrong. Louise felt the boy's forehead. It was hot. She woke up her son. "Armstrong, do you feel sick?"

"No. I'm tired. Can I sleep some more?" Armstrong mumbled.

"Yes. Do you want some water?" Louise asked.

"No."

"Let me get you some water. You need water."

Louise ran to the kitchen and, with trembling hands, poured water into a glass and wetted a morning glory decorated blue kitchen towel. She spilled half the glass's contents in her rush back to the bedroom. After Leo went off to work for the CCC, she and the children had begun to sleep in the same bed. "Here, take a few sips."

"My throat hurts."

"The water will help. A few more sips." The little boy did and then laid back. "Go back to sleep. Call if you need me."

Armstrong's eyes closed before she finished speaking. Louise laid the wet towel on his forehead and examined and listened to his shallow, raspy breaths. The fear that hollowed out her gut moved to her throat. She had to swallow back the vomit. Louise walked to the other side of the bed and laid her ear onto Geraldine's chest, and she listened to her little girl's body. These breaths were natural and deep. Relief made her dizzy. Louise pressed the tip of her nose into her daughter's small belly. She inhaled deep wanting, to suck the reassurance of Geraldine's health into herself.

Louise moved a sleeping Geraldine to the parlor and then she walked to the screen door. Either hand gripped her upper arms and hugged tightly as Louise stared out at the prairie. Did Armstrong have the dust sickness? He needed a doctor. In her mind, she pleaded, not my little boy. Please, no.

Louise hoped one of the neighbors would pass the farm on their way to or back from town. If she could intercept them, she could ask them to send for the doctor. If they didn't come down the road, then she would take the children into town.

It was past one o'clock when she heard a vehicle. She ran out of the farmyard into the road. The Hochhalters' car had already passed the Zints' farm entrance. She kept running. There was a dust cloud between her and the driver's rearview.

They couldn't see her. Louise untied her apron. With one arm waved it in the air and pumped the other arm to keep running. The neighbors weren't going to stop. A sob rushed out of Louise's mouth. She started to heave, and then her sprint slowed to a plod. The vehicle kept going. Louise bent at the waist with her lungs heaving, rested her hands on her thighs, and tried to catch her breath.

Through her gasps and wheezes, she heard gears shift and the car backed up towards her until they were side by side.

"Louise, you need help?" Sam Hochhalter asked.

"Yes. Armstrong needs a doctor. Can you bring him out?"

"Yes. I'll go now."

"Thanks," Louis said and began to stumble home.

CHAPTER THIRTY

The doctor confirmed. "It's dust pneumonia. He'll have a fever, so keep him cool and get him a dust mask. The cough will get worse. Mrs. Zint, are you listening?"

Louise looked up from her sweating son. "I'm listening."

"You know the outlook isn't good. You're going to need to keep Armstrong in bed and away from the dust. Try to keep him as cool as possible. Water and broth to drink and eat."

"How do I reduce the heat and dust storms?" Louise razored the question at the doctor.

The doctor lifted his shoulders and dropped them. "If he gets worse, please reach me in town, and I'll come back out."

"What do I owe you?"

Louise used her egg money to pay the doctor's bill.

She left Armstrong in bed and brought Geraldine into the barn for the evening milking. The demand and necessity of the chores kept her worry about Armstrong shadowed.

It was after eight o'clock when she remembered her gardens. The plants wobbled, tipped, and some had collapsed. Neither garden had been watered all day. Sunburned leaves were stripped brown and tan and curled into themselves or hung limp. The thirsty ground had cracked and split like damaged porcelain. They all needed water and help. Armstrong needed help. Would her little boy survive?

Louise walked to the well and pumped the cloth covered handle up and down until water filled the watering cans and buckets. The well water hadn't been a refreshing cold for a long while. What came out of the ground was tepid. At least the well hadn't gone dry. With a heave and a grunt, she lifted the load and pushed the wheelbarrow of watering containers over to the first garden.

The carrot tops had turned corn kernel yellow. The beet tops had wilted and hung limp. The rest of the garden teetered between the state of living and half-dead. Louise watered the first row and was making her way down the second row. Each step led her to devastated vegetation. If these plants didn't make it, what would they eat this winter?

Louise walked along the rows of sun-burnt cucumbers. Then she turned in a slow circle and viewed the trajectory of the sun's appetite. Her mind saw all the dying. The extent of the losses bowed her legs. Her knees crashed into the dirt. The acceleration of the descent threw her torso forward. She caught herself by planting her hands on the ground. Like an animal, she postured on all four limbs. The fear and rage in her body came spitting and snarling out in howls and sobs.

Wails became crying. Tributaries of tears rolled down her dusty face. The cloudburst of emotion made her tremble. She lowered herself until all of her body was flat on the ground. The earth held her, and she rested.

Louise knew an hour or more had gone by because the sun had almost set. She turned over onto her back and looked up at the dark blue clouds. A wind gusted across the prairie. The cloud cover moved across the sky, caught in a jet stream, and revealed stars. Its outer tendrils creating wind that brushed the garden making the leaves rattle like dry beans in a can. The noisy sound felt alive, and she did not feel alone.

Louise felt the despair, anger, grief, and pain leach out of her body and into the soil. The grit stuck to her skin and in between her teeth sank and fused into her bones. A new space inside Louise waited for her to decide how to fill it. She stood up, and with both her feet planted on that land, she decided to keep going.

It was dark. Louise used a lantern to finish watering her gardens. She shuffled across the yard back to the house. Hardy had already laid in front of the screen door for the evening. He didn't move. Louise was too tired to reprimand. She patted his head and caressed his ears. Stroking Hardy's pelt assuaged any irritation at the canine.

"Good dog," Louise said.

The dog stretched and lumbered to one side so Louise could enter her home. In the bedroom, fully-clothed she lay on the other side of her son. She listened for the sounds of her children's breathing. One well and one ill.

Early the next day Louise milked the cows then fed the children a thin vegetable soup all the while wondering how to help her son get better. On an impulse she decided that they we're going into town to Myra's. When it was time to leave, Louise carried her son to the wagon.

"Armstrong, we're going into town. I've made a bed for you in the back of the wagon."

"I'm hot," Armstrong whimpered.

"I know. Here, drink some water."

"I'm not thirsty."

Louise gently pressed a water jug at Armstrong's lips. "Please, a few swallows."

"Okay," Armstrong wheezed.

Louise swiped loose hair out of her eye. "If a dust storm comes, I'll cover you and Geraldine with the blanket. Please stay under it. I'll uncover you when the storm is over. I have my hat and bandanna to cover my face."

Louise set Geraldine next to Armstrong in the wagon bed. She told Geraldine, "We're going to Myra's."

The little girl's big smile made Louise want to pull Geraldine close and not let go.

Once on the wagon seat, Louise snapped the leather reins to move the horses. When they arrived at Myra's, the doors and windows were closed. Louise left a sleeping Geraldine in the wagon and carried Armstrong to the house. At the backdoor, Louise knocked. There was no answer. Shifting Armstrong in her arms, she knocked again.

"Are you looking for Myra?" a stern voice asked from behind.

Louise whipped around. "Oh hello, Mother Shields. Yes, I was looking for Myra."

"She and Heinrich went to help Sadie."

"I see. Thank you for telling me."

"Your Armstrong is not looking well. When was the last time you all bathed?" Mother Shields asked.

"He's sick," Louise said and as if on cue the boy

coughed. Everyone in the county knew what that cough meant.

"He has the dust pneumonia," Mother Shields said.

"Yes, he does." Louise cradled his head against her shoulder, and the child drooped lower.

"Armstrong should be at home in bed. Make sure he drinks clean water. He eats not just soup, mind you, but bone broth. Don't you have a fresh chicken you can butcher? Keep him cool too. With the fever, he needs fresh clothes. Make sure every crack in your house has a cloth or paper stuffed in it to keep out the dust."

The barrage of orders dropped on Louise's shoulders. She sank onto the top step.

"What are you doing? Stand up for goodness sakes," Mother Shields said.

"I can't."

"Of course you can."

"It's too much," Louise said.

"What are you talking about?"

"How am I supposed to keep my son alive and take care of Geraldine, the cows, the threshing, and all the other chores? I can't."

"Stand up now!" Mother Shields said.

"No."

Mother Shields moved directly in front of Louise. "We may not like each other, but I know you're made of stronger fortitude than this."

Louise leaned back. "It's gone."

Mother Shields pointed her finger. "No, it's not. Now get up, you have work to do."

"That I do, but I'm just going to sit here," Louise said.

"Stop talking nonsense."

A hysterical laugh belched from Louise. "It's your special day. I'm almost on my knees in front of you. Not quite, but close enough."

Neither woman spoke. Then Mother Shields cleared her throat and squared her shoulders. "I'm going to help you."

Louise thought she had misheard her former landlady. "You're going to help me?" Louise asked.

"You will leave the children in town with me. I will care for them until you can. The dust storms aren't as bad here. My house is well-built unlike yours," Mother Shields said.

"You believe I will leave my children in your care? Armstrong is sick."

Mother Shields narrowed her eyes at Louise. "I've cared for them before. I've raised my children. I can tend to yours."

"I will not leave my children overnight to be cared for by your cold, mean person," Louise said.

"I do not dislike your children."

Louise stood up. "It's just me you dislike and are rude to?"

"No. You're still new to this town. You two were

tramps before you came to Bonetrail. No regular church attendance. It takes time to get to know someone."

Louise tightened her hold on Armstrong. "We were not tramps, nor, am I some jezebel. Leo and I were in a traveling band."

"Exactly," Mother Shields said.

"No, it's different. How many years do we have to live in Bonetrail for you to trust us?' Louise asked.

"Are you going to continue arguing with me? Do you take my help or not?"

Louise's anger wanted to strike the woman, but somewhere inside a practical acceptance overrode the desire. "Do you promise on your God and church to treat my children well and care for them properly?"

The matron's chest lifted. "I am offended by your assertion that I would harm your children."

Louise's finger pointed at Mother Shields' heart. "Do you promise?"

Mother Shields nodded. "I promise."

"If Armstrong gets worse you'll send someone out to the farm immediately? I get to see my children whenever I want."

"Agreed."

"We shake on it," Louise said.

"Pardon me?"

Louise repeated, "We shake on it. It locks the deal, or in this case, the promise."

"Fine."

Two strong arms rose, and their hands clasped together in a shake.

"If I find out that you have harmed or even been mean to my children, I will plow you under one of my fields," Louise said.

A harrumph emitted from Mother Shields. Then she went to the wagon bed, gathered Geraldine, and walked back to her house. "Leave the children with me tonight and bring their things tomorrow," Mother Shields said over her shoulder.

A little shaky, Louise carried Armstrong into the house she had been glad to shake loose years before.

The women worked together to settle the children. Armstrong was placed in the bedroom next door to Mother Shields' bedroom, the same room Louise had protested on her first day of meeting the landlady. A makeshift bed for Geraldine was made up in the woman's bedroom.

Louise adjusted the sheet that covered Armstrong one last time. "You're all tucked in. I'm going home now, but I'll be back tomorrow with your and Geraldine's things. Mother Shields is going to take care of you until harvest is over. If she's not nice to you, you tell me."

"Do you have to go?" Armstrong asked in a raspy voice.

"Yes, but I'll be back. I'll miss you and your sister."

"I'll miss you too."

"Close your eyes and rest," Louise said.

Armstrong shut his eyes. Louise kissed his clammy forehead. She used her index finger to trace her son's face and attempted to memorize each curve, color, and all the sweetness it held.

Louise went downstairs and found Mother Shields sitting at the kitchen table drinking coffee. Geraldine sat in her lap.

"Geraldine, I need to return to the farm. You'll stay with Mother Shields for a few days. I'll be back tomorrow to see you."

Geraldine smiled at her mother. Louise knew the little girl didn't understand the circumstances, but she wanted her daughter to not feel abandoned. Leo had left to work for the CCC, and now mother and daughter had to separate while Louise oversaw the farm and Armstrong convalesced. The burden of their circumstance pressed down on Louise and her shoulders bowed in. Then she kissed her daughter's forehead where the skin was dry and fresh.

Louise tightened her focus on Mother Shields. "I'm leaving now. Take care of my children."

"I will."

Louise didn't want to leave. "I'll return tomorrow."

"I should hope so," Mother Shields said.

Before Louise crossed the front door's threshold, she turned back. "Thank you."

Mother Shields nodded.

Louise passed well beyond Bonetrail's border before she opened the valve on her heart and began to sob. There was no drought there.

CHAPTER THIRTY-ONE

Louise didn't remember much about the scenery she passed on the ride home. The horse team knew the way and Louise left them to it. After arriving in the farmyard, she unhitched the horses and fed and watered the livestock and gardens. The cranky cows mooed their dismay at the late milking. A numbness stayed in Louise through all the chores. Hardy followed her around. When she opened the house door, she waited for him to amble inside. He didn't, and instead sat and regarded her.

"Stay outside if you want," Louise said.

In the kitchen, she took off her clothes and let them drop to the floor. Naked, she used the morning water left in the tea kettle to try and remove her day.

Before she went to the bedroom, she walked across the room to the parlor shelf that held Leo's violin. Louise reached up and then set the case on the floor. She knelt down. The release snap of the latch sounded loud and crisp. Louise stroked the strings, releasing notes whose resonance floated through the house and vibrated within her. She plucked, thumped, and strummed fast and loud, trying to shove the emptiness out of the house.

During the Musicale days, Erik had once asked Leo, "When are you going to teach Louise how to play the violin?"

"Whenever she wants," Leo said.

"You'll teach me how to play?" Louise asked.

"Sure. I can also teach you the accordion and some guitar. Erik could teach you some on the horns, but we already have enough hot air around here."

"Have your husband teach you how to play so maybe we can have some real music come out of that violin he likes to carry around."

When the laughter ended, Leo looked at Louise and asked, "Do you really want to learn?"

"It would be nice. My mother had us girls take piano lessons, but our piano teacher was in town. Mother decided it was too far to travel back and forth, so that was over quick enough."

"Well then, we can start you on the violin," Leo said.

Erik snorted. "Finally, seeing to his husbandly duties."

Tonight, Louise wished Leo had taught her to

play. She could use the music to take her somewhere far from her agony, Armstrong's illness, the drought, Leo's absence, and missing her children. Fatigue slowed the violin sounds. When kneeling on the floor planks pained Louise's knees and goosebumps pebbled her skin, she stopped and went to bed.

In the remaining weeks of harvest, Louise worked alongside the other area farmers. What little wheat had come from her fields didn't cover the seed, threshing costs, or the land rent but the CCC checks helped pay their bills and keep the roof over their heads.

She moved at a pace that allowed Louise to immerse herself until she was too busy to feel and her exhaustion at bedtime meant immediate sleep. Because of the heat of the days, she worked early in the mornings and late into the evenings to counter the sun. Her energy was not so much vigor and health, but a relentless determination and grit that overrode weariness and even sense. Every few days she went into town to visit her children. Armstrong was weak. Geraldine was blooming. Both were very much alive. Because of his illness, Armstrong would begin his school year in late September.

A short letter arrived two weeks after the children started their town stay with Mother Shields.

Dear Louise,

We've been out in the field most of August, and

that will continue into September. The CCC job ends sometime in November.

Tell Armstrong and Geraldine hello and that I'm saving up songs and stories for them. I miss you all. I hope everything is going better on the farm.

Love, Leo.

Louise folded the letter and put it back in the envelope. She had wanted more from Leo's message. She knew he would have had to ask John to write the letter for him so practicality would have overridden endearments and worries.

Putting aside the disappointment, Louise reminded herself that tomorrow was her town day and she would see the children.

She pulled up to Mother Shields' and saw Myra pulling spent plants from her vegetable garden.

"Hi, Myra."

"Louise! How are you? How's everything at the farm coming along?"

"Good enough. There wasn't much in the fields. The other farmers were a little put off that I helped with the threshing. But, now that work is done for the year. How's Sadie doing?"

"We're all getting by. Heinrich and the boys are doing what they can at Sadie's."

"I'm glad to hear. Maybe a little something good can come out of all this," Louise said.

"I hope. I miss my cheerful, happy daughter. All that's happened has changed Sadie. Made her harder.

I guess this Depression has made most all of us harder."

Louise nodded. "There's no escaping this decade. It's touched us all. Some worse than others. How are things coming along next door?"

Myra shrugged her shoulders. "From what I can tell, good. That woman may not like the rest of us, but your children are the exception. Armstrong's looking healthier. He doesn't have his pep back yet. In time, he'll be his usual self. Geraldine is growing like a weed."

Louise laughed. "Mother Shields and I have made a strange truce. The weeds did better than any-thing else in my garden this year. The children keep growing, thankfully."

Myra stepped back. "I'd better not keep you. The children are waiting. That chicken and those vegeta-bles you carrying must be getting heavy."

"I'd better get inside Mother Shields'. Take care."

"You too."

"Myra, say hi to Sadie from me the next time you see her."

"That I can do. She might like that."

Louise knocked on Mother Shields's front door and heard, "Coming."

The door opened. The other woman looked over Louise, "I was wondering when you'd finally arrive."

"I just finished my errands."

"Mama," Armstrong called out and the little body half stepped, half lurched to Louise.

Louise knelt to her son and hugged him. "Hello you. How are you?"

"I'm better."

A gentle reprimand followed, "Armstrong, you're still recovering. Why don't you take your mother to the table and I'll get the coffee? Geraldine is there too."

"Mama, come look. I've been practicing school words on my slate." Louise picked up Armstrong and kissed his thin cheeks and pale forehead as they crossed to the table.

Louise reached over to Geraldine and caressed her plump cheeks. "Hello, baby girl."

The little girl smiled, kicked, and chirped, "Mama."

"Armstrong, show me your words," Louise said.

Together they ate an early supper. During dessert, the sweetness included a pinch of sour. Soon it would be time for Louise to return home, alone. The reunions always left her more than a little heartsick.

Louise looked at Mother Shields. "Thank you for supper. As soon as I help wash the dishes, I'll be leaving for home."

"Do you have to go? You can sleep in my bedroom," Armstrong said.

"I need to take care of the farm, but I'll be back. Hardy's waiting for me."

"You promise?"

"I promise."

After kissing the children goodbye, Louise left the house and didn't look back. If she looked back, Louise didn't know if she'd be able to leave.

"Louise!" Mother Shields called from the front steps.

Louise turned around.

"You seem unwell. Are you eating enough?" Mother Shields asked.

"I am."

"You look awful. It doesn't do those children any good if their mother gets sick."

"I'm doing what I need to do," Louise said.

"That's not enough. You need to eat and sleep too. Do what I've said and don't be so stubborn," Mother Shields said.

On the ride home, Louise shouted to the wrung-out beige, ochre, and tan fields and patchy pastures.

"I can't stand Mother Shields. Why is she helping us? Why can't she be nicer? Why, why, why?"

Thoughts whirled in Louise's brain. *Mother Shields tells everyone what she thinks and expects us all to toe her line. She could be kinder. People would like her more. She speaks what she wants.* Louise sucked in deep, understanding the inherent freedom and empowerment that not caring what the towns-people thought of her gave the older woman. Louise still thought of Mother Shields as a harpy, but she needed the other woman's help. In Mother Shields' care Armstrong was recovering and both children looked and sounded well.

Still perturbed by her prairie epiphany and the matron's observation of Louise's self-care, she threw herself into canning the small crop of Will's Pioneer corn from her garden. The hot house had begun to cool a titch, but several hours in steam and heat made her drip with perspiration.

At the washbasin Louise wiped herself down. The reflection in the mirror showed a woman who looked similar to her, but this other woman was weary and colored gray. Hair pulled back so tight that it seemed to strain her facial muscles and framed the bones that pushed up through the skin.

Dang it, Mother Shields was right. Louise looked bad. She needed to start taking better care of herself. Louise felt that last thought hum and buzz in her head.

The children returned home at the end of September. It was Louise again taking care of the children and the farm on her own.

She noticed that Hardy wandered off in the afternoons. Louise figured Hardy was hunting the land as he had when he first arrived at the farm. She never worried about the mutt. Hardy always came home.

One fall evening, Hardy didn't turn up.

"Mama, I can't find Hardy," Armstrong said.

"Did you check the barn?"

"Uh huh."

"Did you check all the shade spots?"

"Yup."

"Hardy's off hunting something good. He'll be back when he's done," Louise said.

"I have to say goodnight to him before I go to sleep."

"You can stay up another half an hour. If Hardy's not back by then, it's bedtime for you."

"Why can't I stay up until he comes home?" Armstrong asked.

"Because you and I need to get to bed. You can talk to Hardy in the morning."

The morning came. Hardy wasn't home. Armstrong was beside himself about the dog's absence. He kept checking in and around the farm and in the fields. Louise found the lack of Hardy's appearance odd. The dog may be lazy, but he was dependable, especially for his mealtimes.

The next day in early evening, Armstrong said, "Mama, Hardy still hasn't come home. Can we hitch up the wagon and go look for him?"

"I don't have time. Evening milking is going to start soon."

"Can we milk now and go looking? I'll milk even faster," the little boy pleaded. Armstrong had started helping Louise where he could around the farm, and that included milking.

"Let's milk now. Afterwards, we'll go looking for Hardy," Louise said.

"Okay," Armstrong yelled as he slow-skipped to the barn. His full vigor still hadn't returned.

Later, Louise and the children walked out of the yard and headed west. According to Armstrong, Hardy liked that direction the best. While they strolled, Louise examined the stubble and dirt of the emptied fields and ditches. There was little green in sight. A breeze was pushing warm air over everything like a constant, turning fan.

They didn't see any signs of Hardy, and a small kernel of Louise's worry was growing faster than any vegetable or field she had ever planted. That night, Armstrong was worried about Hardy and wanted to stay up again to wait. Louise said no and Armstrong sulked to bed.

At sunset, Louise checked that the children were asleep and then picked up a lantern and walked outside. She had decided that she would walk in the pastures northwest of the farmstead. Louise wouldn't go too far. She'd scan for markings or anything to indicate Hardy's whereabouts.

Short of an hour she had no luck and started for home. The receding light made the land shadows bigger. Louise hiked fifty yards when she saw a smaller animal lying flat on the ground. She knew. Louise ordered herself to go over there. *No, no, no,* kept repeating in her mind.

Louise did what she had to. She moved the lantern beams over the body. Hardy wasn't napping. He was dead. On the left leg, there was a wound. She suspected a rattlesnake had bitten him. The dog was beginning to decompose, and small animals and buzzards had eaten off the corpse. She was surprised that a coyote hadn't scavenged and dragged Hardy off.

"Oh, Hardy," Louise said.

Louise and the lantern dropped down beside the dog. It was almost full dark; Louise needed to get home. She didn't want to leave Hardy behind. How would she get him back to the farm? She'd have to carry him.

The smell of decaying animal made Louise's eyes water alongside her escaping tears. She pushed Hardy's eyelids over the vacant holes. Then, she slid her hands underneath Hardy's belly and across prickly prairie and small rocks. As she lifted Hardy, some of his exposed guts dropped and dangled free. Louise sucked back the vomit before it was expelled and stumbled a step. She looped three fingers around the lantern's handle and began carrying Hardy home.

It was a slow, bumbling walk home trying to navigate ruts, small mounds of dry grass and dirt, and the weight of Hardy and her sadness. In the barn, Louise found a burlap sack and placed Hardy inside. She tied the sack closed with string and then put him in an empty wood barrel to contain the smell.

Louise fell asleep that night contemplating how she would tell Armstrong that Hardy was dead.

The next morning arrived as it always does. Louise couldn't and wouldn't tell Armstrong until after breakfast. She moved Geraldine to the parlor floor, and then Louise said, "Armstrong, let's go outside for a bit."

"Can we look for Hardy?"

In the yard, she studied her son, who scanned the landscape searching for his dog.

Louise picked up Armstrong, and he squirmed in her arms.

"Mama, why are you holding me? I'm not sick anymore. I'm a big boy."

"You're growing up." Louise rested her forehead onto Armstrong's forehead. "I found Hardy in a pasture."

"You did. Where is he?" an excited Armstrong said.

"I put him in the barn."

The strangeness of Louise's action and her seriousness had Armstrong asking, "Why'd you do that? Is Hardy hurt?"

"More than hurt. Hardy died."

Louise waited as her son crumbled, and then sobbed into her chest. When the little boy was all cried out, he let his head rest on her heart.

"I'm going to dig a hole behind the house and bury him," Louise said.

Armstrong hiccupped. "Can I help?"

"You can find the big rocks to put on top of his grave."

CHAPTER THIRTY-TWO

A week later, Louise still found herself looking around for Hardy, followed by swift reminders that he was dead and that hard summer over. As much as she disliked the dog initially, he had become a sort of companion to her and a friend to Armstrong and Leo.

In October, Louise could see and feel the land's fertility slow and retract into hibernation. The weather was neither hot nor cold but a comfortable temperature for trousers and sweaters. Louise continued to wear pants around the place and changed into a dress when she had to go into town.

One evening, Louise and the children sat in the farmyard listening to the radio. A breeze holding a soft nip flew through, above, and around the farm. Louise could smell winter was on its way. She admired the sunset as a trailing sheet of peach sky merged with bands of orange and gold while pink fluffy clouds floated across the top.

This year had been unlike any year Louise had known and would want to know. She knew how capable she was. Moving to Bonetrail had been the beginning of hardships and friendships she couldn't have imagined. Louise stood and walked to the middle of her farmyard as the wind carried the sounds of her children's voices. She did not know what the winter or even next year would bring, but Louise had gained and created strength, stamina, and wisdom that would be her life allies.

In November, Louise and the children continued to wait and plan for Leo's homecoming. In the last week of November, she and Armstrong saw the CCC vehicle roll across the hardened scoria road and return Leo to the farm. The truck pulled into the yard with Leo waving to them. Louise and Armstrong dashed to the vehicle before it had come to a full stop. Leo disembarked with his luggage, saluted his CCC co-workers goodbye, and then hugged Louise.

"Hello, sweetheart," Leo said.

"I missed you," Louise replied.

Armstrong grabbed a hold of Leo's leg. "Dad! You're home!"

"I am," Leo said and picked up the little boy and spun him high in the air. When the two stopped spinning, he said to his taller son, "You know where my violin is?"

"Yup, it's on the shelf."

"Can you reach it?" Leo asked.

"If I stand on a chair."

"Get it down, and careful standing on the chair. Put the case on the kitchen table. Your Mom and I will be in in a few minutes."

Armstrong's new shoes kicked and threw up dirt as he ran into the house.

Louise and Leo stepped into each other's arms, laid heads to shoulders, and came back together feeling the muscle and pulse of the other.

They stayed too long in this embrace because Armstrong asked, "When will you be done kissing?"

"I haven't seen your Mom in a long time."

Armstrong rolled his eyes. "Your violin is on the table."

"Thank you, but next I need to see Geraldine."

"Why? She's just a baby. She can stand and walk some."

"I'd like to see that," Leo said.

"Why? It's not like she can run like me."

"Someday she will."

"Did you know I was sick?" Armstrong asked.

Leo grabbed his son's shoulder and looked him over. "What do you mean you were sick?"

Louise touched Leo's arm. "Armstrong's alright. He had dust pneumonia at the end of the summer. He and Geraldine stayed in town with Mother

Shields while Armstrong recovered and I took care of the farm."

"I can't believe that woman helped us," Leo said.

"Sometimes I can't either. I don't know if she likes us, but maybe over the next twenty years, we might become friends?"

"Next twenty years?" Leo asked, and then his eyes searched Louise's eyes. "That's a long time to stay in Bonetrail."

Louise held his gaze. "It's home. I can't wait to hear you play tonight."

The family reunion went inside their house. Leo held his daughter for a time longer than the squirming Armstrong could handle. The violin concert would have to wait until after the evening milking and supper.

As all four Zints were readying to leave the house for the barn. Louise asked Armstrong to run ahead and get the milk cans and stools ready. Armstrong scampered across the yard and into the sun-bleached barn. Sitting down at the kitchen table, she waited for Leo to return from the bedroom. He reentered wearing not a suit or CCC uniform but his farm work clothes. Seeing Leo lifted Louise in an updraft of happiness and the coldness of what she was to do next deflated some of the rise.

Leo passed his hand across the buttons of his work shirt. "I'm ready."

"I sent Armstrong ahead." Louise hesitated.

"Something happened to Hardy while you were away."

"What happened?

"He wandered off one day like he often did. I waited a day or so thinking he'd return. He always came back." The last word hitched onto sadness. "I found him in a field. A rattlesnake bit him and he died. Armstrong and I buried him behind the house. I miss him."

Leo kept blinking his eyes and finally used the back of his hand to wipe his cheeks. "Thank you for bringing him home. You took care of the children and this farm. What's happened these last few years could have blown us apart. You've kept us together. You're a strong woman. I don't know what's going to happen next year, but we'll figure it out together."

"Yes, we will."

Leo strode to Louise and grasped her hands and pulled her up to him. They rested their intertwined hands on the warm expanse of his torso above his pumping heart. His eyes delved into her eyes and he said, "I'm so glad that farm girl fell in love with the young fiddle man."

"Me too."

Later that evening, settled around the kitchen table, Armstrong stood next to his father and rubber-necked as Leo opened the violin case. Louise stepped to her son. With a tender tug she moved Armstrong towards her. Leo had a private moment with his violin. He didn't take it out of the case immediately but instead reacquainted himself by sliding his hands over the carved wood and thin strings. When satisfied with the exploration, he lifted the violin out of its case.

"I tried to keep it free of dust, but sometimes dust just got in there," Louise said.

Leo looked up at Louise. "Thank you. It looks just right."

Leo turned the pegs and plucked the strings and the instrument thrummed, trilled, and announced its annoyance at being left behind while the musician was away. Next, he tightened the horse-hair bow.

The opening scales and chords skittered, leaked, and clunked around the house. Leo practiced until the audible scale was all accounted for. Then came a jaunty jig of a children's tune just for Armstrong and Geraldine. The bow landed and bounced in short pulls and pushes, and fingertips danced and pressed the strings. Geraldine bobbed her head in her version of musical time. Then the jigs were jostled out of place by old country songs and then superseded by American jazz and some new tunes.

After two hours Leo stopped and stretched his fingers. "Not used to playing that long anymore. I'll need to rebuild my calluses and fingers."

"Winter's coming; you'll have time to practice. I like the new music you learned while you were away," Louise said.

"The fellows and I found ourselves in a bar or two. I was there for the music and beer. No monkey business," Leo said.

"Good to hear. Armstrong, time for bed."

"No! More music, please! I can sleep this winter."

Leo and Louise laughed. She relished the sound and feel of it.

"There'll be more music tomorrow. It's time for bed."

"Dad, I'm glad you're home."

"Me too. Get to bed. There's work to do tomorrow. Let me see Geraldine a bit more before you put her to bed."

"Hold her while I help Armstrong get ready? Armstrong, tonight you and your sister are sleeping in the other bedroom," Louise said.

"Why not with you and Dad?"

"You slept by yourself the whole time you were at Mother Shields'."

"Did you know Mother Shields snores?" Armstrong said to his Dad. "I could hear her all the way in my room."

"I did not know that."

Armstrong hugged Leo. "Goodnight, Dad."

"Night, son."

When it was just Leo and Louise, Leo said, "One more just for you."

It was a love song that called to its sweetheart in

stretched notes that beckoned and then pitched high into a galloping longing that raced over heartache and slowed to the low pitch of reunited contentment.

"That was beautiful," Louise said.

"You're beautiful."

Leo played again the next night and many of the nights that came after. In 1937, the weather and farming were bad but not as terrible as in 1936. Because of the CCC regulations, Leo was too old to work for the Corps. In 1938, there was enough moisture to raise crops. Higher wheat prices and small, noticeable weather and economic improvements marked 1939 and 1940. The national and state Farm Bureaus introduced new techniques, programs, and robust seed, which helped combat erosion, dust, and drought and supported efforts to rebuild the land. The calamity of the dirty thirties and the Great Depression was still felt until 1942.

The Zint children grew, and another one came along to wear the clothes outgrown by her older siblings. Louise and Leo continued to farm their Bonetrail land and over time were able to buy it and call it theirs. Most evenings after supper, the violin was brought out and for the next hour or so, a fiddling man would charm a farm woman.

CHAPTER THIRTY-THREE

1999

It was almost time for Geraldine to pick up Louise. The morning coffee was long cold. Lunchtime had come and gone. Louise closed the album heavy with memories and returned it to the drawer. She brushed her teeth and put on a purple shirt that reminded her of the lilacs on the farm. Then she heard the knock at the door.

"Coming," Louise called out.

When she pulled back the door, Geraldine said, "Hi, ready to go?"

"Almost. Let me get my purse and sunglasses," Louise said.Geraldine hesitated at the front door. "Are you sure about this?"

Louise hooked her purse over her shoulder.

"Can't hurt to go back and take a look and consider things. No decision has been made yet about selling the land."

"True, but this is part of who you are," Geraldine said.

"It's time to take care of what Leo and I started. I won't be around forever."

Geraldine crossed the door's threshold. "What would Dad think about this?"

"That I'll know what to do."

"Will you miss it?"

Louise put on her sunglasses. "I haven't visited for a long time. Even for a look-see. You know, I didn't want to be there in the beginning. It started as Leo's dream, not mine. We were very young."

"I'll support whatever you decide about the land. Where's your walker? We should take it, just in case," Geraldine said.

"It won't roll easily on the dirt and grass. I can bring my cane, and I can lean on your arm."

"Mom!" Geraldine protested.

"Fine, then. It's in my bedroom."

From the bedroom, Geraldine brought out Louise's walker.

"I don't need it, but thank you anyway," Louise said.

The women left and drove to the Bonetrail farm. A paved highway branched onto the scoria rock farm road. The car kicked up a red-orange dust cloud that followed them all the way into the farmyard. The old house had been torn down and replaced many years ago. They stopped and parked in the middle of the yard. When the engine was turned off, they sat and looked at the house, outbuildings, corrals, and fields. The wind and songbirds sang to them.

Louise spoke first. "It's nice to see the lilacs are still here. We had to replant them in the sixties. It makes a pretty and nice-smelling shelterbelt."

"Do you miss your gardens and flowers?" Geraldine asked.

"Yes."

"I'm sorry for that."

"What's to be sorry for? I may not get to put my hands in the soil or pick fresh tomatoes, but I have those memories. Sometimes I touch the dirt in the flower pots at the assisted living center when no one's looking."

"Mother, they'll think you're crazy."

"If I'm ever caught, I'll tell them I was checking to see if the soil was dry. They won't know the difference. I'd like to hear the prairie better, let's get out."

"Let me get the walker," Geraldine said.

"Leave the walker. I'll be fine."

Geraldine helped Louise out of the front seat.

Louise took a deep intake of air. "Smell that wind."

"It smells fresh," Geraldine said.

Louise began walking. "Can you hear the wind-mill turning?"

"Where are you going?" Geraldine asked.

"I want to walk over to the west pasture."

Geraldine hooked her arm through Louise's. "The ground's uneven. Let me help you."

Together they shuffled toward a pasture of wheat stalks dancing and rattling in the wind.

Louise patted Geraldine's arm. "That's a nice, healthy crop. I can hold on to the t-post; you can let go."

"Be careful. That's barbed wire fencing," Geraldine said.

"I'm steady. Look at the land around you. It's so wide and big; it can hold the past, present, and future all at the same time. There's hopes and dreams, and even fear, sorrow, and hatred in that soil. It gave us a home, food to eat, and food to sell to make a living. It was here before us, and it will outlast us all."

"I wish Dad was here."

"Oh, he is. He's part of the land and our memories." Louise swayed a bit. She took hold of the fencing, placing her hand between the barb's sharp points. "Can you hear it?"

"Hear what? The wind?" Geraldine asked.

"No. Leo's violin."

Geraldine didn't reply.

"Close your eyes and listen," Louise said.

The women stood at the fence listening to the prairie winds blow and the meadowlarks whistle. Louise regarded the path of her life with deep satisfaction.

Minutes passed and then Geraldine said, "Do you want to look around some more?"

"No. I've seen and heard what I wanted to. I'm ready."

Arm in arm, the women returned to the car. Louise stumbled, and Geraldine yelped, "Are you okay?"

"Just a little hitch in my giddyup. I'll make it."

Seated in the vehicle, Geraldine started the engine and began to drive them to the highway.

Louise looked back and mouthed "thank you." A dust cloud trailed behind as summer sunshine and wind escorted them all the way home.

THE END

Thank you for joining Louise and Leo on and off the prairie!

If you enjoyed the novel, I would appreciate a short review where you purchased the book. Please share the book with a friend!

As a bonus, I created a *Leaving Ordinary* webpage that includes pictures, a soundtrack playlist, and more!

www.billijolink.com/ books/leaving-ordinary/bonus

Interested in updates and more extras?

Please sign up for my newsletter at www.
billijolink.com and find me on social media.

Mistakes happen. If you discovered an error in the
novel, please email me through my website:
www.billijolink.com

AUTHOR NOTES

One of my primary historical resources for this novel was my maternal grandmother Ruby Hoffman. She was born in 1930, and her perspective of the Dirty Thirties, as she calls those years, is through the lens of a little girl and the stories from her parents and community. Ruby told me about the commodity boxes. The time we have spent together harvesting her memories, stories, and thoughts of that period in American Midwest history has been a continuing gift.

I also used weather logs, *Dust Bowl Diary* by Ann Marie Low, and other publications such as the Oscar Will Seed catalog, which reserved a page in each annual edition to include a letter to their customers regarding the previous year's growing season, hope for the upcoming season, and poignant reflections of national and global political and cultural events.

I attempted to be as historically accurate as, and when, possible. I used the weather of both year and season as a guiding timeline. North Dakota farmers and farmers in other parts of the U.S. and other countries, including Canada, experienced ecological, agricultural, and economic upheaval during the Great Depression.

While writing *Leaving Ordinary*, I believed I made up the fictitious town of Bonetrail, North Dakota. After the draft manuscript was written, I learned that a real Bonetrail does exist in northwestern N.D. Memory can be slippery. I've decided that I must have heard the name sometime in my past. My Bonetrail is located in south-western N.D. near the small towns of New Leipzig and Elgin.

I used many of the surnames I heard growing up for the residents of Bonetrail.

My maternal great-grandfather David Miller was a self-taught violin player who enjoyed playing for his family in the evenings. I learned about this during the research talks with my grandmother.

When I was twelve, we went to David's eighty-second birthday. My younger sister had recently begun violin lessons. She was asked to play "Happy Birthday" for Grandpa Miller. Her rendition was more scratches, warbles, and hitches. David silently wept during the performance. My recollection of those minutes is vivid. Years before that birthday party, his violin had been damaged to the extent that he could no longer play his instrument. I never heard him play, but I can imagine it.

Acknowledgements

Thank you to the following: Ruby Hoffman, Carrie Feist, Laura Munson and the Haven Alums, Sarah Hunter, Lisa Triche, Tracey Yokas, Sally Fries, Myrt Scott, and many other hearts. Last, but not least, Donna Link & Lezlie Link, these ladies have the best kind of grit!

ABOUT ME

I'm a Midwestern author who writes comfort reads that uplift, an explorer of hiking trails and neighborhoods, a library power-user, a fanatic sunglasses wearer, a card sender, a daily meditator, and will only own hardy houseplants.

I enjoy caramel rolls with coffee, the sound of

gravel while running under red and gold-leafed Fall trees, Masterpiece Theater on Sunday night, loon calls as evening settles in at the lake, Rainer cherries, and reveling in my loved one's fireworks laughter.

I've nested in North Dakota near prairie and pasture that waves and shimmies in the wind.

What's next?

Bonetrail's next generation, including some cameos by Louise and Leo, continues with the spring 2021 release of an early 1970s historical novel called *Repairing Seams*. The first chapter follows.

REPAIRING SEAMS
(PUBLICATION DATE: SPRING 2021)

CHAPTER ONE

If Geraldine hadn't answered the phone then nothing would have changed. That was what she told herself. This was something she would not tell out loud even to her husband Reiny. Geraldine knew people would think it was crazy. What her daughter Margaret said had to be erroneous. Her daughter was a good girl. She knew better. It was that place and that school to blame. Instead of going to Chicago for college, Margaret should have remained in North Dakota. There were several very good schools here. Why hadn't Geraldine and Reiny pushed Margaret to attend in-state?

The thoughts kept needling Geraldine's mind, stitching her tighter to what should have happened.

Margaret always has to be different. She can't be content with what she has here. Running off to get some big-city education. Why did I let my parents fill her head with all those stories from their vagabond days?

Geraldine had a hard time connecting her parents' traveling band stories of their youth to their present farming life. Her father Leo played his violin with and without an audience, and both her parents still sought out music of all kinds. But they had been rooted to their farm. With all the farm work to be done, gallivanting off to parts unknown just wasn't done.

What will the neighbors think? They didn't know yet and that was a short matter of time. Should I tell mother? Not yet, maybe something will change. What could change? Margaret can't undo what's been done. Could she? Would she? What happens next? Stop it. That's enough, there's work to be done and you need to get the cream cans to the train.

Geraldine's heavy footsteps sounded like crushing glass as she crossed the brick colored clay, shale, and sandstone scoria-front farmyard. The rock made by pressure and heat was becoming a dust that rimmed the bottom of her laced up black work shoes. The Ford sedan's driver door slammed shut enclosing Geraldine and the thoughts she had tried to quiet. They were the passengers that rode with her and the four milk cans to the Bonetrail train platform.

Bonetrail was an Upper Midwest small town whose main street had a stop sign on the north and south ends. In between, there was a grocery, a hardware store, a show theater, a bank, an insurance office, two bars, and a post office. The city hall, elementary school, upper grades school, and sheriff's department were a street over. Spread about town was a wooden church for the Lutherans, another for the Congregationalists, and a brick-built church for the Catholics. The sidewalks were swept or shoveled, and in the summer, residents sat in lawn chairs in their yards or driveways to take in the evenings and the lives of their neighbors.

With a pushed brightness, Geraldine smiled at the railroad porter and they spoke about the weather and how the spring was turning out. The porter traded the full cans for the empty cans sent back by the Mandan creamery.

Geraldine loaded the cans into her trunk, and before dropping the lid, she paused and admired the way the early morning North Dakota sunshine winked and bounced off the galvanized steel. The creamery always sent the cans back cleaned to a high-polish shine. That's how Margaret was supposed to come back: shiny and ready for the world. With both hands flat on the Ford's trunk, Geraldine slammed the lid down.

After arriving home, she returned the waiting cans to the milking barn to be filled that evening and the next morning. Geraldine worked her way through an invisible chore list until she realized she needed to make the dough for the buns. She and Reiny were attending her best friend's Flossie's daughter's wedding this weekend, and she'd volunteered to bring dozens of supper buns. She hadn't finished sewing her dress yet either. Plus, she needed Reiny to try on the new button-up dress shirt she had sewn for him. The cut was good, but it would require slight altering.

Geraldine was looking forward to her sewing. That was her joy and her show. They could have bought new. They had been doing well with the farm. But Reiny liked mending and repairing the farm equipment and Geraldine creating the family's custom-made clothes. That is, until the kids had left home.

Their son, Allen, a young Army soldier stationed in faraway Germany for now, didn't need Geraldine's sewn gifts, and Margaret preferred mini-skirts and bell bottoms. Margaret had once told Geraldine, "The bigger the bell, the better the jeans."

Margaret never did like to sew. Sewing was Geraldine's art and hobby. It was the respite from the farm hours. She pinned, snipped, and stitched yards of fabric into wearable, high-quality clothes.

Geraldine was proud of her homemade clothes. She could sew everything better than any company, except for factory-made blue jeans. For church and special occasions, the kids had to wear the slacks and skirts she'd sewn them; no blue jeans. The clothes

Geraldine made also had to look as good on the inside as they did on the outside. There were no slap-dash creations from her.

The two o'clock brighter sunshine filled the converted bedroom that Geraldine had turned into her sewing room. The room had a rounded wood headboard with a matching dresser. The top drawers stored sheets and pillowcases. The bottom drawer had been reserved for storing Allen's yearbooks, childhood mementos, pictures, and the wintergreen and white high school graduation tassel. Geraldine would keep them safe until Allen came home. Her son and other mother's sons, and even a few daughters, were learning first-hand about the war in Vietnam. That Southeast Asian country was now more than an outlined land section on a basketball-sized, bumpy surfaced, blue oceans globe.

Geraldine had previously cut out fabric pieces using the tissue paper pattern. Multi-colored ball point pins held the fabric, and next came the sewing. Instead of taking the warm peachy chiffon off the upright dress form, she stared at the waterfall of unfinished dress.

Geraldine felt unraveled. What was she going to say when people inquired about Margaret? The truth wouldn't do. Should she tell Flossie? Not now. Geraldine itched to talk to someone other than Reiny about Margaret. She wanted reassurance that it was going to be alright. Geraldine wanted someone to side with her, to tell her that Margaret's actions were reckless and couldn't be taken back. The world and Bonetrail would teach her daughter in a way her parents never could, or would, have.

Heated tears fell from the corners of Geraldine's eyes. Using her forearm, she swiped at them and felt the ungentle touch press into her eyelids. When the crying was over, Geraldine hung as limp as the dress on the mannequin form. She knew she should get started on the sewing but her hands were still damp and she didn't want to mark up the fabric.

Geraldine looked out the window onto the western side of the farmyard. She saw the new barn they had built a few years ago to replace the sagging, grey barn that had come with the farm's purchase. In its place was a two-story barn painted white with black trim around the doors and windows and even the hayloft window. Reiny had wanted to paint it traditional red, but Geraldine had wanted something different. She liked the contrast between the white and black.

Further past the barn's cattle corrals were the sunflower fields. Those fields had rotated spring wheat, barley, oats, and this year sunflowers. Since it was late May, there was not much to see in the field. At the end of summer, those fields, minus any hail storms, would have sunflowers rising, turning, and lowering as they followed the sunlight. That was something Geraldine could look forward to.

Geraldine, with her hands now dry, stood before the soon-to-be dress, and with a gentle deftness gathered and moved the fabric to her sewing machine. In firm and light dips and rises her foot moved the treadle as the spool, bobbin, and needle worked together, transforming fabric into a ready-to-wear frock.

It took all afternoon, but Geraldine's party dress was ready. After she hung the elegant flowing chiffon on the door she inspected the puffed-up collar that extended out into a long-draped scarf. Her eyes worked down across a tailored bustline and cinched-in at the waist and stopped at the billowy full skirt with an above-the-knee hem. Inspection complete, she smiled her appreciation at the finished garment and felt more confident for what lay ahead, at least for this weekend's wedding.

(Publication: Spring 2021)

www.ingramcontent.com/pod-product-compliance
Lightning Source LLC
Chambersburg PA
CBHW020241110726
47898CB00004B/1345